Timekeeper

Julie Parker

Contents

Chapter One

"Okay, you're going to feel a slight pinch..." the doctor said as he placed my wrist underneath the machine.

I knew he was lying. I had seen people go through this before. I looked down at my wrist under the device; it looked so strange. I guess you could describe it as a massive stapler, because that's what it was going to do. It was about to insert a countdown on the inside of my wrist. You didn't have a choice if you wanted it or not, once your sixteenth birthday came, that thing was embedded into your skin.

The doctor began to count backwards from ten. I looked over at my mother outside the viewing window and gave her a weak smile, receiving a nervous grin in return. Thanks, Mother. Thank you for making me feel even more frightened. I gazed at my blank wrist, thinking that this will be the last time I see it untouched and free. He was down to five. I took a deep breath and closed my eyes, hoping it would be over soon. I wished they could just give you a bracelet instead, telling you how long you have. It would be a lot easier, and much less painful.

"And one," he exclaimed, pushing a big green button on the control panel that sat in front of him.

The machine began to rumble, a light shining onto my tied down wrist. I squeezed my eyes shut, having little hope that it would decrease the pain I was about to experience. I felt a heavy weight against my wrist before a piercing, agonising pain shot into my skin. I let out a scream, wanting to rip my arm away from the machine. My mother rushed through the doorway and over to my side, getting a tight grip on my free hand.

The pain shot up my arm, going through my entire body. It was the worst pain I'd ever experienced, and I couldn't even describe what it felt like. Just imagine feeling a tiny needle being stabbed into every inch of your body, and then multiply that by like a million. I may have been over exaggerating, but it really was excruciating.

The horrid pain subsided a little and I opened my eyes, blinking at my new wrist. The countdown read 0000d 00h 00m 00s. I looked up at the doctor, confused as to why it didn't say anything.

"Don't worry sweetie, it need's time to work and connect to your system." He smiled blankly, grabbing a clipboard from the desk in the corner of the room.

"Now. Just a few things you should know," he began. "Firstly, it will take about six hours for the Timekeeper to connect to your nervous system and brain. So, when you wake up in the morning, it should be working."

"And if it isn't?" my mother mumbled, still holding a tight grib on my hand.

I looked up at her wrist, her countdown only displayed a big red horizontal line. That was what happened when your soul mate passes away.

My mother met my father about a year after her sixteenth birthday, and would say how they instantly connected. People around them were jealous of how in love they were; how perfect their relationship was. I wish I were alive to see it; it would've been so magical. But my father died when my mother was pregnant with her third child; me. My older brothers were both lucky, they got to spend time with him and see him. But I didn't, which hurt like a stab to the heart. I wished for my relationship to be like theirs, so magical and unforgettable.

"-Make sure that you follow these rules, the consequences can be terrible," the doctor finished as I realized that I had zoned out for half of his talk.

But I guess it was alright. I knew how it worked anyway. I had always been so fascinated with the Timekeeper, and couldn't wait to have my own. I would always ask mother about it and how it worked. I watched both my brothers get theirs and find their soul mates as well.

I knew that the Timekeeper could control you. That's what it had to do. It leads you to your soul mate, even if they are across the ocean. You would just end up buying a plane ticket and not have any idea of where you were going, all because of the little device implanted into your wrist.

"Are there any other questions, Candice?" the doctor asked, opening the door for us, signaling that it was time to go.

I stood up from the dentist-looking chair that patients have to sit in and walked towards the door. My eyes met those of the old man, and a smile came to my face before I shook my head.

"Very well then. If you have any questions in the future, please don't hesitate to call."

He closed the door, leaving my mother and I out in the hallway of the clinic.

* * *

"How do you feel?" my mother asked as we pulled up in the driveway of our home.

I shrugged. "Fine. It doesn't hurt anymore."

She gave me a warm smile before walking into our family home. It was such a big house, especially now that my eldest brother Daniel had moved into his own home with his soul mate. It was only my mother, my brother Jacob and his fiancée Patricia, and I.

We lived on a massive property out by the beach; every room of the house had a stunning view. Whether it is of the beach, the hillside or our own property, it all looked so beautiful from our home.

"Hey Sis. Let's take a look," Jacob called, running up to me and grabbing my wrist. I let out a little yelp; not knowing it was still painful to the touch.

"Jacob, watch it." Patricia came over, gently taking my arm out of his strong grip.

Sometimes, I wished I was like Patricia, or could at least look similar to her. She had long black hair, startling green eyes and was the perfect height. But, I was me. Light brown hair, and hazel eyes.. Just boring sixteen year old, Candice Smith.

"Sorry Candy," he replied.

He let go and the duo walked back into the living room.

"I'll start to cook some dinner okay? It should be ready in half an hour." Mother smiled, giving my shoulder a light squeeze before walking towards the kitchen.

I let out a sigh, glad to be finally alone, and went upstairs to my room. I sat on my bed, looking down at my wrist and wondering how long I'd have to wait, until I met him. Well, to be fair it could be a girl, but I was pretty certain that I didn't feel that way towards girls. My brother Daniel once said that one of his friends found their soul mate, and turned out to be a guy. Daniel's friend never even realized he was gay until he met his soul mate.

I found myself brushing my fingers along the Timekeeper, which caused me jump a little. It felt so strange, a little metal strip just sticking out of your skin, especially since I was so used to feeling only skin there. I lied down, trying to imagine what my soul mate might look like. Whether his skin is pale or olive, whether his hair is golden or dark, whether his eyes are electric blue or chocolate brown. I couldn't picture a face, how tall or if he would be, skinny or toned. I couldn't think of anything. My mystery soul mate is just an anonymous, blurry figure in my mind.

"Candy, dinner will be ready in five minutes!" my mother called from the bottom of the staircase.

I sighed; everything in this darn world revolved around time. Time surrounded all of us, whether we were cooking, working, at school, or even eating. Time is everywhere. It controls our lives. Even love; the one thing you thought you could control and you thought was full of choices, is way out of our hands.

* * *

Once again, I had fallen asleep on the couch. We had been sitting in the lounge room, watching movies and snacking on popcorn. It was a classic Friday night, except for the fact that Daniel wasn't there. He had been so busy planning his wedding with his soul mate, Lucy, that we had hardly seen him the past few weeks. I was so happy for him though. Lucy was stunningly gorgeous, not to mention that she was also very smart and funny- she was everything you could want in someone. Their wedding was in a month's time, so they were extremely overwhelmed with the planning and hadn't been around for a while now.

I stretched myself out, yawning as I sat up and rubbed my eyes. I could usually smell Mum's cooking in the mornings, but not today. I was pretty certain that she was out getting some food to cook for breakfast, but there was the slight chance that she could still be in bed. Sighing, I got up and walked towards the staircase. The sunlight shining through the windows caught on my wrist, confusing me at first, because I never wore much jewelry. But then I remembered, and raised my hand up to my face, staring at the small countdown embedded into my skin.

013d, 022h, 042m, 045s

"Oh my gosh," I gasped, still staring at the numbers on my wrist.

The seconds slowly went down, bringing me even closer to my soul mate. If it's the eighth today, than thirteen days from now it will be…the twenty-first? The twenty-first of March. That's when I was going to meet my soul mate. But that wasn't including the hours or minutes or seconds, so maybe it would be even later? It felt so surreal already. I had dreamed about the day forever, and now it was almost two weeks away.

I ran upstairs and into mother's room, hoping to find her, but she was nowhere to be found. 'She must be getting food,' I thought to myself before running out and to the other end of the hall. I burst into Jacob's room, hoping I didn't interrupt anything in the process. Jacob and Patricia were still sleeping, though I had no idea how Patricia could put up with Jacob's snoring. I walked over to the window and pulled their blinds open, filling the room with sunshine.

"Turn off the light." Jacob groaned, burying his head into his pillow. I giggled before running over and jumping on him.

"Jacob, wake up. Look at my Timekeeper!" I chirped, bouncing up and down on him.

His eyes opened to look up at me. He rubbed them, before pushing his soft, dark hair off of his forehead.

"What does it say?" Patricia asked sleepily.

I held my arm out in front of me, showing them both my wrist. They looked at each other and smiled, before turning their attention back to me.

"Only thirteen days, Candy! That's a new record!" Jacob grinned, pulling me into a hug.

Daniel and Jacob's countdown's were fairly similar; they both had around six months before they found their soul mates. This really was a record. Even my grandmother had to wait longer than me. And her countdown was only two months.

I was still buzzing with excitement when we walked downstairs to help mother with all the food. Of course, she bought much more than just breakfast for us. She hated going to the supermarket all the time, so usually she just went once a fortnight and spent like four hundred dollars to get enough food to last us until the next time she went shopping. There were a heck of a lot of bags, but we ended up packing all of it away in no time.

"Take a look at Candy's Timekeeper, Linda. It's pretty exciting!" Patricia smiled at my mother, who seemed to have forgotten all about it.

Her eyes grew wide with excitement as she rushed over to me. I held out my arm, showing off my modified wrist. She looked at the countdown, tears filling her blue eyes.

"Oh Candice, this is wonderful!" she said as she squeezed me into her arms. I was so glad everyone was happy for me. I guess it was a pretty big thing, finding your soul mate.

"Have you worked out when it will be?" my mother asked, finally releasing me from her motherly hug.

I sat down at the table next to Jacob, while mother and Patricia began to cook breakfast. "The twenty-first or second I think. But I didn't work it out to the very last second." I smiled, rubbing my fingers over the Timekeeper.

It gave off a very faint vibration; all around it my wrist felt numb. I wondered if that normal the day after you got it, but I didn't want to worry mother. She seemed so happy and pleased that her youngest child, and only daughter, was finally going to meet the love of her life.

I think I was more nervous than anything. I was going to meet the one. My soul mate, my future husband and the future father of my children; it was too crazy to even think about.

"I worked it out!" Jacob yelled, startling us all.

He had been busy scrawling down notes on a notepad, which I thought was just something to do with his work. All eyes were on him. He was the smartest in the family, which he hated to admit but we all knew it was true.

"Candy will meet him on the twenty-second of March, at seventeen seconds past quarter past one," he announced triumphantly. I could never understand how my brother worked things like this out; it was beyond me.

"How on earth?" Patricia and mother said in unison, before laughing at themselves.

I wasn't the only one who was amazed at his seemingly magical abilities. Everyone seemed to be so thrilled about meeting my soul mate, but I couldn't stop myself from thinking about it. What was he going to look like? Will it be love at first sight like mother and father's was? What if something happens before I even meet him? I shake the questions out of my head. There was only one way I would find out, and that was when I would be face to face with him.

Patricia placed a big plate of mum's famous homemade pancakes in front of me, which was when I realised just how much my stomach was nagging at me. Breakfast at our house was always filled with a lot of talking and laughing, with the occasional accidental food spitting, which were usually quite funny, unless you were on the receiving end. I would sometimes wonder what my father would be doing at times like this. Whether he would be sitting with his eyes glued to the morning paper, or maybe he would be the main reason for everyone's laughter.

Mother said that he was quite a funny man; she said he would always make the silliest jokes. Most of the time they never made any sense, but that's what made them so hilarious. She said he was always outside, working around the garden to make everything look beautiful. The rest of the time he spent outside with my brothers, playing football or working on car parts. Mother would always be watching through the kitchen window, smiling at how lucky she was to have such a beautiful family. She would be rubbing her stomach, thinking that her beautiful family was going to get even better in several months time.

But unfortunetly, that's not how things turned out.

Chapter Two

It was a typical Monday morning. I was up at seven to shower and get ready for school, while the rest of the family was rushing around to get to work on time. Mother was up first; she would wake up at six and was usually gone before I was even up. Patricia and Jacob were up the same time as I was, so it was always pretty crazy with everyone trying to use the bathroom or toaster at the same time. They would take their cars to work, going their separate ways out the driveway. Then, it was lonely ole' me; I was left to walk to school by myself every morning.

It wasn't too bad though- school was only a few blocks up the road. I didn't mind walking; it was calming and peaceful. I clutched the straps of my electric blue school bag as I walked along the footpath, kicking at the stones that were closest to my ugly school shoes. Our school colours were electric blue and yellow, a terrible match I know. I was wearing our summer dress even though it was Autumn, and the air had become a little fresher. I could see the top of the school building through the trees in front of me; the noise of school kids running around and laughing was just audible.

I stood in front of the open school gates, sighing as I went through them. A few moments later I spotted Claire reading Looking for Alaska, for what had to be at least the fiftieth time. She was a sucker for John Green novels.

Her head shot up as I approached her, a smile plastered on her rounded face.

"Hey Cand. Oh, you won't believe what happened on the weekend!" She started, rambling on about her boyfriend Alex and how she finally lost her virginity.

"I mean, it wasn't that bad. But people make it sound as if it hurts like hell...I beg to differ." She was a very unique girl, I must say. She was one of the smartest people I knew; yet she was also popular.

It was quite strange, because even though I was her best friend, I wasn't popular. I could be with her all day, and people would come up to Claire and ask her who I was. To be honest, I didn't mind it. Being somewhat invisible was fine by me.

"So, how was your weekend?" Claire asked as we arrived at our lockers.

I was still surprised that she didn't remember that it was my sixteenth birthday, and what that actually meant. I wasn't much of a party girl. Most of the time, I preferred to sit at home and read or go on the internet.

I pulled my jumper sleeve up to my elbow and flashed my wrist in front of Claire's face, grinning at the numbers. Claire's eyes widened and she grabbed my wrist.

"Oh my gosh, how could I have forgotten? I'm so sorry! Happy sweet sixteenth girl!" She squealed, before examining my Timekeeper.

"Wait a second, this is like next week. That's so exciting. You're going to meet the man of your dreams and he's going to sweep you off your feet–it'll be love at first sight. Just you wait until you get into bed together...oh my. I can't begin to describe–"

"Please, Claire, no more," I groaned as the bell rang, signaling that class was starting.

Lucky for me, Claire was in my first class, which was English. And when I said lucky, I meant it with sarcasm. Every chance she got, she was talking about my soul mate. What he would look like, where we would meet, and then the more personal details, like if he would be good in bed and how big his junk was. Like I said before, she was an interesting human being, but she was still my best friend.

After double periods of English, it was time for recess, which just involved Claire telling more people about my Timekeeper. After our short break, we had psychology and math. Psychology was super interesting to me. At the moment, we were learning about mental illnesses like Schizophrenia. I found it to be a fascinating subject, but could never concentrate with Claire's high-pitched voice right in my ear.

When lunchtime finally came around, I was so relieved. Mister Collins droned on and on about the Pythagorean Theorem for the entire class, and I was beyond bored. Math was definitely not my favorite subject, but I was still pretty good at it. So in a way that was a plus, because it meant I didn't have to pay as much attention and I could still ace all of my tests. Being smart had its perks, but it also had its downers. It meant that Claire and I were targets of the less intelligent students, which was in fact, most of Claire's popular friends.

I walked into the cafeteria to find a spot in line and grab some food. I didn't buy lunch at school much. My mother didn't like wasting money on food when she could just make something for me at home that was cheaper. That day was different though. Mother decided to give me money for lunch, as like a reward or something. I figured that it was because of my birthday. It's not like I didn't get anything for my birthday, because I got plenty. My mother bought me a new Nova phone, since I had been complaining for a while about my old one. My new phone was able to do everything I could think of. The commercials weren't kidding when they called them "smart phones."

Lunch went by with even more talk about my Timekeeper and soul mate. I seemed to be the gossip of the whole school, which annoyed me a little. This happened to another girl about two years ago. Her Timekeeper showed that she only had like twenty-four hours until she was going to meet her soul mate, and the entire school was ecstatic for her. The next day came and she had about six hours to go, when her Timekeeper flashed with a blood red horizontal line. The whole school was silent and staring at her for the rest of the week; the poor girl never even got to meet her soul mate.

As you could guess, she didn't take what happened well. She dropped out of school about a month after it happened, and nobody had seen or heard of her since. I didn't blame the girl though. The event was horrible. I only have to wait a week to meet my soul mate, and it's already getting to me. But to have your soul mate die only hours before you're about to meet them would be so terrible. All the waiting and wondering was for nothing. It would have driven me crazy; never knowing who he was or what he looked like, the colour of his eyes to the way he walked. She would never know any of it; she would never get to meet the one that she belongs to. All she would ever be able to do was imagine him and think about what he would have been like.

That, I thought, had to be the saddest thing imaginable.

* * *

006d, 020h, 051m, 054s

It was only a week away now. It's crazy how fast things come isn't it? Even though when you're waiting for something to happen and it feels like it takes forever to finally come, you know that it has actually come so fast. Maybe it's just me though. I guess I've had a crazy week already. I had suddenly become known at school, which was extremely weird and made me slightly uncomfortable. Everybody seemed to know me now though; I've been labelled 'The girl with the shortest Timekeeper', which I was sure wasn't true anyway. I had read somewhere that the record for the shortest countdown so far was only about 5 hours. The longest however, was over 10 years. Imagine waiting that long to meet your soul mate? I think it would be pretty frustrating.

I had not long got home from school and was spread out along the couch when I heard a car pull up outside. I knew it could only be my brother Daniel. I still hadn't seen him since I had gotten my Timekeeper, so I was super excited to see him. I ran to the front door, opening the door to see my tall and skinny older brother.

"Hey lil' sis." He smiled, pulling me into his long arms.

"Hi Daniel, I've missed you!" I said into his black shirt, squeezing my arms tighter around his chest. We stayed like that for a little while before he pulled away and we walked inside.

"So how's my little sister been?" He smiled, sitting on the grey suede couch in front of the TV. He flicked his hair out of his eyes before grabbing the TV remote and switching it on. His hair was almost at his shoulders, chocolate brown, straight hair. We had all told him that he has to get it cut before the wedding, which was only about a month or so away.

"I'm good, Dan. I've become almost popular at school." I giggled, turning Daniel's attention from the TV screen to me. He laughed, before raising an eyebrow.

"And how did you suddenly become so popular? I thought you liked being the quiet one?" I got up off the couch to his left and skip over to his side, baring my wrist in front of his face. His eyes lit up, and I could tell he was excited to see his little sister finally getting her Timekeeper.

"Six days! Candy that's next week!" He grinned, in a way that almost resembled the Cheshire cat from Alice in Wonderland. He had one of the biggest grins you would ever see. He would always get complimented on his "award-winning smile" as he called it.

His eyes started to tear up, and I knew this was likely to happen. Daniel is my oldest brother, and since dad passed away he has taken over his role for me. Daniel has been like a father to me, and I know that may sound a little weird, but it was true, and he was good at it as well. He had always taken care of me, always been there for me, and now that his little sister wasn't really so little anymore, well he was bound to cry.

"Daniel please don't cry! I can't be your little sister forever." I mumbled, as he wiped his eyes with the hem of his shirt. He let out a small chuckle, followed by a sigh.

"You'll always be my little sister, even when you're 45." He smiled, before pulling me into a bear-like hug.

At the dinner table, most of the talk was about Daniel's wedding. I didn't mind though, not at all. I was actually going to be in the wedding, as one of Lucy's bridesmaids. I was beyond excited for it, and I was going for a dress fitting some time next week, which had me even more excited. I was so happy for Daniel; his life seemed to work out so perfectly for him already, I just hope mine turns out the same. But I guess only fate can decide, if you believe in that. Or maybe God decides, or maybe you decide. I don't think anyone really knows the answer to that question; just a bunch of philosophers making up theories about life. In my opinion, I think we get some choice in life. Well, a lot less than we used to.

I mean, the Timekeeper wasn't something that had been around for centuries, oh no. People didn't have the technology or mind power to discover how these things worked back then. They were quite amazing creations I had to agree, but sometimes I wish things were all natural. For instance, I sometimes wished you could just go through all your frogs, to find your prince. I know that sounds so cliché' and just plain stupid, but it would be nice, you know? To feel like you have a choice in one of the biggest parts of your life, rather than being told who and that's it. But I guess it wasn't all bad. I mean if we didn't have the Timekeeper then we might never meet our soul mate, and we could end up with somebody completely different instead.

"Candice! Are you okay?" My mother raised her voice to get my attention. I had obviously zoned out for a while; I now had no idea what everyone was talking about.

"Uh, Ye-Yeah I'm fine. Just daydreaming that's all." I blushed, a little embarrassed. All eyes were in my direction now, trying to get the truth out of me. I had always been a terrible liar, especially around my family. They always seemed to know when I was lying or not, which was most unfortunate for me.

"Candy, what's wrong?" Jacob said, with quite a serious tone. I looked down at the plate in front of me; spaghetti bolognese was usually my favourite, but I had hardly touched it tonight. I put my fork down, before letting out a sigh.

"I guess I'm just afraid. I'm afraid that my soul mate's not going to be who I expect. What if it's not how it's supposed to be? What if we don't have love at first sight? Or love at all? Is that even possible? What if he hates me? Or I hate him? I just, I don't know. I know what I'm thinking is stupid and you're all probably think I'm crazy. But I'm scared that when I meet him, he's just not going to feel like the one. And we just aren't going to connect the way we should." I said, unable to stop the words from coming out of my mouth.

"Is it even normal to think like that? Or am I just overthinking the situation way too much?"

They all looked at me with sympathetic expressions, and I began to wonder if I really was going crazy. My mother put her arm around my shoulder and kissed my forehead.

"Of course it's normal to think those things before you find your soul mate, sweetie. It's one of the biggest moments in your life so it's completely fine to feel worried about it." She said reassuringly, while my brothers' head's nod in agreement.

"Stress less Cand, I'm sure he will be perfect for you." Daniel smiled.

"Yeah and I can see you two falling in love at first sight, just like our mother and father did." Jacob continued, making mother tear up a little.

I guess they were right. It was normal to be nervous about things that are going to have a big effect on your life. For instance, if you were scheduled for a life-saving surgery in a few months time, of course you would doubt the doctor's abilities and whether it will work out because you're nervous for it, but in the end it will be worth it. Was that a bad comparison? I don't know, but I do know that whoever my soul mate is, and whatever happens to us, that we can make it work. I guess we had to, since it wasn't in our control anymore. It was in the Timekeeper's.

Chapter Three

O 00d, 000h, 000m, 000s

I looked up, at the empty space surrounding me; I was alone in a completely white room. Where was he? He was supposed to be here as soon as the Timekeeper reached zero. When it rings like wedding bells, you're supposed to see your soul mate. But all I could see was white. There was no furniture in the room; no windows and I couldn't even see a door. How did I get in here? Where was I?

My Timekeeper started to buzz, which couldn't be normal. I should've seen him by now, where on earth was he? He wasn't dead, because my Timekeeper would've shown a big fat red line, but it didn't. At the current moment, it was blank. There was nothing on it at all, like it should be when I meet him. But he's no where to be seen.

"Hello!" I yelled, my voice echoed off the walls.

"Where are you!" There's no reply, no sound at all. I was all alone, and I felt like I was going to be that way forever.

I woke up; sweat trickling down my face and the back of my neck. Oh thank god, it was only a dream. I checked my wrist and see that it's not blank, it's still counting down. I let out a sigh of relief, knowing that he was still out there somewhere, and I was going to meet him in under a week. I wiped the sweat from my face and neck, before getting up and walking across the hallway and into the bathroom. I turned the shower on, stripped down and hopped in, letting the warm water immerse my skin.

I stared at the countdown on my wrist, which I seemed to be spending a lot of my time doing lately. Why did we have to have them embedded into our wrists anyway, you might ask? I would sometimes wonder that as well, although I actually knew, I still found myself wondering why we needed them.

It was well over 50 years ago, when technology started to evolve into the wonders we have today. Scientists began to get creative and mix unknown chemicals to create cures and solve all the mysteries of science. One group of Scientist's though, weren't working on a cure for cancer or a way to live on Mars; they were trying to figure out how love works. Crazy right? Who cares how it works, it just does.

Anyway, they worked on this project for at least 5 years, saying it would be 'life-changing', before they finally finished the device. There were tests done and experiments to make sure it would all be perfect and work exactly how they wanted, and I guess it did. People were notified and there was news about it everywhere, making people of all ages rush to the nearest clinic to get one. At first it was only optional, but then they realised that it wouldn't work if only a few people had them, so they made it compulsory.

Of course they had problems with it. People were getting their children done when they were only a few days old, and unfortunately the Time-keeper malfunctioned and the babies got long-term damage, which is quite horrible I know. That's when they realised you should be a certain age before you get your Timekeeper, and they chose the age of sixteen. Why? Mainly because they did more tests that somehow proved that most people meet the one they will marry at the age of sixteen. That seemed a little crazy to me, but I guess so does the Timekeeper.

As I walked out of the bathroom, I heard my family talking quietly downstairs. Eager to find out what had gotten them up so early on a Saturday morning, I rushed into my bedroom and slipped on some denim shorts and a plain black t-shirt, before hopping down the stairs and into the kitchen. The whole family sat around the dining table, Mother, Daniel, Patricia, Jacob and Lucy. They seemed to be talking about the wedding that was only about a month away now, and I for one, was beyond excited for it.

"Hey Candy, you're just in time." Lucy smiled, which showed off her pearly white teeth.

Daniel called me over to sit next to him, and I took in the faces of the people around me. They were all such wonderful people living wonderful lives; they've met the ones they are meant to spend their lives with, to create futures together. I don't understand how other people could stay sane waiting longer than a month to meet their soul mate, I was going crazy and I only had to wait a week!

"Just in time for what?" I asked, too lost in my own thoughts that I almost forgot Lucy had said anything. She tucked a loose strand of short blonde hair behind her ear, with a look of annoyance that it had fallen out of her tight bun. She was so beautiful, I would give anything to look like her, but no. I was stuck with brown wavy hair and I was just, me.

"We've been talking about the wedding, and how exciting it will be to have your soul mate there." Daniel grinned as he patted me lightly on the back. Were they being serious? They were basically inviting a total stranger to their most precious and beautiful day?

"I know he's my soul mate and all, but you don't have to invite him to your wedding." I said; receiving some very confused looks from my family.

"Cand, he'll practically be apart of the family. Why wouldn't we invite him?" Lucy laughed a little nervously.

"I know that. But he's still going to be a stranger to you guys, and maybe even to me as well. What if we don't have that magical connection? Or love at first sight? What if somehow something went wrong with his Time-keeper, and he doesn't end up loving me at all? I just- I think it's your special day, not mine. You shouldn't worry about my love life on your wedding day." My mother gives me one of her sympathetic motherly smiles.

"Honey, no matter who he is, what he's like or how your relationship starts off, he will always be welcome in our family. He is already welcome in this family!" The others all nodded their heads in agreement, while my mother reached across the table for my hand.

"You don't need to worry your pretty little mind, things will work out beautifully and one day we will all be gathered around here to talk about your wedding." She said, squeezing my hand in hers as she tried to blink the tears out of her eyes.

My mother always knew what to say. She seemed to be as wise as an owl, which I wasn't exactly sure how wise they are, but the simile seemed right. The Timekeeper had a certain way to draw the two soul mates closer together, even if they didn't want to be near each other. I guess if you kept trying to get away from your soul mate, and you just kept getting drawn back to them, then you would probably just put up with it right? Just suck it up and get to know them better, or do something fun together to find out what they're like. And after it all, that's when you might start to fall for each other, and maybe that's even more magical than love at first sight.

"Don't forget little sis'," Daniel began with a wide grin. "Nobody hurts you, not even when you're 45. Not if I have anything to do with it." He mimicked an evil chuckle, which made me laugh.

"Especially if I have anything to do with it." Jacob added, joining in on the evil laugh as well. I gave Daniel a playful punch on the arm, before he wrapped his arm around my neck and kissed me on the forehead.

It was times like these I wished my father was still around, to be sitting next to my mother and joining in with his sons. Because there's nobody who want's to protect their little girl, more than her father.

* * *

"So how are you feeling, Candy?" Claire said as she appeared beside me while we walked to class. She twirled her finger through her hair and chewed her gum quite loudly as we walked. She had tight blonde ringlets that always fell so effortlessly around her face, that I was also extremely jealous of, since my hair was a boring mixture of wavy and straight.

"Feeling about what?" I asked, trying hard to balance the books in my arms before I dropped them all. My books were so heavy; this year seemed to already be taking its toll on me. I guess I was lucky that it was the two-week break that split the year up into terms next week. It was actually perfect timing for me.

"Tomorrow!" Claire squealed, slapping me on the head as if to jog my memory of what tomorrow was.

That's right, tomorrow was the big day. The day that everybody lived for, waited for and hoped for. I was so unprepared for it; I just kept trying to avoid the fact that I was going to be meeting my soul mate tomorrow, because I was scared to death. It's not that I didn't want to meet him, I mean of course I did, why wouldn't you want to meet your soul mate if you had the chance? No, it wasn't because of that, it was the mystery and suspense that was killing me. You know when you were younger and it was Christmas Eve and all you could think of while you lay in bed was that Santa was coming. You knew that if you didn't get to sleep then he wouldn't come, but you were way too excited to sleep because the next morning is Christmas Day and you'll be getting presents and what's not exciting about that? I guess what I'm trying to say is, when you're excited or nervous for something that's happening the next day, you try not to think about it so that you can focus on other things, like sleeping for instance.

"I'm so nervous, Claire. What if he isn't who I think he is? What if I don't even like him? Or he doesn't like me?" I whispered as we take our seats in our History class, relieving my arms from my bulky textbooks. Claire let out a little giggle, before the teacher began to drone on about how Australia was discovered; I think he lost me as soon as the words left his lips.

"You worry too much, Candy. Seriously stress less! You should be thrilled about tomorrow, not over-analysing the situation!" She said quietly, though her eyes never left the teacher. I guess she didn't want to get in trouble, and she always had a soft spot for history, even if she wouldn't admit it. I nodded, remembering that she couldn't see me anyway and turned my attention back towards the teacher.

"Remember when I got my Timekeeper?" She smiled as she flashed back through her memories. I did remember actually. It was late last year when she turned sixteen, so she's basically the oldest in our year level. Her Timekeeper gave her two months, which was pretty exciting and we both thought that there was no time at all to wait. It was about a week before she was going to meet him, and she had a panic attack about it. She was stressing and asking me all the same questions I had been asking everyone lately. I was there for her though, and told her not to worry about it and that everything would work out perfectly for her, which it did. She met Alex at a beautiful park while she was walking her dog; he was doing the same. She had told me that there was an instant connection between them, and that she had worried for nothing because it turned out perfectly. I could only hope mine would be the same.

"I was so scared and nervous about meeting Alex, and I know now that it was such a stupid thing to do. You'll be the same Cand, it'll be magical and one of the most perfect moments in your life." Claire sighed dreamily, as she stared off into space. She did have a point though, and my god I hoped she was right about this one.

It was almost the end of school, which I was quite thrilled about. Usually I could handle school; the work was fairly easy for me, I didn't have to worry about drama much due to my lack of friends, but this week was far from a normal one for me. I struggled to concentrate in my classes, which had never been a problem for me, but I couldn't stop thinking about him, and he was controlling my thoughts at the moment. And it wasn't only that I couldn't keep my focus in class, but I had also met so many people that I had never talked to or ever thought to talk to before, and I seemed to have a lot of people want to know me. I know right? It had been so crazy.

There was this one girl that I had a few classes with, her name is Meg, and she has been constantly trying to talk to me and I don't know what to think about it. Like, she seemed like a nice girl, but why was everyone so interested in me all of a sudden? I just couldn't wrap my head around it.

I was in my art class, which was one of the only classes I didn't have with Claire, which I really enjoyed. Of course, I love Claire, she's my best friend, but I did like having my own time, and art was the perfect time for it. I was too busy sketching in my book to notice that a boy had made his way over to me, and had sat down beside me. It wasn't until he cleared his throat that I looked up from my book and noticed him. I had seen him around before, but I had never spoken to him. He had tousled, thick brown hair, and piercing green eyes. I had to admit he was pretty attractive, but what did he want?

"Hi, Candice." He smiled, his voice low but pitchy. He looked down at my book, staring at the page I'd been drawing on.

"May I?" He asked, gesturing towards my sketchbook. I nodded in reply, and watched as he slid the book in front of him and started flipping through the pages.

"You're probably wondering why I'm over here talking to you, seeing as we've never spoken before. But I've always watched you in this class, without sounding like a creep, but you seem like an interesting girl. Oh, and I'm Ryan by the way." He said as he looked up at me, before sliding the sketchbook back to me.

"I've heard a bit about you these past few days, about that stupid thing on your wrist. A lot of people are talking about it, aren't they?" He asked, staring out the window.

"Uh yeah, it's getting pretty annoying now actually." I said honestly, as I began to draw again.

I didn't know what it was about him, but he was mysterious and intriguing. He didn't have to say much about himself for me to know that he had been through some rough times. He was like me in a way actually, we were both outsiders at school, although I was becoming more known as the word about my Timekeeper spread. But he didn't seem to like being in the spotlight, which we seemed to have in common.

"Hmmm." He mumbled, before standing up as the teacher told us it was time to pack up our things and get ready for the bell to sound. I began to put away my things and lean on the table, mystery boy Ryan still by my side.

"You're a good drawer you know. And don't let this little moment of fame change you into one of those popular girls, it's not worth it." He whispered, his lips so close to my ear it made me shiver.

He pulled away and gave me a mischievous smirk, just as the bell rang to signal the end of school. He walked past me then, brushing his shoulder against mine. I watched as his arms swung by his sides, and that's when I noticed it. His jumper sleave was pulled up just enough to see his Time-keeper. Just enough to see that big fat red line; the line that so many of us dreaded to see appear on our wrists.

Chapter Four

O 00d, 001h, 000m, 000s

In exactly one hour, I was going to meet him. One hour, that's all that stood between us. After all this time, it was finally here. The day I had been waiting for my whole life. I couldn't concentrate, couldn't eat, and couldn't sleep. All I could think about was him. Although it was quite a struggle as I had no face or name to think about. All I could do was imagine what he would be like, which is all I'd been doing lately.

School so far couldn't have droned on for any longer; I felt myself getting impatient as each class went on. I couldn't focus in any of them; nothing was getting through to me. I spent most of my classes in my own little world, apart from when Claire had to snap me out of it or get my attention, which was almost every five minutes. I found myself watching the seconds tick down in math class, my heart beating a little faster as the minute dropped as well. This stupid thing was driving me insane, and I couldn't wait until it was bare.

The school bell sounded, which brought me out of another daydream, but it meant that it was lunch time. I kept wondering where we were going to meet; maybe he was already at this school? I wasn't sure what or how it was going to happen, but most people say your Timekeeper controls your body and takes you to your soul mate. I always thought that was crazy; how could a little piece of metal on your wrist control you like that? Well I did think it was crazy, until I noticed I had walked out of the school gates and was heading towards the city. I could hear a familiar high-pitched voice yell from behind me, but I couldn't turn around. I was physically unable to control my own body, but the Timekeeper could.

"Candice! Candice where on earth are you going!" Claire puffed as she caught up to me, holding her hands on her hips.

"I have no idea Claire, it's the Timekeeper!" I replied nervously, almost forgetting how to speak. Well maybe that was in the Timekeeper's control as well, it seemed to be controlling everything else.

"What? Already? Oh my god Candy!" She squealed, as she turned on her heels to make her way back to the school grounds, "You better tell me all about it tonight okay?" But before I could reply she was off, leaving me alone with no idea where I was going.

* * *

The city was busy, but not as busy as a city usually is, so this was unusual. I didn't come into the city very often, but now I wondered if this is where my soul mate lived, and maybe I would have to come here more frequently. It wasn't like it was a really long walk from my house, only about fifteen minutes maybe? But walking was quite exhausting; I just wanted my feet to stop for a second. As if I had triggered something in my body, my feet stopped moving. My heart skipped a beat. I checked my wrist, but I still had half an hour and felt quite hungry now. I didn't even get to eat lunch at school, and my Timekeeper seemed determined to get me to this spot on time, or half an hour early by the looks of things.

I took a look around, but everyone on the street was busy walking and talking or rushing to get somewhere. He wasn't here, so why had my feet stopped all of a sudden? Did I make them stop? Maybe I could make them go again, but go where? I was so confused, which added to the list of other moods and emotions I felt. What if my Timekeeper couldn't find him? What was I supposed to do then? All these questions rushed through my head and I could feel a headache coming on. I had to stop over thinking this; everything was going to be alright. As if on queue, my feet began to move again.

I could feel myself smiling; maybe everything was going to turn out alright after all. No more negative thoughts Candice, I told myself, hoping it would create a wall inside my head to keep those thoughts contained. I only had fifteen minutes to go now, and I could feel my nerves really kick in. I think if I was to stop and I stood completely still, my whole body would shake like one of those Chihuahua dogs. I wonder if he would be feeling the same way right now? If he was as excited to see me, as I was to see him.

I kept on thinking about Ryan, the guy in my art class. I wonder when his Timekeeper showed that awful red line, the line that means your soul mate had passed away. I wonder how close he was to meeting her, what if he only had fifteen minutes like I did? The thought sent chills down my spine; I couldn't bear to see that line appear now. I knew I didn't have to wait as long as some people did, but being this close to meeting him only to see that red line, now that would be completely heartbreaking.

I had been so lost in my thoughts that I didn't even realise I had come to a stop in front of a small antique store. The structure of the shop looked very worn and fragile, like it could collapse at any second. It was an off yellow kind of colour, and the sign above the door was almost too faded to read, but I could just make it out, Little Knacks. Although I only came into the city a few times a month, if that, I had never seen it before. It sat on one of the main streets that ran through the city, so it was odd that I hadn't come past it before.

I liked to collect vintage things; I don't know if that made me weird or seem way older than I actually was, but it was so interesting. You could almost guarantee that you would never find the same thing twice, and the things you would find were from before our technology was so advanced. These days our phones had everything built into them. They weren't just for calling people anymore; you could do anything on them. I loved the new technology we had, but I could never go past a good book or finding a cute little antique.

I looked down at my Timekeeper and gasped,000d, 000h, 005m, 013s

Five minutes, five damn minutes! I could feel my heart pounding against my ribcage, my whole body shook like crazy. I couldn't believe it, I was about to meet him. I was only 5 minutes away from meeting my soul mate, and I felt like I was going to faint. I spun around, trying to look at the faces around me. Nobody was standing still; nobody even looked my way or seemed to be looking for someone like I was. Everyone was too busy to even notice I stood in the middle of the footpath, but just walked around me as if I was a tree.

Without my control, my body turned back towards the antique shop. He must be in there, I thought to myself. I could feel sweat trickle down my neck, the palms of my hands clammy in the warm autumn air. This was it. I was about to come face to face with my soul mate. It was almost like I could feel his presence, like an invisible chain was pulling us even closer together. I walked through the shop door, chiming a small bell that hung above it. All I could see was a hooded figure at the register at the back of the store, but nobody else was in sight. I must have startled the figure, because he began to run towards the door, only to crash into me instead.

We both fell to the floor, my vision blurred from the impact. It was as we both got to our feet when the ringing began. At first I thought it was a phone, but then I realised exactly what it was. I snapped my wrist over to see twelve zeros flashing at me. I looked up at the figure in front of me and see he was looking at his wrist as well. I then noticed that his hood had fallen and his face was now visible. His messy, dirty blonde locks sat just above his blue eyes that were tinted with specks of green. His jawline was lined with stubble and he had angular cheekbones. He was about a head taller than me, and although he wore baggy clothes, I could tell he was lean and athletic.

Our eyes finally landed on one another's, but he wasn't at all like I had imagined. He seemed to be hiding from something, almost like he was too frightened to open himself up to somebody. I took a deep breath and smiled, only to be shoved aside as my soul mate ran out the door and onto the bustling street. My mouth was wide open; I couldn't even piece together what had just happened, until I looked down at my feet to see a bag full of cash and golden jewellery.

I had no idea what had come over me, but I begun to sprint after him. What kind of girl can say that when they met their soul mate, he ran away from her? Well my name was at the top of that list now. I could just see the top of his head through the now overcrowded street, and boy did we get extremely odd looks from bystanders. I didn't blame them though; I would do the exact same thing if I were one of them. I wanted someone to stop him, to jump in front of him so he wouldn't be able to run away any longer.

We had come to the end of the street, where he made a swift turn down an alleyway hoping I wouldn't have seen him. But I did, and we ended up face to face again, the only way out was behind me. I held my hands on my hips, as I gasped for air. I couldn't remember the last time I had run so fast, not even for school. I had never been very sporty, believe me, but I was quite proud of my effort to corner him. I felt a little better about myself when I noticed that he was puffing as well.

"What the hell is wrong with you?" He puffed as he leant back onto one of the brick walls that surrounded us. I noticed sweat trickle down the side of his face, his blonde fringe sticking to his forehead.

"With me? I should be asking you the same question!" I shouted, trying not to show that I ached all over from the race we just had.

"You're the one that just chased me down the street!" He replied, his voice husky and deep. I had to admit, he was definitely attractive, but so far I wasn't very fond of his personality.

"And you're the one that ran off on me in the first place! I'm not sure if you realised back there, but that ringing sound signalled that we're soul mates!" I yelled, as I got more and more frustrated with him.

So far, this had definitely not been at all how I imagined meeting my soul mate would turn out. I mean so much for love at first sight; this was almost the opposite. And if that wasn't bad enough, he was a thief. Out of all the wonderful guys that the Timekeeper could have chosen for me, it chose this guy. This ignorant, yet attractive guy that stood in front of me was apparently meant to be my soul mate. I didn't even know his name yet, or anything about him really, except that he stole.

"Who cares? It's only a stupid timer thing, it means nothing to me." He hissed. Hearing that, really got to me. How could someone care so little about the one they are meant to spend the rest of their life with? I didn't want to be here anymore. In fact, I wanted to be as far away from him as possible. I just wanted to curl up in a ball and cry, but I tried to fight back the tears.

"How could you even say that? You don't even know my name yet." I whispered, taking my gaze from his face to the dirty concrete ground.

I hoped he could tell I was hurt, so he could tell me this was all a big misunderstanding and we could go get lunch and talk about each other. But he just stood there, not making a sound. It felt like it was silent forever; the two of us avoided each other's eye contact, as we hoped the other would say something. I had almost lost all hope, until he broke the silence.

"Jase." He said quietly, looking up at me. There was something in his eyes that wasn't there before. They were glassy and he seemed to be hurt, although I didn't think I had insulted him.

"What?" I asked in confusion, not sure what on earth he had said.

"My name, its Jase. Jase Williams." He said softly, before he slipped past me and ran off through the crowd of people, for the second time today. I sighed, but didn't bother to run after him. Firstly, I was still, sadly, worn out from the first run, and secondly, I didn't think it would do much good if I managed to catch up to him anyway.

* * *

Walking home seemed to be taking even longer than walking into the city, but it was mostly because I was tired, hungry and couldn't stop crying. I knew I sounded like a baby, but I was still trying to wrap my head around today's events. I was so excited for today, as anyone was on the day they meet their soul mate. Everything that I thought could go wrong actually did. I kept hoping that it was all just a dream and that I was going to wake up any minute now and be able to do the day all over again. But I knew this was reality, and as much as I could try and ignore it, it would constantly bug me.

My eyes were still filled with tears when I noticed a blurry figure come into my vision. My heart skipped a beat, hoping that Jase had followed me and had come to say sorry so we could start over. But as my vision began to clear, I noticed that where I expected blonde hair, there was brown. It was

Ryan. I tried to wipe my tear-stained cheeks as I got closer, but I knew it was pointless. I could tell my face was red and my cheeks were puffy, so he was definitely going to notice.

"Candice? Are you alright?" Ryan asked as he approached me, still in his school uniform, which is when I realised that school had probably just finished, meaning that there would be school kids everywhere along my walk home.

I nodded; not wanting to speak since I knew my voice would sound hoarse. He gave me a polite smile, before he sat down on the bench beside the bus stop.

"No offence, but you don't look okay." He said gently, as he waved me over to sit beside him. I sighed as I sat down, knowing that he probably wasn't going to let me lie my way out of it.

"That's still pretty offensive." I joked, putting on a small smile.

We sat there for a little while in silence, both waited for the other to speak. I knew he wanted me to say something, to tell him what was wrong, but I didn't know if I was able to. Honestly, I didn't even want to tell my family about my day, but I knew it would come up. Of course it would come up, they were expecting my day to have been fantastic and probably hope I'll be bringing my soul mate home to meet the family already, but that wasn't going to happen. Not for a while, if at all. For some reason, I felt like I could tell Ryan, and he wouldn't judge me. Maybe it was the fact that he had that big, fat red line through his Timekeeper, and when people saw that, you'd be the talk of the school. But it was strange that I hadn't heard anything about it before, unless it only just happened so the students hadn't been able to get the information around yet.

"I met my soul mate today." I said, though I hadn't even realised it slipped out of my mouth.

"I know, you we're all everybody was talking about at school today." He said, pretending that it didn't interest him by faking a yawn. I bumped his shoulder with mine, a small smile spread across my face.

"It was horrible though. He ran away from me, and was nothing at all like I imagined. I-" I was cut off by an outburst of laughter. Ryan was almost in tears, when he realised what I had just said was actually serious.

"Wait, seriously? He ran away from you? Why?" He said in quite a serious tone, as if he hadn't just erupted in laughter only seconds ago.

"I wish I knew." I frowned, as I went over today's events for the millionth time in my head. I couldn't think of anything to explain what had happened today, no reasons, nothing. I was so confused; I just couldn't figure out my soul mate at all.

"Hey, look on the bright side." Ryan smiled, but it didn't last very long. His face filled with sadness and his eyes became glassy. He looked down at his wrist, which I notice has been exposing his Timekeeper. The red line seemed to stared up at me, sending shivers all through my body. Without taking his eyes off his wrist, he continued to speak, "At least you got to meet your soul mate."

Chapter Five

I lay in bed, refusing to get up. My mother kept calling me from downstairs to say that breakfast was ready, but I kept pretending to be asleep. I didn't want to leave my bed at all today; I just wanted to lay there and try to forget everything that happened yesterday.

Once I got home last night, after my chat with Ryan, I was bombarded with questions from my family. The funny part is, I wasn't even exaggerating. As soon as I stepped through the front door, the questions began. But do you want to know the worst part? I lied to them. Lying was a big thing in my family; we never lied to each other and would always tell the truth no matter what it was or how bad it might be. But I couldn't tell them what Jase was really like, or that I would probably never see him again. I tried to keep things as close to the truth as I could, and hoped that they would leave it at that.

After the family had settled down a little, Claire called. Even though I didn't want to tell her about my eventful day, I did. I felt like I needed to get it off my chest to someone that would actually understand, and I knew she would. She told me not to worry though, and that the Timekeeper has a way of always bringing soul mates together, no matter how badly they wanted to stay away from each other. The Timekeeper seemed to be getting more advanced and smarter the longer it was stuck to my wrist, and I still couldn't completely understand how on earth it could control you.

"Candice?" A polite voice called as my door opened slowly, revealing my mother. She walked over to my bed and reached across me, opening the window and letting sunshine flood into my room. I squinted my eyes and let out a groan, before pulling the covers over my head.

"Come on sweetie, time to get up." She laughed, pulling the covers back and blinding my sight.

"Your breakfast is going to get cold." She said before walking out the door, leaving me to follow after her.

As I got to the kitchen, I noticed that the whole family was sitting at the dining table. I couldn't remember the last time I had seen the table so full, or seen so much food. It looked like a feast! As I sat in my seat, I noticed that everybody was smiling at me.

"What?" I said, as I spooned food onto my plate. They all looked down at their plates before looking back up at me again.

"What is it?" I asked, putting my fork down and resting my elbows on the table. There was definitely something up. It was weird enough that the whole family was here, but they seemed to be hiding something from me as well.

"When are we going to meet Jase?" Lucy announced, before covering her mouth as though what she had said could have insulted me. Now it all made sense. They were all here expecting to meet him, my soul mate. They wanted to meet him, the one that I had tried so hard to forget about and hoped that there was a big mistake. I wanted it to be a dream, and that my wonderful, loving soul mate was still out there waiting to meet me. But no, it wasn't a dream and no matter how much I wished for it to change it wouldn't.

"Yes, Candy, when are we going to meet this special boy?" My mother grinned widely. I knew they were expecting to meet him soon, but I wasn't ready for that. How was I supposed to introduce him to the family if he didn't even want to know me? And how was I supposed to tell them that he was a thief? I would rather them never meet him, but that was highly unlikely.

"Uh, I'm not sure yet." I said, hoping there will be no more questions. But of course, it didn't stop there.

"We want to meet him, Candy! You can't keep us waiting forever!" Patricia said excitedly.

"I just want to make sure he won't hurt you." Daniel said sternly, which I knew was no joke. Everyone started to pick on him for being so protective, which is when I began to leave the table.

"Where are you going?" Mother asked as I began to walk out of the dining area.

"Um, I'm meeting up with Jase." I suddenly blurted out, unsure of where that came from. It wasn't the truth, but it wasn't entirely a lie either. I wanted to see him again that was for sure, but I had no idea how I was going to find him. I mostly just wanted to get out of the house and away from the curiosity of my family; I hated having to lie to them and I knew Jase was going to be a common subject most of the day.

Mother's face suddenly lit up. She was about to talk but I cut her off. I knew exactly what she was going to ask, and it was not going to happen.

"No mum, I'm not inviting him over today. Can we at least get to know each other a bit more first before he gets bombarded by the family?" I snapped, instantly feeling a little guilty for the bitter tone in my voice. She gave me a sympathetic smile and nodded, before walking back into the kitchen.

* * *

I grabbed a book off the shelf and found a small table at the corner of the cafe. This was where I spent majority of my time, in this small book cafe. I liked the concept of drinking coffee or tea whilst being able to dive into a good book. The warmth of the drink and the intensity of a good book always seem to go well together. Combining the two in one place was an even greater idea, which was why I was always here. It was quite antique looking, the lights quite dull and the floor lined with wooden floorboards. The counter was off to one side of the room, while the bookcases and shelves filled with wonderful stories filled the back half. It was a small yet, adorable space, and I loved the fact that there was never really anybody in here.

I guess what I loved the most, apart from their steamy hot chocolate which was to die for, was the chalkboard wall. The wall sat at the very back of the room, in the 'library' as I liked to call it, where nothing was leaning against it, nothing in front of it or hanging from it. The wall was filled with people's names and quotes, small drawings and patterns; it looked beautiful. Every time I came in here, I'd vow to write something up there, but I never knew what to write. I didn't just want to write my name; that would be boring. I wanted to leave a mark, my mark.

It may have sounded strange, actually I knew it was strange, but one day when I'm up there with all these other amazing quotes and names, I hope people will look at mine and be inspired just like I had been. There was this one poem up there that I found utterly beautiful. It didn't have a name, and when I asked one of the waiter's about it, they told me that nobody knew who had written it either.

'I don't know if you've ever had one of those dayswhere you'd rather be hit by a trainthen take another breathor not get out of bedbecause you've forgotten how to loveor how to be loved where each step is like a warzonenot wanting to go onbut knowing you have toI don't know if you've ever had one of those daysbut I hope you never do'

I didn't realise how long I had been standing in front of the wall, staring at the poem I found so intriguing, until someone cleared their throat from behind me. "I see you're admiring my work." A deep husky voice spoke, sending shivers through my entire body. I turned around and gasped. If a jaw could literally drop to the floor, mine would've dropped so fast that it would've dented the floorboards. I was utterly speechless; why was he here and how did he find me?

A smirk crept up onto his plump lips as he stood in front of me. He wore all black for what I could see, but I found it strangely attractive and it seemed to suit him well. His black jeans and black leather jacket clung to his frame perfectly, and his hair was pushed back off his forehead, unlike yesterday. His eyes looked green in the daylight, and they seemed to stare straight into my soul. I kept constantly wondering if he was analysing me, as I was to him.

"Jase? How did you-" He cut me off before I could even finish my question.

"The Timekeeper controls us, love. We're connected now, remember?"

I took a seat at the table I always sat at; Jase followed, sitting across from me. I looked down at my entwined fingers before looking up at him, but he wasn't looking at me. In fact, he seemed to be trying to look anywhere but towards me, which annoyed me a little.

"How did you know I was here?" I said, finishing off the question that Jace interrupted before.

His eyes finally met mine, as he leant back on the wooden chair. And did you really write that poem? It lingered in the back of my mind, but I figured it would be pointless and stupid to ask. I mean I saw him try to steal, and he did it like he had been doing it for years and had mastered it. He had mastered the art of stealing; it was highly doubtful that he had any interest in poetry.

"Like I said, the Timekeeper. We're soul mates. We can't ignore each other or try to hide from one another even if we wanted to; it brings us together." He sighed, which made my heart drop a little more.

He didn't want to see me, he wished he could stay away and never have to put up with me. All these small thoughts kept rushing through my mind, but I had to shake them off. I couldn't let him see me as weak, not again. I needed to try and at least pretend that the Timekeeper wasn't such a big deal, when in fact it was. But to Jase it didn't seem to be. He seemed like he couldn't care less about having a soul mate, and that was what hurt me the most.

"Are you here to explain yourself?" I said, not meaning to sound so bitter.

He called over to Ruby, the petite waitress with a pixie cut, and ordered himself a hot chocolate. Well at least I found one thing we had in common, but our love for hot chocolate couldn't possibly be why we were soul mates. We must have more in common, or this was just a big mistake and the Timekeeper had gotten it all wrong.

"What was your name?" Jase asked, completely ignoring my question yet again.

I guess I was kind of glad that he actually wanted to know my name though, but I still needed an explanation for what took place yesterday. "You didn't answer my question, Jase." I said with clear annoyance in my voice.

He chuckled before resting his elbows on the table that separated us, "I don't need to explain anything to you." He hissed just as Ruby came back with his steaming hot chocolate.

"Would you like another drink, Candice?" She grinned as she placed the cup in front of Jase. I shook my head, receiving a small smile this time, before she walked back to the counter.

I glanced around the room and noticed that there was only one other couple in here, but unlike Jase and I, they were laughing and holding hands. The couple looked to be in their mid twenties, but you could tell they were in love. The smiles on their faces and the way their eyes seemed to sparkle when they looked at each other told me that they were so happy and very much in love, a love I longed to have.

I glanced back at Jase to notice that he had been staring at me."What?" I asked, feeling a little self-conscious.

Was he checking me out? Was he admiring my long hair, my eyes, or was he looking at me in disgust? Maybe he was picking out all my flaws; the flaws I saw every time I looked into a mirror. He shook his head as if to get out of a trance, before taking a sip of his hot chocolate.

"Nothing, nothing. Just enjoying this hot chocolate." He said sarcastically, taking another sip before he continued, "How old are you, little Candy?"

His smirk grew wide across his face, obviously pleased with himself that he now knew my name. I could tell he was trying to make me crack, trying to break me down to the weak, pathetic girl he saw when we first met.

"I just turned sixteen, and don't call me that." I said, trying not to let him get to me.

I couldn't let him see that side of me again, I needed to be stronger than that and stick up for myself. I could tell he thought of me as a child and I hated that, especially since I was probably only a year or two younger than him.

"Oh, cute." He said, using a tone you would talk to a five year old with. Who did he think he was?

"How old are you then, Jase?" I hissed, my frustration growing with each word that was coming out of his mouth. He could tell I was starting to get annoyed, but he seemed to like it, as if that was what he wanted all along.

"Seventeen," he said triumphantly, as if being seventeen gave him some kind of power and more respect.

I began to look around the cafe again, trying to calm myself down a little before I exploded. Why was he treating me like a child? And why did he want to purposely make me upset? Did he think that if he did then I wouldn't want to see him? Maybe he was trying to break the chain that connected us together? I didn't know what it was, but thinking about it all seemed to make me even more frustrated. Soul mates weren't supposed to hate each other, but the way this day had been going it was turning out to be just that.

"What's wrong Candy is something bugging you?" He said with a wide grin spread across his face.

He knew exactly what was bugging me, and he was still trying to make it worse. I couldn't understand what I had done to make him act like this towards me. We only met yesterday and already he was making me want to slap him repeatedly across his attractive face. Soul mates are supposed to like each other, tell jokes and go on cute dates to the movies or the beach, but not Jase and I. So far my dreams of having a perfect relationship looked very slim, and they were only about to get worse.

"Nothing. Nothing at all." I smiled through gritted teeth, trying to hold my anger and frustration back.

He took the last sip of his hot chocolate, keeping eye contact the whole time. He placed his elbows on the table, before resting his head in his rather large hands. His plump lips turn into that mischievous smirk, and I knew that he had more to say. I knew he wasn't finished trying to torment me yet, and I also knew I was going to crack any moment now.

The rest of the cafe could feel the tension between Jase and I; they kept glancing over every now and then. The young couple were no longer laughing, but whispering just as the rest of the cafe seemed to be. I knew exactly what they were all whispering about, it is all about the same thing, that thing being Jase and I. They were all waiting for somebody to crack, and I knew that sooner or later, and that somebody was going to be me.

"Candy, you don't seem okay. Do you want me to call your daddy to come take you home?" He said in a childish voice.

But I couldn't reply, I was speechless. All the sadness and frustration I had been feeling had completely vanished, and all that remained was anger. But it had grown and now it seemed to have turned into rage. I could feel my face burning up, and I just couldn't help myself. I stood up so fast that the chair I was sitting on fell behind me, crashing loudly on the floorboards. Jase couldn't even prepare for what was coming, and honestly either could I. I couldn't control myself, and before I knew it my hand had made contact with his cheek.

"How dare you talk to me like I'm some immature child. I am one year younger than you, Jase. Being seventeen doesn't make you some sort of king that gives you the right to treat me like shit. You hardly know me, and you think you're better than me and think you have a right to treat me this way and talk to me like I'm a five year old. Well guess what, it doesn't." I yelled, but I couldn't stop the words as they poured out of my mouth. I had never been so angry in my life; the words just kept piling out one after the other.

"You are the most ignorant asshole I have ever met and I feel sorry for you because being like that is going to get you nowhere in life. I just hope you realise what a terrible person you are and fix it before it gets you into serious trouble and you end up getting arrested or worse, you end up dead."

I turned away and headed towards the door, noticing that all eyes were on me, except Jase's. I turned back towards him just as I reached the cafe door; my eyes began to fill with tears.

"And just to make you feel like an even bigger arse, my father died before I was even born, so I never got to know him. You should watch that mouth of yours, Jase. It's going to get you hurt one day."

I walked out of the cafe in such a rush that I almost knocked a young man down as he was walking past."I'm so sorry." I tried to say, but all he would have heard were sobs.

Tears fell from my eyes and ran down my cheeks; I couldn't believe what had just happened. My hand was red and stung, I didn't realise how hard I had slapped him. Oh my god, I actually slapped him. The person I was supposed to love, I had just slapped across the face so hard my hand hurt. I was never a violent person; I never thought I could hurt anybody until now. But, my god did he deserve it.

As if him being a thief wasn't enough, he was selfish, ignorant, and an absolute asshole. I couldn't care less if I was never to see him again, because I would be much happier without a soul mate than with Jase as one.

(Disclaimer: The poem is not mine.I give full credit to whoever wrote it, as I found it on Tumblr.)

Chapter Six

"Congratulations sweetie, you passed." The lady behind the desk smiled as she handed over a pink slip of paper with a checklist of things that had been ticked off, and my new drivers licence card.

Even though I was only sixteen, I was now old enough to drive on my own. It had always been that when you turned 18 you could get a probationary licence, but that changed ten years ago to the age of sixteen. I guess it's not really very different to America, but we had to get a probationary licence before we got a full one. It's pretty similar to a full licence, just with harsher penalties and a few different rules we had to follow. I didn't care though; I was just so happy that I would be able to drive myself wherever I wanted, whenever I wanted.

"Thank you so much!" I grinned, before walking out and spotting my mother waiting patiently for me in the car park.

She looked nervous until she saw the huge smile spread across my face, then her expression instantly matched mine. I ran up to her and she wrapped her arms around me, squeezing me tightly into her chest.

"Congratulations, Candice, I'm so very proud of you." She whispered into my ear, before letting go and walking over to the driver's side of our car. I gave her a strange look that made her laugh.

"Can't I drive you since it will probably be the last time you'll need me to?" She pouted; the realisation of her baby girl growing up finally seemed to hit her.

I sighed and gave in, knowing that she was right. I had been the baby forever and now that I was getting older mother didn't know what to do anymore. Soon enough Jacob and Patricia would be moving out and it would just be me left, and I won't want to move out and leave our poor mother on her own in our huge house. The thought of my mother being alone made my heart break, I couldn't possibly leave her when she had given so much to our family. I pushed the thoughts aside just as we pulled into our seemingly endless driveway, our house barely visible from the road.

She parked the car and we both got out and began to head towards the house, before she paused. I turned around and opened my mouth to ask what was wrong, but she spoke before I could get a word out.

"Wait here, Cand, I have something for you." She smiled softly and started walking towards the back of the house.

I stood there puzzled at what she could be doing, wondering what on earth she could have for me. Maybe she was grabbing one of those beautiful lily flowers that grew over near the great gum tree in our scenic backyard. When I was younger she would always come inside with what seemed like millions of different flowers, and we would sort through them all and put them into vases and spread them all around the house. Our house would always smell just as it did every spring when the flowers bloomed and the garden looked so elegant and peaceful. Even in the autumn when the flowers seemed to disappear and the leaves turned to red's and orange's, the garden still looked enchanting.

Mother always told me of the time when we were in the garden together picking out flowers, and she was sticking them in my hair and I told her I felt like a fairy princess. She told me I had told her that when I meet my soul mate and we were to get married, it would be in the spring time right here in our backyard, because the flowers were so beautiful and it always looked perfect.

I knew my mother would want that to happen more than anything, but that was because she still had no clue about the awful soul mate I had been stuck with. I knew that if I told her she would think I was just exaggerating and being stupid, that my soul mate couldn't possibly be that bad because I am 'special' and would have a 'perfect' relationship just like her and my father did. My relationship was far from that though, so far away that I wouldn't even call it a relationship to begin with.

At that moment, an engine started to roar, bringing me out of my thoughts and back to reality. It was definitely the sound of a car, but what was she doing in the car? Did she forget something? I couldn't even begin to think of an explanation for what my mother was up to, my thoughts had become so puzzled that I don't even think a champion puzzle maker could fix them. Just as I was about to go around the back of the house, a sleek blue car came rumbling around the corner. I could see my mother in the driver's seat grinning from ear to ear, as she honked the horn repeatedly before coming to a stop and jumping out.

"Surprise!" She screamed as she walked over to me, holding the keys in an outstretched hand. But before I could even attempted to say anything, she continued although in a much more serious tone.

"This car used to be your father's; it was his pride and joy. Every night when he would come home from work he would be working on this car, right up until he started to get sick. Daniel and Jacob used to sit in his shed and pass him tools and would always watch him as he worked on it. It was his baby, and now it's yours." She paused for only a second, then continued.

"When we found out that I was pregnant with you, he was very sick and he couldn't work on the car anymore. I remember one night when he couldn't sleep because of the pain; he turned to me and put his hand on my stomach. He sighed then, as if he knew he wasn't going to make it to see you when you were born. Then he moved his hand from my stomach and cupped my face; he said to me that no matter what happened he wanted you to have the car, even if it sounded a little strange then, but that way, at least you would have a part of him, even if you never got to see him."

She was crying, but I could tell they were tears of joy. I tried to be strong as I took the keys out of her trembling hand, but I wasn't strong enough. I burst into tears as my mother pulled me into her arms holding me firmly. I couldn't believe that this car had been here all this time, and I had never seen it or known about it. I felt slightly angry at my family for keeping this from me for all these years, but then I figured out that if mother had have tried to give it to me any other time in my life, I knew I wouldn't have appreciated it as much as I did right now.

* * *

I think mother already regretted giving me the car; I hadn't been home all day. The freedom that came with driving alone was wonderful and something you wouldn't understand unless you had driven by yourself I suppose. I spent most of the day driving through town and out to the countryside, even past the beach where the smell of salt engulfed my car through the open window. There was only one place I really wanted to go, but I couldn't bring myself to it. What if Jase was there again? I couldn't deal with another showdown like the one from the other day. But even if he wasn't there, I couldn't face the staff after that either.

Every time I drove past, I could feel something pulling me towards it, like the pull that drew Jase and I together for the first time. It had to be him, and I couldn't deal with his arrogance today. I was still quite mad and upset at the fact that my soul mate and I seemed to hate each other, though I had no idea what I had done to make him loathe me in the first place. I mean, he was rude to me from the very beginning and never even gave himself a chance to get to know me.

I pulled up out the front of the cafe, finally deciding that I had to come back sooner or later. I got out of the car and locked it, turning around to face the cafe and a very familiar face. He sat by the window where I always sat, where we sat and argued the other day. He looked different though, and I couldn't quite work out what it was that I hadn't noticed before. Perhaps it was the sad expression that masked his face, that made him look lonely and vulnerable, but I still couldn't be sure.

He looked up then and spotted me. He began to walk towards the door but I wasn't going to put up with this again. It was my turn to run without an explanation, my turn to leave him wondering what on earth he had done wrong. Except for the fact that he knew exactly what he had done wrong, unlike me.

I quickly jumped in the car and turned the key, the engine revved but it wouldn't fire up. I tried again but it was too late, he was by my side and my car didn't seem like it was going to start anytime soon.

The Timekeeper controlled a lot more than humans, it seemed.

I jumped out of the car and walked around the front to open up the bonnet, completely ignoring Jase's presence. Smoke leaked out as I opened the bonnet, causing both of us to cough.

"What on earth did you do to it?" Jase asked, attempting to wave away the smoke from his face. He leant in and began to play with a few parts of the engine that I had no clue what were called or what they even did, before I pulled him back by his blue shirt.

"No, Jase. I don't want your help and I don't need it. Now please leave before I leave a handprint on your other cheek this time." I hissed. I was already beginning to get mad, and I didn't want his help, even if I actually needed it. I will admit, I had no clue how to fix my car, or what was even wrong with it in the first place. Even if Jase was capable of fixing my car, I wasn't going to let him. I couldn't give in to him again, not like the last time.

I could just see that his face had saddened dramatically, and I wasn't sure if it was due to the smoke or something else, but it looked as though he had tears welling in the corners of his eyes. He turned towards me, the smoke had begun to disappear slightly so I could see him more clearly now. He avoided eye contact, and started to kick at a loose stone at his feet. He seemed like a completely different person than the one I had met only a few days ago. This Jase seemed shy, quiet and very lonely, whereas the other Jase was fierce, cocky and extremely egocentric.

"Candice, just listen for a moment. Let me fix your car, then we can talk and I promise it won't be like the last couple of times we bumped into each other." He said, almost desperately.

"Fine." I said coldly, though a small smile appeared on his lips. It wasn't a smirk that I had received from him the other day, but in fact a genuine smile.

After sitting in the drivers seat, turning the key over and over again, the engine finally roared to life. I contemplated for a second or two driving off without a chat or even a thank you but I shook the thought out of my head almost as soon as it had entered. I turned off the engine and got out of the car just as Jase pulled the bonnet down and dusted himself off.

"Thanks, Jase." I said, giving him a half-hearted smile. Was I being too harsh on him? He just helped me fix my car, and all I do in return is treat him poorly. But he deserved it, didn't he?

We walked over to the park adjacent from the Cozy Cafe' and sat at a park bench that sat in front of a beautiful oak tree. Being Autumn, the leaves were a mixture of dusty orange and deep red's, but the tree was still full of leaves, only a few were scattered across the lush, green grass that lay below it. We sat in silence for a few minutes, but it didn't seem awkward. I was waiting for him to speak first, since he was the one that needed to apologise and explain himself to me. Jase cleared his throat then, sighing before he began to talk.

"Look, Candice, I am really sorry about how badly things started between us, and I know that none of it was your fault, it was all mine. I don't know why I did and said those things to you, but I really am sorry and I hope we could possibly start over?" He paused for just a moment, now looking into my eyes.

"I know I'm not what you expected for a soul mate, you don't deserve someone that treats you the way I have been. Nobody deserves to be with someone as arrogant, rude and troubled as me, and I'm sorry that you're stuck with me."

"Thank you for apologising, Jase. You can't be that bad of a person if you can manage an apology," I smiled softly, seeing the guilt through his alluring blue-green eyes and knowing that he was truly sorry.

"I still have to know something though." I murmured, drawing Jase's attention back to me.

"And what's that?" he asked, a hint of worry present in his husky voice.

"Why do you steal?" I whispered, afraid somebody would hear me and I would get Jase in trouble. But the coast was clear, seeing as there was barely anybody around us anyway. He sighed then, running his hand through his soft blonde locks.

"My family has been struggling with money for some time now, and I told my aunt that I would get a job and help her out. I really did plan on getting a job, but nobody would hire me. I then resorted to stealing, then selling the things I stole and giving the money to my aunt. She's done a lot for me, so I thought it was okay because she was so happy. I had become so good at stealing things and I could do it so easily."When we first met, that was the first time I had been caught, which is why I was so awful towards you when we met again. I blamed you as the reason I got caught, and I was angry because of it, which I know was stupid of me. I really can't tell you enough how sorry I really am for it." He said with sorrowful eyes.

"It's okay Jase, it's in the past now," I said, trying to act positive but failing miserably.

"I promise though, I am trying to change. I know you probably won't believe me now, but I have to change because if I don't, well like you said Candice, I'm going to get in a lot of trouble and I'm going to start losing the people I care about." He stated, before looking down at his hands as they fidgeted in his lap.

I began to really evaluate him then; I know that sounds really creepy, but he gave off a much happier vibe then when we had met previously. His skin tone was naturally bronzed, and made his messy blonde locks stand out even more than they already did. He had dark, long eyelashes that any girl would kill for, and they framed his eyes that resembled the colour of the sky so perfectly. I wanted to stare at him all day, taking in every inch of him and memorising it. He was so enticing, and the fact that he seemed to be trying to become a better person made my dreams of have the perfect relationship now seem possible.

"You hear that?" He smiled, startling me and bringing me out of my daydream. I tried to listen to something in particular, but all I could hear was cars zooming past, and the sound of birds chirping in a nearby tree.

"Hear what?" I asked, raising an eyebrow, still trying to pick out a unique sound.

Jase chuckled then, before he grabbed my wrist and flipped it over, exposing my Timekeeper. His touch made me flinch, not expecting it to be so gentle. His hand was warm and a little clammy, but I didn't mind. The fact that his touch made my heartbeat quicken had to mean something, he had to be the one.

"It's our Timekeeper's, don't you hear it? We're soul mates." He smirked, that same cheeky smirk I had seen the other day. I was still so confused at to what he was trying to do, until it finally hit me. He was trying to start over, trying to recreate how we were supposed to have met.

"My name is Jase, Jase Williams. And what's yours?"

Chapter Seven

I was still trying to figure out if yesterday actually happened, or if it was all just a dream. I now had the slightest hope that Jace and I could actually have the relationship I had dreamt of since I was a young girl, but we were still very far off that. He was so different to the boy I had first met, and now I wasn't sure which one was the real him.

"What's on your mind, Candy?" My mother asked, not taking her eyes off the road that stretched out in front of us.

We were on our way to meet Lucy to try on dresses for the wedding, as it was just over a week away. I was so honoured to be apart of the wedding, and I was beyond excited for it. There was only one thing that kept creeping into my mind, no matter how much I tried to push it away.

"It's about Jase. I still don't think he should be invited to the wedding," I sighed, which caught my mother by surprise.

"Why do you think that sweetie? He's your soul mate after all, and we're all so excited to meet him," she replied with a look of reassurance.

I didn't bother replying to that, it was pointless trying to argue with my mother. She still didn't know what my first couple of encounters were like with Jase, and I really didn't want her to know either. I hated lying to her, but it was best left with her believing my relationship was just like her and my father's. Of course my hopes seemed to be higher than when we first met, but I knew Jase and I still had a long way to go before we could even be classed as 'love'.

We pulled up next to a small bridal shop and I pushed all my previous thoughts to the back of my mind, before hopping out of the car and following mum into the shop. It was quite a small shop, and only Lucy, Patricia, Lucy's mother Louise, and an employee filled the store as we walked in. Lucy was as bubbly as ever; she had already found several dresses she wanted to try on.

"Linda! Candy! I'm so happy you're here!" Lucy squealed as she ran over to us. She was so full of excitement, it reminded me of a child in a candy shop.

She ran into one of the change rooms, dragging my mother and her own along behind her. Patricia gave me a small wave before disappearing behind the red velvet curtain where Lucy was. I started to walk around, skimming my fingers along the dresses that covered the walls of the small store. I knew we were supposed to be trying on bridesmaid dresses as well, but I didn't expect to be the one to choose what dress we were going to wear.

The bell that hung over the door chimed then, as a short blonde-haired woman strutted in. I guessed she was the maid of honour, and Lucy's best friend. I had never met her before, but Lucy had mentioned her a few times at the wedding planning days she had organised. She was never there for them though, which I thought was a bit strange since she was the made of honour.

"Hi, you must be Lucy's best friend? I'm Candice," I smiled, receiving a small smile in return.

"Hazel," she answered bluntly, before disappearing behind the curtain with the others.

I sighed, and began to look through the endless supply of dresses. Some of them were hideous, and I just prayed that the other two girls wouldn't pick them to wear. Lucy wanted us to pick the bridesmaid dresses, but I knew that really meant that Hazel and Patricia were in charge of choosing the dress.

"You two go find a bridesmaid dress! I don't want to waste anymore time!" I heard Lucy growl as Patricia and Hazel left the change room and began filing through dresses. I decided it was best if I stayed out of their way, my opinion wasn't needed anyway. I sat down on an elegant, velvet-covered sofa with gold framing. Although it was appealing to look at, it wasn't very comfortable.

I wasn't sure how long I had been sitting there, but I must have been off in my own little world because all of a sudden I heard screams come from the change room beside the one Lucy was in. Hazel stormed out of the change room wearing a funky green silk gown with a long cut that reached up to her mid thigh and a very low 'v' that showed off her quite obvious fake breasts. Patricia came out then, wearing something the complete opposite. She had a red silk gown that hugged at her curves, but only went down to her knees. It had a straight neckline and then lace that went up her neck and down her arms, finishing at her tiny wrists.

Lucy came out then, wearing a stunning white gown with detailing all over the bodice and a very low-cut back. The straps looked like snow-covered petals, and the rest of the dress was chiffon with the same flower detailing scattered through. It was absolutely gorgeous and fitted her like a glove, except she didn't look very happy.

"What is going on?" She snarled at Hazel and Patricia, who were glaring at one another.

They both began trying to explain their side of the story, which I didn't bother waiting around to hear. I walked over to the back of the store and started rummaging through the gowns, trying to mute the heated argument behind me. I pull back a black Cinderella dress and find a gorgeous, strapless lavender gown with a ribbon tied around the bodice, just before the chiffon skirt began. It was nice and simple, but it was still so beautiful.

I grabbed the dress and slipped into one of the change rooms, somehow not being noticed by anyone. I slipped my denim shorts and white shirt off, before sliding into the soft material. It was a little too big around the waist, and was definitely too long for my petite body, but it still looked gorgeous. I walked out of the change room then, holding the dress up so I wouldn't stand and trip over the bottom of it, and cleared my throat.

The girls stopped arguing and looked at me. I didn't know what I was expecting from them; honestly I didn't even think I would've gotten their attention so easily.

"What do you think of this one?" I croaked, suddenly becoming nervous as all eyes were on me. I felt like I had just dropped a lit match in a room filled with explosives. There was complete silence, and I wanted to wrap myself up in the thick curtains that were behind me.

Lucy smiled then, and gave me a tight hug. I could now see that she had tears streaming down her rosy cheeks, as she pulled back and twirled me around.

"Thank you Candice, it's perfect," she whispered, before pulling me into her arms once again.

* * *

We had decided to get some lunch at a small restaurant just up the street from the bridal shop. After deciding on the dresses, the employee took our measurements and we were good to go. Hazel left from the store, saying she had to be somewhere, so it was just Lucy and her mother, my mother, Patricia and I.

Patricia was still a little annoyed about the whole dress situation, but she did tell me she liked the dress I picked, which made me feel a bit better. I felt bad for picking the dress, which sounds awfully strange I know, but I felt as if I wasn't supposed to choose. I was glad that Lucy liked it though, but I still felt as though I was out of line.

"You ladies ready to order?" A familiar voice asked as he appeared at the end of the table. I looked up from my menu then, spotting the familiar head of dark curls and those enchanting green eyes.

"Oh, hi, Candice," he grinned, which caught the rest of the table's attention as well. My mother's eyes grew wide, and I knew exactly why.

"Hi, Ryan," I smiled back, noticing the disappointment flick over my mother's expression once she realised he wasn't my soul mate.

Once we had ordered and Ryan had left, mum began questioning me. I knew it was coming, and I knew half was because she was getting impatient with me. She wanted to meet Jase as soon as I found out he was my soul mate, and she had expected him to come over straight after we had met. I wasn't sure if her relationship with my father was like that or not, but I knew ours wasn't going to be like theirs once was, not even if we ever became a real couple.

Ryan came back with our food, giving me a shy wave as he walked away. I never even knew he worked here, but then again, I still didn't really know that much about him at all. He was in my art class, and he didn't have a soul mate, that's basically all I knew. I couldn't understand how he could be so calm and generally happy all the time, after the horrid red line appeared on his wrist. I wondered what he was doing when it happened, and what his instant reaction was when it did happen. It would've been so hard to deal with.

After plenty of arguing, my mother paid for the meal and we began to walk out when Ryan called out to me. I spun around as the others walked outside and into the cool autumn air, waving them to go without me. Of course my mother waited behind, a hint of curiosity spread across her expression.

"I finish in about ten minutes. Want to go for a walk?" Ryan proposed, his green eyes sparkling in the afternoon sunlight.

"My mum is waiting for me, I can't-"

"I can take you home. I have my licence," He practically begged. I sighed, and walked outside towards my mum.

"Ready to go now?" She smiled as she pulled the car keys out of her tan-coloured handbag.

"Actually, I was going to chill with Ryan for a bit. He said he can take me home," I stated.

"If that's okay with you?" I added; realising what I said came out a bit too demanding. She sighed then, but nodded and kissed me on the forehead.

"Don't be home too late then!" She yelled as she walked off to the car.

Ryan was out within a few minutes of my mother leaving, and we started off in silence as we walked the opposite direction that my mother had only moments before. I noticed his sleeves were rolled down, so I couldn't see the dreadful red line that caused so many people pain. He must have noticed that I was looking at his arm, because he sighed then, breaking the silence.

"Everyone looks at me like that. I hate it," He groaned, tugging on his sleeve as if it would make the Timekeeper disappear.

I think I would rather have it removed, than have the red line always there for the world to see. It was just a constant reminder that your other half no longer exists, and for people like Ryan, a reminder that you will never get to meet them.

"I'm sorry, I didn't mean to-"

"Don't be, I suppose I'm used to it," He sighed again; the cool breeze flicked his curls back, revealing a pale forehead that was usually hidden.

We walked in silence again, but it wasn't a horribly awkward silence, it was quite a relaxing and calming silence. It was nice to be able to be with someone that you didn't feel awkward around, even though I hardly knew Ryan.

"So where are we going anyway?" I asked, curiosity finally taking over.

"Oh, just some secret place I love to go to when I'm alone." He smiled, almost mischievously.

I raised my eyebrow, which just made him chuckle.

"Don't worry, we're already here," He grinned, coming to a stop at what looked like an abandoned apartment building.

Now I was really freaking out. Why would he be taking me to a place like this? Had I gotten the wrong idea about him? Was he actually a serial killer and this was going to be the end for me? He chuckled again then, my face obviously giving away my paranoid thoughts.

"Stress less Candy, this is where I come to do my artwork. Come on, I'll show you." He reassured as he grabbed my hand and lead me up a quite unstable stairway.

(A/N: I'm so so so so SO sorry about the extremely late update! I know I am a horrible person and you are all very welcome to come and attack me, I will allow it (that is, if you can find me hehehehe). The picture on the side is Lucy's wedding dress (ooooh so pretty) and for the bridesmaid dress well you just have to use your imagination my little friend. I hope you guys liked this chapter I am sorry if it's boring it's kinda a filler-inner-ra chappie but hey at least it's an update right??? Please vote, comment, read x20 (apart from vote coz you can't sigh) and let all your pretty wattpad friends know that danielle has updated and her story needs some lovin! (I'm totally kidding, but I won't stop you if you do...) Thank you for the ongoing support you're all beautiful creatures mwah xoxoxox)

Chapter Eight

The view from the apartment was actually stunning. It was abandoned as I had thought, but it wasn't a complete dump. There were old, worn-out couches placed in the centre of the dark wooden floor boards, and there was an old dining table in one of the corners. Two of the walls were made up completely of windows, and all that could be seen was the sun setting over the beautiful skyscrapers.

It could've been a pretty romantic moment actually, not that I wanted to admit it. But Ryan seemed to think so as well, and maybe he even planned for it to be. He sat on one of the couches, picking up a sketch pad before gesturing me over. I sat down beside him, noticing that the couch was a lot smaller than a normal two-seater couch; we were sitting quite close together. He opened the sketch pad then, and pulled out a couple of greylead pencils from his pockets. He handed them to me, along with the sketch pad.

"Draw me," he grinned, before pushing his dark curls out of his eyes.

I raised my eyebrow; surely he wasn't serious? I wasn't an artist, and I definitely wasn't good at drawing portraits. I could never capture exactly what I saw, and it always bothered me. So instead I would draw landscapes or create my own pieces; I found it a lot easier and it was calming at the same time.

The serious look that spread across Ryan's face told me he wasn't joking, which only made me laugh.

"I can't draw portraits Ryan, I'm hopeless at it," I sighed, but Ryan didn't reply. He was staring at me, his startling green eyes filled with emotion. I couldn't tell if it was sadness or confusion, but they looked so enchanting. I suddenly wanted to draw them, or at least try. Eyes were complicated to draw, but I had been practicing lately.

I picked up one of the pencil's and let it glide across the page. All my surrounding's became non-existent. The busy street with car's zooming past, the birds or the sound of people chattering, it all vanished. All that I could see was the paper and Ryan, staring intently towards me.

I hadn't even realised that I had finished his eyes and moved on to the frame of his face. I wanted to draw all of him, and I wanted so badly to capture everything perfectly. From the small dimple on his left cheek when he smiled, to the soft curls of his hair that seemed to frame his face in a way that I could only express through perception. He was intriguing and mysterious, and I was taking in all of his features one by one.

The light caught at his wrist then, reminding me of his Timekeeper. The blood red line stood out so much with his pale complexion, and I realised I had completely forgotten that he didn't have a soul mate. How on earth could I forget something like that? The realisation dawned on me then that while studying Ryan, I had completely forgotten about my own soul mate. I looked down at my half-finished work, and was actually impressed. Of course, it wasn't like a photograph of Ryan, but I had portrayed him in the way I saw him. I had noticed the small details about him, and somehow made them stand out on the paper.

I was still in a daze, until I realised it was almost night outside. The city lights were illuminating and made everything else around it seem to glow. I stood up abruptly, which startled Ryan.

"What's the matter?" he said as he stood up, sounding genuinely concerned.

I shook my head, before handing him the sketch pad, "nothing. It's getting late, I should probably go."

His eyes widened when they fell on the drawing. He looked shocked, and I was afraid he hated it. But he looked back up then, and grinned. It was a clumsy sort of grin, but it suited him perfectly.

"I thought you said you couldn't draw portraits?" he laughed, which made me smile in return.

We left the apartment then, and began silently walking along the street. We stayed silent for a while, but I didn't mind. I liked taking in our surroundings. The city at night seemed to come alive; it was such a different atmosphere to what I usually saw during the day. We lived too far out to come into the city at night, well so my mother always said. Honestly it wasn't that far, but mum didn't like going into the city after dinner. It was strange really, she was missing out on all this beauty, because she thought it was dangerous at night.

I glanced over at Ryan, only to catch him staring at me. He looked away, and I was sure I could see his cheeks turn a rosy pink. Although it was dark, the streetlights casted enough light to see his face, and see that he was now trying to hide behind his curls. I began to wonder why he was staring at me, or how long for. He clearly didn't want to be caught though, as I noticed from his reaction.

I didn't want to ask about it though. It wasn't like I hadn't caught people staring at me before, although usually it was because people at school had never seen me before, and were trying to figure out if I was new or not. Something told me that Ryan wasn't doing the same kind of stare, so I was still a little curious about it. There was something else I wanted to know a lot more then why he was staring at me though, and before I knew it, my mouth had already began to blurt it out.

"What's it like?"

He looked back at me then, his cheeks no longer tinged pink. He raised an eyebrow, clearly confused as to what I was actually asking.

"What's what like?" he questioned, before letting out a brief chuckle.

I could have thought of something else to ask him instead; I should have thought of something else, but every time I thought about Ryan, the question would always linger in the back of my mind. I wished it was an easier question to ask though, and I wished I hadn't asked out of the blue.

"You know, um. Knowing you won't ever meet your soul mate," I said, instantly regretting it once it had left my mouth.

He flinched at the word 'soul mate', and I knew it was still an extremely touchy subject. Of course it's a touchy subject, Candice! How stupid can you be? I didn't know what I was thinking; how could someone want to talk about this? About they're soul mate dying before they could have even met them, and knowing they will never get to meet them. A pang of guilt rose in my chest then. All this time I had been complaining that Jace couldn't possibly be my soul mate; I never really thought about what it would be like if I didn't, and never could, have a chance to meet my soul mate.

"Ryan, I'm sorry I didn't mean to-" I started to apologize, finally realising what a stupid idea it was in the first place, but Ryan cut me off before I got the chance to finish.

"No it's fine, really," he said, no obvious signs of sadness evident in his expression.

He walked over to a park bench then, which coincidentally happened to be the same one Jase and I sat on yesterday, and sat down. It felt like it had been days ago, and I was still so confused about the whole situation. I wondered what our next encounter was going to be like. Would it be like the first few times we met, or more like yesterday? I didn't know, and honestly I was afraid to find out. Of course, I was going to sooner or later, but I hoped it was going to be later, rather than sooner. Maybe it would give me more time to think about what to do, but then again all I had been doing since yesterday was thinking about him.

Ryan sighed then, bringing me out of my thoughts and back to reality. I cursed myself for thinking so much about my soul mate troubles, when Ryan's were ten times worse.

"It's been hard, really hard. But it's so strange at the same time. Like I feel as though a piece of me will always be missing, but then again, I never even met her. How can you miss someone you've never met?" He sighed again, before I sat beside him.

I opened my mouth to say something; I wasn't sure what I was going to say, but I had to say something, didn't I? I could have said that it was going to be okay, but I wasn't sure it was. I knew life wasn't all about your soul mate or the Timekeeper, but sometimes that's what it felt like. If you didn't have a soul mate, you were kind of disconnected to the rest of our world. It was accidental, and no one meant for it to happen, but if you didn't have a soul mate, people looked down on you. Not in a way of disgust, but a more sympathetic and sometimes, superior way. I thought it was awful, how could people like Ryan or my mother have any say in what had happened to their soul mates? Why should people with soul mates look at them any differently?

I closed my mouth then, knowing whatever I could say wouldn't really be much help. Ryan didn't notice though; he was staring down at his lap where his hands sat, curled together.

"I guess-" he began again. I watched as his fingers twirled around one another, his Timekeeper barely noticable in the darkness.

"-I guess it will get better eventually. I mean, there's bound to be other mateless girls around, right?" he chuckled, but I could still hear the sadness in his voice.

I gave him a half smile, still not sure what to say. I wanted to comfort him, and I wanted him to find another girl, but how could he? If he ever did find another mateless girl, he'd always know that they weren't supposed to be together. He'd know that they were meant for two completely different people, and that would always be at the back of his mind. I knew it would always be at the back of mine if I was in his situation, which I hoped would never happen.

"You're a great girl, Candice," Ryan smiled, causing my cheeks to flush.

"And I think you deserve a better soul mate. You know, one that doesn't run away from you or infuriate you on purpose," he sighed, before looking down at his lap again.

I had almost forgotten that I had told Ryan about what had happened with Jase. I didn't know what it was about him, but I felt like he wouldn't judge me or think I was just overexaggerating the situation. I still hadn't mentioned it to my mum, and I had hardly spoken to Claire about him. I knew they both wouldn't have believed me if I told them. I mean, it was still pretty hard for me to believe, and I was the one who witnessed it. But it felt good to tell Ryan, seeing as he didn't treat me like I was fragile and still a child.

I hadn't told him that I had seen Jase yesterday though, and that Jase had apologised for his behaviour. I guess I just didn't have the time yesterday, and I wanted to try and figure out what to do on my own. Not that it really mattered what Ryan thought; Jase was still my soul mate and there wasn't much I could do about that.

"We should probably go, my mum's probably worried about me," I sighed, brushing myself off as I stood up from the bench.

Ryan looked up at me, before nodding and standing up beside me. We walked back towards the restaurant Ryan worked at, and turned down the next street over. I didn't even know he could drive, or that he had his licence. But there was a lot I didn't know about him, even though I felt like he knew me so well. We hopped in the car, the engine roaring to life, before he drove off, leaving the city behind us.

It was silent once again, and I was worried I had made him upset with something I had said. Or hadn't said, I suddenly realised. I hadn't replied when he talked about meeting another girl, and I hadn't replied when he complimented me either. I didn't even say thank you, or explain to him that Jase wasn't as bad as I had originally thought.

We pulled up at a set of traffic lights then, and I was about to say something to Ryan, when something outside caught my eye. The police station was on the corner closest to me, and a few officers were standing beside one of their cars. It looked like they were trying to pull someone out of the car, someone who was clearly intoxicated. After a few seconds, the guy was out of the car and was being pulled towards the front entrance of the station. The guy was still struggling in the two officer's hands, clearly trying to get away. His head shook back and forth, along with the rest of his small body. Well it looked small compared to the policemen beside him.

And that's when I froze. I recognised the blonde hair, the strong jawline, the broad shoulders, everything. His face was hidden by the shadows, until he was inside the building and I could see him through the glass doors. I couldn't believe it, and I didn't want to. I thought-

The car began to move again, but we didn't make it very far before I screamed.

"Stop the car!"

I felt the brakes lock and was jerked forward, the seatbelt cutting into my neck. Ryan spun the wheel and pulled over to the side of the road, turning the car off before glaring at me.

"What on earth-" He began to say, but I was already out of the car and sprinting towards the police station before he could say anything else.

I reached the glass doors, trying to catch my breath. I could hear Ryan yelling after me; he probably thought I was crazy. I opened the glass doors and walked in, ignoring the sick feeling in my stomach. I hoped I had been wrong, that the person I had seen wasn't actually who I thought it was. I began heading towards the counter where a lady sat, typing at her computer, before someone grabbed my arm and spun me around.

"What are you-" Ryan began to say, with enough anger that it sent a shiver through my entire body. I had never seen him so angry before, and to know it was caused by me made me feel ten times worse. But he stopped talking; why did he stop?

I noticed then that he was looking past me, over my shoulder. I spun back around, hoping it wasn't who I thought it was. But there he stood, hands in cuffs and blue-green eyes peering back at me.

"Oh," Ryan whispered then, clearly understanding why I had made him stop the car.

"Jase?" I stuttered, still unable to believe my eyes.

(A/N: a massive thank you to @perfidy for making me the beautiful cover on the side and for being such a dedicated reader! you should all go follow and love her kk?i hope you guys enjoy this chapter! please leave me comments and stuff, it makes me feel good hehe mwah xxx)

Chapter Nine

"Candice?" Jase stuttered. He was clearly just as surprised to see me, as I was to see him.

He looked over my shoulder then, obviously just noticing Ryan for the first time. For a second, I had completely forgotten about him as well. All that I could think about was what was going on in front of me, and why Jase had lied to me yet again. I could feel the anger rising inside of me, and I wanted so badly to slap him across the face again, but I figured it wasn't going to do much. And being in a police station surrounded by police officers wouldn't really be the best place to do it either.

"What did you do?" I wanted to sound angry, I was furious believe me, but all that I could manage was a nervous whisper.

It must have been scarier than I thought, or maybe I was just over-analysing him, but he bit his lip. I hated to admit it, especially in the situation we were in, but he looked so vulnerable, which made him look so attractive. You're supposed to think he's attractive; he's your soul mate. And what a good soul mate he was. Running away when we first met, stealing from shops, abusing me, and now he had been arrested for God knows what. But before I could find out, one of the police officers stepped forward.

"Excuse me Ma'am, but may I ask who you are and what you're doing here?" His voice was deep and had a slight European accent.

"Oh, um. I'm Candice Smith and-" I wasn't sure what to say next. Why was I here?

"Well I'm here because he's my soul mate," I sighed then, before looking down at my feet.

It was wrong of me to feel slightly ashamed that Jase was my soul mate. But I felt like I was allowed to be ashamed. He had been so awful to me, and really he had brought it on himself. So maybe it wasn't really that bad of me to be ashamed. I hated the feeling though, and I still felt like a horrible person for it. Why couldn't he just have been an ordinary seventeen-year-old boy that went to my school and liked to play football or something? I could deal with ordinary, but not this.

"Wait, did you say Smith?" the other police officer asked then.

"Um, yeah I did." I replied, raising an eyebrow.

The two guards looked at each other then, still keeping a firm grip on Jase's arms. He hadn't looked at me since I first got here, and I hoped it was because he felt ashamed. I still had no idea why he was here, no idea what he had done. My first guess was that he had been caught stealing, even though he told me he was done with that. All that he had said to me yesterday had been utter bullshit; how could I have thought he could change so quickly?

"Are you, by any chance, Malcolm Smith's daughter?" the European officer asked then, which really caught my attention. How and why did he know my father?

"How do you know my father?" I said softly, before looking down at my feet.

"We used to work with him, or for him I should say. He was the Constable here, and a good one at that," European said, before gazing off.

He must've been reminiscing, thinking back to all the good times he had spent with my father. It was strange really, but it made me jealous and a little bit angry. He had memories with my father, he actually knew my father, unlike me. I'd kill to have at least one memory with him, but all I had were old photos that were scattered throughout our home.

"He was a good man, Candice," the other officer said, as if reading my mind and seeing how much it hurt that I had never actually met him.

I always wondered if it would've been worse if I actually did know him, like my brothers did. They had real memories with him, parts of him they could cherish forever, or would always bring them grief. But I suppose that would still be better than not having any memories at all, wouldn't it?

The two officers began to walk Jase down a narrow hallway, but I couldn't just let him go. I had too many questions that needed to be answered, and I had to at least try to get Jase out of the situation he was in, eve if he did most likely deserve it. I turned to face Ryan, telling him to wait, before I ran down the hallway after Jase.

"Stop!" I yelled once I had caught up to them, which gained me strange looks from the other people in the long hallway.

The officers turned around then, still holding Jase with a firm grip. Jase had a confused look on his face, and I could tell he was exhausted. Dark circles had appeared underneath his eyes, and he looked as though he would fall asleep at any second.

"Candice, we have important things to do. If you want, I can talk to you about your father tomorrow?" European was clearly tired as well, which made sense since it was almost midnight. My mother was going to kill me when I got home.

"Tony's right, Candice. Go home and get some rest now, and we'll talk to you tomorrow," the other officer sighed.

"No this isn't about my father, it's about him." I pointed towards Jase, which caught their attention, including Jase's.

They all raised their eyebrows, and Jase gave me a warning look, like he knew what I was planning. I didn't even know what I was planning, I just knew that I had to at least try and get Jase out of whatever mess he had gotten himself into. It wasn't because I cared about him, because he had made it very hard for me to, but it was more for my own benefit. I couldn't bring my family to a jail cell to meet my soul mate, now could I? I was being extremely selfish I know, but if it got him out of trouble, I doubted he would care what my reasons were.

"What about him?" Tony asked, curiosity evident in his tone.

"I know that he's probably caused you a lot of trouble in the past. Well he obviously still is, but I was wondering if, just this once, you could maybe let him off? For me?" I asked, in the nicest, most innocent way I could manage.

The men looked at each other, and I thought they were about to burst into laughter, but they didn't. Did what I say actually work?

"Candice, do you even know what he's done? If we let him go we'd be breaking the law, and making the streets dangerous."

Oh great, he's probably killed someone. Thank you Timekeeper, out of all the millions of boys in the world, you had to choose this guy to be my soul mate? You couldn't have paired me with someone caring and nice and funny, with the same interests as me? Someone like Ryan, you mean? A small voice chirped from the back of my mind, but I pushed it back instantly. I couldn't think about Ryan like that, even if he didn't have a soul mate and my soul mate was a complete douche.

"Make him do community service instead of throwing him in a cell, or making him go to Court," a voice piped up then, which I realised was actually my own.

Jase's eyes narrowed on me then, clearly not agreeing with what I had just said. He would rather go to jail, than do community service? What was his problem? I was surprised at how sober he appeared to be ever since he was dragged through the front doors of the station.

"That's not for us to decide, Candice. He'll still have to go to Court and let the Judge decide his fate," Tony sighed.

It was clear he was getting annoyed at me constantly bugging him, but I felt like I could crack him. If I pulled the right strings, I was sure he would be able to let Jase go tonight, without another mark on his record.

"Give him community service for a couple of weeks, and I'll make sure he won't bother you again."

Tony was about to reject my offer, I could tell. So I had to keep going,

"Please, if not for me, then do it for my father? I'm sure he would've pulled a few strings to let him off for me," I pleaded.

I didn't even know what I was saying anymore. How on earth was I going to make Jase change his rebellious ways when he didn't even want anything to do with me? I guess I'd just have to cross that bridge when I got to it, if the officers would ever let me get to it. I also knew it was wrong to bring my father into this situation and I felt guilty as hell for using him like that. How would I know if he would help me save my soul mate? What if he cared more about the law and doing what was right? Those were things I'd never know about my father, along with so many more.

The two men stayed silent for a moment, before turning towards each other to speak. I couldn't hear what they were saying, which had to be intentional. I didn't know what the big deal was; it wasn't like they had to hide anything from me. Jase was the person they were discussing after all, and he still stood right between them. There was no doubt that he could hear every word they were saying, but he didn't seem interested in them at all. His eyes seemed to bare right into me, which made me feel extremely uncomfortable. I was trying to help him, but it seemed like it had only made him hate me even more.

"Okay, Candice. You have a deal," Tony sighed finally.

He looked nervous, as though he could get in big trouble for helping me. He probably would get in trouble if he got caught, and I hadn't thought of what the consequences would be during my 'Save Jase' mission.

"But there are certain rules that we will have to enforce to make this work, alright?"

"And if Jase doesn't follow them, then he will come straight back here."

I nodded, before the other officer, who I now knew was Paul, began to tell us the rules. Well, he mainly spoke to Jase, but I guess I was the one that had to make sure this would actually happen. I knew they didn't trust Jase to keep this community service thing going, they just expected him to go back to his old ways. I couldn't let that happen; I had to at least try and make him do the right thing.

"You'll start at nine in the morning and finish at three. It'll be at the homeless shelter on Nixon Street, and you'll be there for ten days. We will check up on you every day to make sure you're there, and if you're not, then the deal is off. Got it?" Tony said, as he unlocked Jase's handcuffs.

"Yeah, whatever," Jase shrugged, before rubbing his wrists.

The officers said a few more things, before walking off down the hallway, leaving Jase and I alone. Before I could even say a word, he had already brushed past me and began to walk back towards the entrance. I wasn't letting him go that easily though, not after what I had done for him and not without knowing why he was here in the first place. I was about to follow him out the front door when a familiar face stepped in front of me.

"Ryan! I'm so sorry I didn't think you would still be here!" I said surprisingly.

"Well I couldn't leave you without a ride home, and I wanted to make sure you were okay-" He began to say, but I couldn't wait any longer.

"I'm sorry Ryan, I have to go after Jase. I'll be like ten minutes!" I was already through the front doors and walking down the few steps out the front before I could hear his reply.

The night air had dropped dramatically since I was out here last, and I had to hug myself to keep some body heat in. I began to look around for any signs of Jase, but he was nowhere to be seen. My heart sank; did I really just miss my chance? I started walking right, hoping that the Timekeeper would lead me towards him.

"What do you want now?" A voice sounded from behind me moments later, making me jump.

I turned around, somewhat happy to hear his voice even though he clearly didn't want to speak to me. The dark circles underneath his eyes seemed even darker and bigger than before. I wondered how I must look right now, seeing as it was the middle of the night. I pushed my hair behind my ear, suddenly feeling self-conscious of how I looked. It shouldn't have mattered to me, and I tried to focus instead on the reason I had followed Jase.

"I want to know what you did. And don't talk bullshit to me either, Jase. I want to know the truth. Now," I demanded, which surprised Jase, heck I even surprised myself.

"I didn't murder anyone, if that's what you're thinking," he sighed, before stifling a yawn and continuing.

"I just, I stole again. And then I got caught, end of story."

"No, Jase. It's not the end of the story. It's only just started actually," I began.

"This is serious, Jase. If you don't do this, you'll end up in jail. You can't want that, it'll ruin your life forever. You'll struggle finding jobs, because well, who would want to hire a criminal? And how would your family feel if you end up in prison? You should be thanking me for getting you this deal."

"My family?" Jase scoffed, before continuing.

"Let me tell you a little about my family. My mother left my dad and I when I was five, and I haven't seen or heard from her since. And well, my dad was an abusive alcoholic, who wanted nothing to do with me when I was eleven. Then my dad's sister took me in, and now I live with her and her daughter."

He became quiet then, and I wanted to comfort him. I wanted to be able to hug him without it being weird or feeling wrong. That's what I was supposed to do; I was his soul mate. I had never thought that maybe he acted this way because of his past. I couldn't imagine what it must've been like for him growing up; it would've been awful.

"They're the only family I have, and I just wanted to give my aunty something back, for putting up with me. I felt like I owed her, and I think I'll always feel that way. She saved me from him." He said so quietly I hardly heard him.

"Hey, it'll be okay. Just get through ten days of community service, and then find yourself a job, okay? I'll help you out if you need, Jase. Promise."

"Candice, I know you're just trying to help, but just stop it, okay?" He snapped, which caught me by surprise.

"Wh-what?" I stuttered.

I hadn't expected that kind of reaction from him, not at all. It was only about a minute ago that he was basically pouring his heart out to me, and now he seemed angrier than I had ever seen him before. How could he have changed so quickly?

"This isn't your life, it's mine. I know you don't like the way I've been living it, but you can't decide what I can and can't do. You can't treat me like I'm your child! We may be soul mates, but that doesn't give you any fucking right to try and control my life. So please, just stop!" Jase yelled, and began to walk away.

"No, don't you dare run away from me again, Jase! I'm not trying to control you, I'm trying to get you to do what's right!" I shouted back at him, all feelings of sympathy for him had vanished and were replaced with anger.

"You don't get to choose which path I take, just because you think it's the right one! Let me make that choice on my own!" He took a step closer this time, and I could see now how angry he really was.

Was I really trying to control his life? I just wanted him to do good things, to be a better person. So, yes you are trying to control his life, Candice! You're trying to make him into your idea of a perfect soul mate. I shuddered. How could one small part of my be right, and the other be so wrong? I was trying to make him into something that was impossible, something perfect. I was wrong to try and make Jase change, he had to learn to become a better person on his own.

It was too late now anyway, Jase had already started walking away. I couldn't manage another word; the truth had hit me hard. I was so caught up in thinking that I could change Jase, that I didn't realise what I was actually trying to do.

I also had no idea how badly I had just made things for us.

Chapter Ten

I woke to my phone buzzing near my ear, and somehow I still managed to answer it in my half-asleep state.

"Hello?" I said groggily, unsure of who had called despite having caller ID.

"Candice? Gosh, you were still asleep? Come on girl, it's past midday!" Claire's voice rang through the phone.

"I had a late night last night," I yawned, rubbing my eyes to try and wake myself up a bit more.

"With your boy toy? Oh, this is exciting! We're going on a shopping trip, and I want all the goss!" She said excitedly, before continuing.

"I'll be around in fifteen. Be ready!" She squealed, before hanging up the phone.

I sighed, before putting my phone on my bedside table. I wasn't in the mood to do anything today, not after last night anyway. After Jase left, I walked back to Ryan's car and waited for him. We didn't talk the whole ride home, which I was thankful for. I didn't want really want him to know this time, but he could probably tell what had happened anyway.

As I thought, my mother was furious when I got eventually home. It wasn't easy trying to make up an excuse for why I was so late. I didn't want to tell her it was because my soul mate had been arrested, and that I had bribed the officers to let him go, possibly just causing everyone much more trouble. I still hadn't told her much about Jase; I just didn't know what to tell her. I thought it would all be best left unsaid.

I slipped out of bed, before walking down the hallway and into the bathroom. After taking a quick shower, I hurried back to my room and pulled on some denim shorts and a simple loose-fitting black t-shirt. I threw my hair up into a ponytail, and had just finished putting on a bit of make-up when there was a knock at the door. Taking one last look in the mirror, I sighed, knowing that this was as good as it was going to get, before walking downstairs to answer the door.

"Hey Candy! Oh come on, that's all you're wearing? I gave you plenty of time to get ready!" She laughed.

She always judged my sense of style, though I wouldn't call it a style really. I never wore skirts or dresses, well apart from my school uniform, but that was different. Claire always liked to call me 'Plain Jane', because I never wore anything bright or pretty, whereas she was the complete opposite. She was wearing a bright floral sundress that looked gorgeous on her, not that much didn't look good on her anyway. She had the body that all teenage girls dreamed of, and although she was quite pale naturally, you never saw it. I think she would possibly die without fake tan.

"I'd like to see you get ready in under fifteen minutes, Claire," I teased, before walking out the door.

It felt like I hadn't seen Claire in forever, and we seemed to have a lot to catch each other up on. She told me all about her romantic week away at the beach with Alex, her soul mate. Unfortunately for me, she didn't try and refrain from telling me every little detail either. She had just started telling me about what they did at the beach in the middle of the night, when we pulled up at the shopping centre. I had never been so eager to get out of a car before in my life, until that moment.

"Okay, we're on a mission to get you something cute to wear. Or maybe something sexy, you know, for your man." She wiggled her eyebrows at me, which only made me laugh.

I hadn't realised how much she really didn't know about Jase. She only knew about when we first met; I hadn't spoken to her about much else that had happened between us. She must have thought that we had made up, and everything was fine. Why shouldn't she think that's what happened? It would've been so much easier if it had.

We walked through the huge glass sliding doors then, and I could practically feel the excitement coming from Claire. She was constantly buying new clothes, new handbags, and new make-up. I don't think I had ever seen her wear the same outfit twice, or even just the same shirt. Her family was quite wealthy, and I suppose the fact that she was an only child meant she got whatever she wanted. I did get jealous of her sometimes, not because she was an only child, I loved my brothers more than anything, but because she was so wealthy.

It wasn't as if my family wasn't well off, because we had it pretty good and I would never complain, but my mother is constantly battling bills and trying to make us a wonderful meal every day. I had overheard her talking to Daniel one day; he was trying to make her sell our home. She had gotten quite upset about it, but I knew Daniel had a point. If she sold the house, and downsized, she wouldn't be struggling like she was.

"Hello! Earth to Candice!" Claire said, her manicured hands waving in front of my face.

"Sorry, Claire. I've just got a lot on my mind," I sighed.

"All the more reason for some retail therapy then!" She grabbed my arm before I could respond, and dragged me into one of the stores.

Usually shopping trips with Claire started with clothes shopping for Claire, then shoe shopping for Claire, and then finishing up with jewellery or make-up shopping for Claire. I would buy a shirt or two in between, but I was never really the main focus of the shopping trip. Today though, Claire seemed to want to shop for me. It was strange, and although she was still shopping for herself as well- if she wasn't I would've been worried- it was nice of her to make me try on things and actually include me in her shopping trip.

"Come on, Candice! I want to see what it looks like on you!" Claire called from the other side of the curtain.

I looked at myself in the mirror, struggling to believe I actually liked what I saw. Claire had given me a black tight-fitted dress that hugged my body and somehow accentuated the little curves that I had. It ended at my mid-thigh, and was quite low-cut, which felt extremely revealing to me, although Claire would've said it wasn't revealing anything at all. Turning around, I pulled the curtain aside and my eyes met Claire's, which grew wide when she saw me.

"Holy! I knew it would look good on you, but Candice! I didn't know you had curves like that!" She exclaimed, grabbing at my sides.

"Oh please, Claire. You'd look ten times better in this dress, and you know it," I said, but she didn't seem to be listening.

"I found some more things for you to try on! They will look great on you, trust me!" She handed over a pile of clothes, before heading into the change room beside mine.

I sighed, before closing the curtain. There was no way I could afford all of this, I wasn't sure I could even afford this dress. My mother had given me fifty dollars before I left, telling me to spoil myself with it. I don't think she realised the Claire had such expensive taste. I still tried on all the items she had given me, and she had been right. They actually did look good on me. I had never really tried to look good or dress up this nicely before, but Claire did it every day. Even at school, she always seemed to have a different hairstyle, whereas I just pulled it up into a ponytail every day.

I tried the last item of clothing on, which was a skirt. Claire hadn't given me any shorts or plain t-shirts to try on, to my disappointment. The skirt was short, reaching to my mid-thigh, and seemed to flow outwards. The teal colour made my skin tone look darker, to my surprise. I felt pretty in it as well. Not that I wanted to admit it to anybody, and I wasn't trying to sound conceited, but I did feel pretty in it. I think it was just because when I spun, the skirt flew out around me. It made me feel like a little girl, carefree and full of joy.

I pulled my own clothes back on, and decided to buy the black dress I first tried on. It was under fifty dollars, to my surprise, so I would still be able to get something to eat later as well. Claire came up behind me as I bought the dress, and she seemed to be very pleased with herself that I was actually buying it. But then she noticed that I hadn't bought any of the other clothes she had made me try on.

"Candy, what about the other clothes? The skirt? The cute crop top?" she said with what sounded like a disapproving tone.

"I can't afford it all, Claire. You know that," I sighed, before grabbing the bag carrying the dress from the employee.

I walked out then, waiting for Claire to follow. She had almost an armful of clothes, which made me a little jealous. I shook the negative thoughts out of my head as she walked out and joined me, a wide grin spread across her face.

"So, tell me all about Mister bad boy," Claire said as we sat down in a small cafe to eat lunch. Well really, this was my breakfast. I hadn't had a chance to eat before we left.

"Where do I even start?" I laughed, before sighing.

I started from the start, which Claire had already heard. I felt like I was retelling a story from months ago, but it was only a week ago. So much had happened between then and now; it was actually quite hard to believe, even though I was the one who had lived it. As I recounted the events that had happened, I found myself getting angrier. Not just at Jase, but at myself for being so stupid. Once I had finally finished, I was almost out of breath.

Claire hadn't stopped me once; she just let me ramble on and on, taking in what I was saying and nodding every once in a while. Our food had come, although I wasn't sure when and I was yet to eat any of it. I just pushed the food around on my plate, seeming to have lost my appetite. I knew I had to eat though, and my stomach thanked me when I did.

"So-" Claire began, after what felt like several minutes had passed. "You're telling me that you aren't happy with your soul mate? That he isn't what you wanted or pictured just because he's a bad boy?"

"Well I-" I began, but Claire was already speaking before I could finish.

"Do you really think you're the only person in the world who has a soul mate that's a criminal? There are thousands of criminals in the world, Candice. And most of them would have done a lot worse than just stealing. There are people out there who have soul mates who are murderers and rapists, how do you think they feel?" She said, before taking a bite of food.

"You know, you can't change the fact that Jase is a thief. It will always be apart of his past, even if he does change in the future, which we can only hope. But you can't force him to change, especially if he doesn't want to.

You'll just have to change the way you are towards him, the way you see him. Otherwise he will think he cannot be loved for being himself."

I stared, wide-eyed, at my best friend. She was right, as she always was. I should've come to her about Jase so much earlier. Maybe I could've avoided some of our encounters. I was lucky that Jase was only a thief, and it wasn't like he had robbed a bank, well I suppose he could have, since I still hardly knew him. I had to get to know who he was, instead of trying to change him into something I wanted him to be. I was wrong to want that, and I understood now why he had been so upset about it.

"When did you become so wise?" I asked sarcastically, but Claire only laughed in return.

We left the cafe, and headed back towards the car park. I had to help carry some of Claire's shopping bags, but I didn't mind. All I could think about was Jace starting his community service tomorrow at the homeless shelter, and I wondered if he was actually going to show up. I really hoped he would, but like Claire said, I can't change him. Jase even said it, it's his life and I can't control what he does and doesn't do.

After finding Claire's car- we couldn't find it for about five minutes, Claire was beginning to freak out and my hands had started to ache from all her shopping bags- she drove me back to my house. When we pulled up in the driveway, Claire looked over at me with a goofy grin on her face.

"What?" I asked, unsure of what she was smiling about.

She grabbed one of her shopping bags from the backseat and handed it to me, the same grin still on her face.

"That's not my bag, Claire." I laughed, before handing it back to her, but she just shook her head.

"It is your bag. I bought you some of the clothes you tried on, seeing as you couldn't afford them," she grinned, pushing the bag back towards me.

"Claire, I can't take this," I said.

"Of course you can, Candy! Consider it a late birthday present, okay?" she smiled, and I knew she wasn't going to take no for an answer.

"Fine." I sighed, before hopping out of the car.

"Thank you for today, and for the clothes," I said as I started closing the door, but not before I heard Claire reply.

"Yeah yeah, I know. I'm the best." An even bigger grin was spread across her face as she drove off back down the driveway.

(A/N: ola my lovely amigos, i know this chapter isn't really exciting or anything, but i felt like we didn't really know much about claire, and seeing as she is candice's biffle, i figured she needed to be in the story a little more. i like her anyway, she's a pretty cool cat. and i kinda also needed a filler chapter, i promise the next one will be better coz it'll be a jace and candice one hehehe are you excited coz i am

i hope you guys enjoyed this chapter anyways, pls vote and comment and all that jazz coz i know you wanna make me happy and smile kk?)

Chapter Eleven

As I walked along Nixon Street, I couldn't help but think what Jase was going to do when he saw me. I knew he wouldn't be happy, but if I told him I hadn't come to check on him, and that it was actually the Timekeeper's fault I was here, then maybe he wouldn't be as angry. It wasn't exactly true, but Jase didn't have to know that.

I knew I shouldn't be checking in on him, but I was afraid he wasn't even going to show up. All I was planning on doing was checking if he was there, and then I was going to leave. He might not even see me there, which was what I was hoping for.

I stopped at the door of an old brick building, a sign above the door telling me I was in the right place. I had driven passed this building hundreds of times, and I had always thought it was abandoned. It was strange really; some people would call this place their home, yet I would never have thought it could be someone's home from the outside.

I pushed open the door, which opened into a reception-like room. A lady sat behind the counter, smiling at me as I entered and neared the desk.

"Hi there! Are you here to volunteer today?" She exclaimed, though I wasn't sure if she was trying too hard to be nice or if she was just genuinely nice.

"Um actually-" I began, but I couldn't tell her why I was really here. I couldn't say that I was spying on my soul mate, and I guess it wouldn't hurt to actually volunteer anyway. Maybe it would help me to get into a good college in a few years time.

"Yes. Yes I am," I smiled, before she handed me a form and gestured me towards the couch on the left side of the door I had come through.

It wasn't an elegant couch, nor was it very comfortable, which was the vibe I seemed to get from the whole place. I hadn't expected it to be like a five-star hotel or anything, but I imagined it to be a little more, cosy. Once I filled out the form, I was guided down one of the hallways and into the cafeteria. It was pretty deserted when I got there, but only because they hadn't started serving food yet.

I began walking across the room, weaving through the long tables and benches to get to the kitchen on the other side. I was about to push open the door, when a strong hand gripped my arm and spun me around. I had to quickly try and regain my balance, before looking up to see who was now in front of me.

Jase.

"What on earth are you doing here, Candice?" He hissed; trying to make sure nobody would hear him.

"Did you come to check up on me, huh? Making sure I would actually show up?" His grip on my arm tightened. I let out a gasp, before he noticed and let go completely.

"I- The Timekeeper controls us, Jase. We're connected, remember?" I tried to mimic what he had said to me, back in the cafe on our second encounter, although Jase had managed to sound a lot more sarcastic than I had.

He glared at me, which made me feel a little proud inside. It mainly made me feel nervous though, like coming here had been a bad idea. We already weren't on very good terms; I didn't want to make it even worse.

"Oh good, you two are already making friends." A man in his early forties spoke as he walked over to Jase and I.

"I'm Stephen, and I'm the one who runs this place," he smiled, before shaking both our hands.

"You must be Jase," Stephen said as he handed Jase a mustard-coloured apron and a hair net.

"And you must be Candice!" He handed another apron and hair net to me, before guiding us through the kitchen door.

We were introduced to some of the other volunteers, and I was by far the youngest. There were four other volunteers, all over thirty years old. Three of them were women, and the only man there had a long grey beard that was wrapped in a hair net, which made me want to laugh. They all seemed to know each other though, like they did this on a regular basis. I guess it was a good thing, at least the people here would always have people to help them out.

Stephen gave Jase and I some jobs to do then, and I could tell Jase was regretting walking through the doors of this place already. We had to collect all the dirty dishes from the dining area when they were finished, and then clean the dishes afterwards. It didn't really bother me; I would do the dishes all the time at home to help my mother out, and I was actually looking forward to meeting all these different people.

Jase on the other hand, well he didn't really strike me as the type who would want to engage in a conversation with these people. He had hardly spoken to me all day, which I guessed was because he was mad at me. Who knew what for though, maybe it was a mixture of me getting him into this, and me just being here? I could tell he wanted to leave already, and I knew that if he actually decided to, I couldn't stop him. I had given him this chance, and if he threw it away, well there wasn't anything more I could do.

The doors, adjacent to the one I had come through earlier, opened then, and people started pouring in. There were a lot more than I had expected, around fifty or so. My heart broke knowing that all these people were left with no home. Most of them were older than me, but there were some families with young children walking through the doors, even teenagers like Jase and I, which was awful.

They started lining up before the serving area then, which reminded me a lot of the cafeteria back at school. Once they had been served their food, they all sat down and began eating. Most of them laughed among each other, and it seemed like they had all known one another for years. I couldn't imagine how they all ended up here, and how awful it must be to not have a home. I guess this shelter was their place to call home, and most of them seemed perfectly okay with that.

The day seemed to go by so quickly. We stayed there until dinnertime, which was the last meal of the day. They seemed to love having new people around, and Jase and I were bombarded with questions majority of the day. It went well though; most of them were pretty friendly and a lot of them seemed genuinely happy, which I hadn't really been expecting. Even Jase and I got along well, which wasn't exactly what I thought would happen at all.

After we had some dinner, and said our goodbyes, we walked out and into the chilly autumn air. Although it was silent as we walked, it was nice to walk beside my soul mate and imagine that our situation was somewhat normal. I still had no idea how anything was going to work out between us, but I really hoped it would. We were a fair way away from being lovers, even a fair way away from being friends at this point. Surely it could only get better from here though, right?

"I didn't think it would be like that," Jase said suddenly, which caught me by surprise. I thought I would've had to be the one trying to make conversation.

"Didn't think what would be like what?" I asked.

"The shelter. I didn't think it would be so clean. And I didn't think the people would be so- so, nice," he admitted, lifting his gaze to meet mine. It was silent for a little while again, but this time, I was the one who broke it.

"Can we promise each other something, Jase?" I said, looking away suddenly. He stopped walking then, and raised his eyebrow.

"Promise each other what?" He asked curiously. I stopped walking then, and turned to face him.

"That we will speak the truth to each other from now on. No more lies."

He gave me a funny look then, before stuffing his hands further into his jacket pockets. The temperature had dropped since we first walked out into the evening, and it had gotten a lot darker already. The streetlight above us cast shadows across Jase's sharp cheekbones, which somehow made them even more prominent. His dark blonde hair almost looked brown from the shadows, and his eyes were jet black. I had admired his looks before, but now I just couldn't help doing it.

"Are you sure you want to hear the truth, Candice?" He murmured, making me shiver.

"I'd rather hear the truth, than be lied to," I said quietly, so quiet that I thought he didn't hear me. I was about to repeat myself, but Jase spoke before I could.

"What if the truth hurts? What if you're being lied to for your protection?" He took a step closer, and I felt my heartbeat quicken.

"I- I don't need protecting. I'd still rather know the truth, even if it hurts," I whispered. We held each other's gaze for what felt like forever, before Jase stepped backwards and looked away.

He almost seemed shy, but I knew he wasn't. He had shown a softer side just then, and I knew he hated himself for it. I could practically see him rebuilding the walls, and it was only a second before he was back to the arrogant Jase.

"Yeah, whatever. No more lies, I can do that." He shrugged.

We started walking again, and I wondered why he hadn't made a run for it yet. I knew he wasn't fond of me, and hanging around me seemed to just irritate him even more. So why hadn't he left yet? It's not like he had never run away from me before. He sighed then, before clearing his throat to speak.

"Did you see me talking to that old man, the one with an eye patch?" Jase asked. His voice was soft again, like he had decided that he didn't care about me seeing his softer side.

"Yeah, I did," I replied.

I actually had seen him talking to the guy. They were talking for a while, and I had wondered what they were talking about. I looked over at one point, only to find them both already looking at me. I'd been meaning to ask him what it was about, but I had almost forgotten about it until just now.

"Well he knew we were soul mates, and told me not to throw away the chance to love," he said, running his hand through his messy locks.

I stared wide-eyed at him. I could see his cheeks turn a slight pink, even though the dark shadows tried to conceal them. I never expected that they were talking about that. I really hadn't thought too much about what they were saying, only that it had concerned me somehow. How did he know that we were soul mates? We sure didn't act like it. Jase turned to face me again, the pink now gone from his cheeks.

"I've never really been great at making friends, and I thought that this whole Timekeeper thing was just some stupid thing the government made to try and make more money. But now that I have a soul mate, well- Oh god I don't even know what I'm fucking saying anymore!" He paused, taking a breath, before continuing.

"I've just never done this kind of thing before, alright? I don't know how to act or what to say. I just don't know how to deal with this."

Before I knew what I was doing, I grabbed his hand. I half expected him to push me away, but he didn't. His eyes were full of emotion as they stared down into mine. I hadn't really ever noticed our height difference, until now.

"I'm new at this too, Jase." I squeezed his hand then, trying to reassure him that it was going to be okay.

"How about we just try and focus on being friends first, then see where we go from there?" I gave him a small smile. We both knew this was the best way to go about our situation.

He smiled then, and it was one of the most beautiful smiles I had ever seen.

Chapter Twelve

- -

"So, how'd it go yesterday? Did you kiss and make up?" Claire's voice rang through the other side of the phone.

"No, Claire," I sighed. "But I think thing's are going to get better between the two of us from now on, which is a good thing."

Things had gone pretty well yesterday at the shelter, to my surprise. I hadn't expected to be on good terms with Jase so quickly, but I knew we still had a long way to go before we could call ourselves a 'couple'. We had exchanged numbers though, which was another step closer to what we were supposed to be. Now we could try and make plans instead of hoping to bump into each other around the town.

"So you two are taking things slow? That's such a boring approach, Candy. Just jump straight in the deep end and hope for the best! And by the deep end I mean his pants, of course." Claire had turned into a crazy sex addict since her and her soul mate had first done the deed. It seemed to be the main thing that occupied her mind nowadays, which I admit did annoy me a little.

"Claire, sex isn't the answer to every problem," I groaned, before putting the phone down beside me and placing it on loudspeaker.

I picked up one of my granite pencils then, and flipped to the page I had been working on for the last few days.

"It's the answer to all my problems!" she exclaimed. We talked for a little while longer before hanging up a few minutes later.

I loved Claire, but sometimes she just got too much and it was hard to put up with her. She was crazy and outgoing, whereas I was the complete opposite. Our differing personalities didn't always see eye to eye, and this meant we seemed to get tired of each other rather quickly. It wasn't too bad though, both personalities ended up showing on in the other person anyway. Sometimes Claire liked to be alone and quiet, and sometimes I enjoyed being a bit loud and crazy. She was my best friend, well really my only friend, so I had gotten used to her crazy outbursts and overall crazy personality. It's what made her, her, and although she was overwhelming sometimes, she was still a good person.

I had almost finished the drawing now, even though I had been in a complete daydream most of the time. I didn't even know the pencil had been still moving, until now. The drawing was of a boy, but I couldn't tell who the boy was. All of his features were familiar to me, but the person wasn't. I realised then that I had mixed Jase and Ryan together into one person, and drawn it. I ripped the page out of the book, tossing it into the mountain of crumbled papers by my wardrobe.

There was a small knock on the door then, before my mother walked in.

"Sweetie, I need to ask you something," she said as she sat down on the edge of my bed. Her tone worried me a little; she rarely ever asked much of me.

"Sure, Mum. What is it?" I put my pencil down, spinning in my chair to face her.

"Is Jase coming to the wedding tomorrow?" The words seemed to tumble out of her mouth before she could stop herself, as if she was afraid to ask.

I knew they were all worried about me, seeing as I hadn't brought him home or spoken much about him. I had been asked every day at least three times about Jase since we first met, and well I hadn't really had much to tell them. I hardly knew Jase; sometimes I would even wonder if his name was actually what he first said it was.

"You know we're all dying to meet him, and tomorrow would be perfect for us to meet him!" She smiled, finally looking up at me.

"I haven't mentioned it to him, but I can ask him and see if he wants to come. He might be busy tho-"

"Oh, that would be wonderful!" She grinned, jumping up from the bed in what seemed to be a rush of excitement. I knew my mother was dying to meet him; I was her baby girl after all. It wouldn't hurt to ask him, would it? After last night, there might actually be a chance that he will come. As my mother left, I grabbed my phone and began typing a message.

Hey Jase! I don't know if you actually saved my number last night, but it's Candice. I was just wondering, and I know it's super late notice and I'm sorry I haven't asked you sooner. Well anyway, do you want to come to my brother's wedding? It's tomorrow, and I figure we can try to get to know each other as friends there. It's at my place, not that you know where that is yet, but well let me know anyway! From Candice.

I deleted the whole message before I could hit send and embarrass myself. How hard was it to send a simple text message? Why couldn't I just send 'Hey Jase, it's Candice. I forgot to mention before, but you're invited to my brothers wedding. It's tomorrow at my place, I hope you can come!' Why did I have to make things so awkward and embarrassing? It took me way too long to get the right message. After multiple tries and a lot of frustration, I finally hit the send button.

I wasn't sure what to expect in return; maybe I thought that after last night we both wanted the same thing, but when Jase's reply came I was pretty disappointed. 'Hey, sorry I don't think I can make it. Hope you have a good time.' was all it said. I sighed, before falling back onto my bed. I guess I shouldn't have expected things to change so quickly.

* * *

After helping my mother with some of the cleaning for tomorrow, I walked back into my room. The screen on my phone was lit, and my heart skipped a beat. Maybe Jase had changed his mind about tomorrow? I grabbed the phone, sliding my fingers across the screen to make the message appear. Unfortunately, the message wasn't from Jase. But I was just as surprised when I saw Ryan's name above the message.

I hadn't spoken to Ryan since the incident at the Police Station. I half thought he hated me for making him wait around for so long, but I guess not. 'Hey Candice, wanna do something today?' I smiled at the phone. I didn't have anything planned for the rest of the afternoon, and Ryan was always good to hang out with.

After replying with a yes, I went downstairs to tell my mother what I was doing before walking back into my bedroom to grab my things. I took a glance in the mirror just as I was about to walk out, and stopped. I was wearing an old, oversized Metallica t-shirt and some ripped denim shorts, not the cute type you buy in the store's these days, but old, worn shorts. The shirt wasn't mine; I wasn't a fan of Metallica or the genre of music at all actually. I decided I needed to change, not that I was trying to impress Ryan, but this outfit definitely was not supposed to be seen in public.

I grabbed the first thing that I could find in my wardrobe, which just so happened to be a cute dress that Claire had given me. I looked at it for a while, before throwing it back in my wardrobe and slipping into a pair of white denim shorts and a loose blue t-shirt. I threw on my Converse sneakers before walking out the door, down the stairs and out to my car.

Ryan was already there when I pulled up, the wind pushing his curly locks across his face. I hadn't realised how cold it had gotten since I was outside helping my mother this morning, and silently cursed myself for not bringing a jacket or wearing more clothes. I hopped out of the car, the cool breeze hitting my bare skin like tiny needles as I walked towards Ryan.

"Aren't you cold?" He asked as I reached him. I didn't need to answer, he already knew it without me having to reply. "Come on, let's go inside."

The warmth of the cafe hit me as soon as Ryan opened the door, the wonderful smell of coffee hit me soon after. I hadn't been in here since Jace and I had argued, and I was hoping that none of the staff had remembered it, even though I was extremely doubtful that they would have forgotten. Nothing much happened at the cafe, and I was quite well known with most of the staff, so I wasn't surprised when Ruby came up to me as soon as I walked in.

"Hey, Candice. How are you? Everything okay?" She began. "I haven't seen you since, well, you know."

"Yeah I know, and I'm fine," I said with a genuine smile. I really was fine.

Things hadn't turned out exactly the way I wanted them to, but when did that ever happen? Nothing that happens in life is certain, and for me to try and plan out what would happen with my soul mate just made it harder to accept Jase for who he was. Ruby gave me a sympathetic look, and I knew that she didn't believe me.

"Really, I'm fine." I tried to reassure her, but I don't think she wanted to believe me. She shrugged, before taking our orders and leaving us to find a seat.

"I've never been here before," Ryan said as we sat at the table closest to the heater.

I stared at the wall down the back, trying to find the poem that still nobody had claimed as their own. I remembered then what Jase had said to me when I was reading it. 'I see you're admiring my work.' It did make me wonder if he had written it, or if he was even interested in poetry or writing. Surely he had some hobby other than stealing, and I was yet to find out what it was.

"I come here all the time. It combines my love of books and coffee together, it's perfect." I smiled as I looked back at Ryan.

When our drinks came, we moved to the back of the cafe and sat against one of the bookshelves. It was a pretty busy afternoon, actually it was probably the busiest I had ever seen the cafe. It was always a quiet place, but today it wasn't.

"Here." I broke out of my thoughts as Ryan handed me a book from one of the shelves we were leaning on, though I wasn't really sure what to do with it. I looked at the cover; 'Lost Soul' in big letters covered most of the dark picture.

"It's about a guy who spends his whole life searching for his 'soul mate', only to get to the end and realise that it was his best friend. But then it's too late and she ends up dying of cancer."

"Gosh that sounds awful. Why would you want to read that?" I said in horror, but Ryan only chuckled.

"He still ends up happy, which I guess it shows that you don't need a soul mate to enjoy life. It's one of my favourites."

I understood why now. Ryan felt like he could connect with the book, because he too had lost him soul mate. He wanted to move on with his life, and be happy even in a society that revolved around being with the person you belonged to. It was heartbreaking, but at the same time, I could tell he was starting to get through it.

"Do you ever wonder what she would've been like? Or what her name was?" I asked without much thought. It was still a touchy subject, and I had just caused all those unwanted feelings to rise to the surface for him.

"Of course. I don't think there will ever be a time when I don't think about her," he sighed, before continuing. "I dream about it, what meeting her for the first time would have been like. What her name was, how her voice sounded, the way she walked, everything. Sometimes her face is visible, and it's nobody I have seen before that I think it must actually be her. But other times, it's just another girl's face I see instead of hers."

He looked up at me then, his green eyes glassy through fallen strands of his tousled hair. I hadn't realised that the distance between us had shrunk, and I wasn't sure when it had happened. My heart had sped up as well, but I wasn't sure why. The words that left Ryan's lips didn't help my heart either, but made it a lot worse.

"Sometimes, the girl I'm staring at is you."

Chapter Thirteen

"Mum! Mum!" I yelled from my bedroom.

"What is it, sweetie?" She said breathlessly as she appeared at my door, looking frazzled.

Today was Daniel and Lucy's wedding day, and my mother was clearly extremely stressed out for it. They were having it the backyard, and mum was in charge of most of the day. It's not like we all didn't want to help out, she just insisted that she would do it all.

"I can't get the zip done up at the back, could you-" She was behind me before I could even finish asking her, and I felt the dress tighten around my back as the zip slid up my spine.

"Thanks, Mum." I smiled as she spun me around to face the mirror. Claire had come over earlier to do my hair and make-up, since I had no idea what to do or how to do any of it. My long brown hair was curled and fell down over my bare shoulders, a pretty clip encrusted with diamonds pinning part of it back from my face. I hardly ever wore my hair down, let alone put any effort into it. I could feel it tickling my bare shoulder blades; it was an unusual feeling for me.

Thankfully, Claire hadn't put too much make up on; I still somehow looked natural, just with much longer eyelashes, rosier cheeks and pink lips. I hardly recognised myself. I had never worn make up, apart from when Claire wanted to give me makeovers. It wasn't like I didn't need it; it was more to do with the fact that I had no idea how to use it.

"You look beautiful, Candice," my mother said as she stared at me through the mirror.

I smiled back at her, before taking in my full appearance. The lilac dress flowed freely all the way down to my toes, but was fitted around my chest quite tightly. It gave my breasts a nice lift surprisingly, which made me feel a little exposed. Overall, I was shocked at how nice I looked, though I didn't actually look much like myself.

I looked back up at my mother then, her eyes looked glassy, like she was about to cry.

"Mum, are you alright?" I asked as I spun around to face her, the dress spinning outwards as I moved.

"I'm fine, I just- I can't believe my eldest boy is getting married, today. And there's still so much to be done. I still have to-" she began to ramble before I stopped her.

"Mum, you know you don't have to do this all by yourself." I said. "We're all here to help out."

She sighed, before giving a small smile.

"I know, sweetie. I just wanted to make sure everything was perfect."

"It's going to be perfect, Mum, no matter what." I smiled as she handed me my flats. The other girls were wearing heels, though I refused. I had never worn heels before, so I wasn't about to start trying on my brother's wedding day. Knowing my luck, I'd end up falling over in front of everyone.

Mum helped me as I slipped them on, before pulling me into a hug. She left then, probably to go check on the bride for the tenth time already. I grabbed the bouquet of flowers from my bed, taking one last look in the mirror before walking out the door.

*　*　*

The backyard was filled with people in suits and dresses, laughing and smiling and just generally having a good time. The ceremony had been beautiful, just how I imagined my own to be. It was perfect really. They said their "I do's", in front of all they family and friends, and were finally about to start a new life together.

Daniel couldn't wipe the grin off his face the whole day, and wouldn't leave his wife's side. They were the perfect couple, and I was so happy for them to finally tie the knot. My mother had been in tears ever since the ceremony, of course, they were happy tears. She was so happy for Daniel and Lucy, you could almost see her glowing with pride and happiness.

We were gathered around one of the tables now, everyone laughing and sharing stories about their soul mates. It made me sad, though I know I shouldn't have been. I guess it didn't help that Jase wasn't here, or that our first encounter wasn't nearly as sweet and wonderful as everyone else's. But that was when I saw him standing alone across the yard.

He was dressed in a fancy grey suit with a light blue collared shirt underneath it. The first couple of buttons were undone, and he hadn't bothered with a tie. His hair was still a blonde mess atop his head, as usual, but taking in his whole appearance, he was almost unrecognisable. I couldn't believe he had actually turned up to the wedding, and also couldn't believe how nicely he scrubbed up.

He looked so different, not just the clothes, but there seemed to be a whole new aura about him. His eyes locked with mine then, and he smirked. This was it, I had only just realised. My family was finally going to meet Jase, my soul mate. This time when I thought about it, I didn't feel worried or scared. I knew they would accept Jase, because that's just the type of people they were.

"You didn't steal that suit, did you?" I teased as I reached his side.

He chuckled then, before looking down at his appearance and smoothing down his shirt. He looked handsome, attractive; I couldn't even find the right word for it. I had always thought he was good-looking, but today, right now, was something else. I felt like this was the first time I had actually seen him stripped back of his bravado and arrogance, and it seemed to be physically showing as well.

"Maybe I did. You didn't give me much time to get a suit ready," he said as he looked up at me. "Wait, did you just make a joke about stealing?" He raised an eyebrow, but his mouth grew into a smirk.

"I didn't think you would come. You said you weren't going to," I said then, looking down at my feet.

"I didn't think I was going to either, honestly. I didn't think it would be a good idea, you know, me meeting your family already when we aren't exactly like most other soul mates." Jase said, avoiding my eyes.

"So, what changed your mind then?" I asked as we began to walk over to a long table filled with finger food.

"I'm here now, does it really matter what changed my mind?" Jase smirked, his guard going up once again.

In a way he had a point, at least he had shown up. But I was still curious as to what did make him change his mind. I highly doubted it was because he wanted to see me, but I knew what ever it was, he wasn't too keen on telling me. What if he was here to sabotage the wedding? Or steal from me? Several negative thoughts ran through my mind then, but I shook them out almost as soon as they appeared. Jase wouldn't do that, would he? He knew he couldn't get caught stealing again, so surely he wouldn't be stealing from me.

"Candice? Is that- is that who I think it is?" A voice called from behind me. I turned around to face the beautiful bride, and my new sister-in-law. She was practically glowing, and to me she looked like one of those models in a bridal magazine. I turned to Jase then, who had gone slightly pale. Was he nervous to meet my family? Because if he wasn't, I for sure was. I knew I didn't have anything to worry about, my family would welcome him with open arms, but I still couldn't shake the nerves.

"Lucy, this is Jase. Jase, this in my sister-in-law, Lucy." I smiled nervously as Jase looked up. Lucy's eyes lit up, though I didn't think I could see her get anymore excited than she already had been the whole day. She almost squealed, before pulling him forward into a hug. Jase looked taken back and quite confused, but hugged her back nonetheless.

"Oh my, it's so good to finally meet you! Candice has been keeping you hidden for much too long!" She exclaimed as she let go of him. "The rest of the family is going to be so thrilled that you came today!"

We walked over to the table my family sat at then, although no one noticed us for several moments. We stood there, almost awkwardly, until finally my mother noticed my presence.

"Oh, Candice. I was wondering where you-" My mother began, stopping as she spotted Jase by my side. Her eyes flickered from Jase to me, and back again to Jase, before her mouth spread wide. She stood up abruptly, which caused the whole table to suddenly quite down. They all looked up at Jase and I then, Daniel, Jacob, Patricia, Mum, and even some of my aunties and grandparents.

Jase's hand grabbed mine softly, almost making me jump. His fingers locked with mine, and my heart began to race. He had never done something so intimate before; we had hardly even touched. So this was strange, but I didn't want to let go; they felt like they belonged together, our hands, just like our souls did.

"Everybody-" I announced, "meet Jase. Jase, meet everybody," I grinned, though nobody moved or said anything straight away. It took them a few seconds to register the words, but then it was chaos. Everybody jumped up from their seats, practically pouncing on Jace with questions and handshakes and more hugs. My mother was the worst though, which I had half expected. She hugged him so tightly I thought he might suffocate, but he was fine.

In fact, Jase took it all extremely well, which surprised me. After we sat down at the table, he answered their questions confidently and quite openly. He hadn't answered all the questions truthfully, but he wanted to make a good first impression, which made the nerves and butterflies vanish, leaving nothing but happiness.

"Candice never told us exactly how you two met. Would you mind telling us?" I looked from my mother to Jase, wondering how on earth he was going to get out of this one. He couldn't tell them what really happened, surely not.

"Well, it's quite a funny story actually." Jase smirked before looking at me. He was actually going to do it; he was going to tell them what really happened. I wasn't sure what my face looked like, but I was sure I looked ill. I should have been prepared for this question; we should have rehearsed it. But when? We had hardly spent much time together, and when we had it was mainly spent arguing with each other.

"But I think that's a story for another time. Do you mind if I use your bathroom?" Jase said as he pushed his chair back, before standing up.

"Oh of course not. Candice, will you show Jase the way?" My mother said, though she didn't say it like a question.

We walked towards the house, Jase a step ahead of me. He opened the door, before guiding me through like a gentleman would years and years ago.

"After you," he said with a smile, and I finally realised that this was all an act.

"You don't have to act anymore, nobody's watching you," I sighed as we walked down the hallway. Jase raised his eyebrow at me, before looking ahead.

"What?" he said as we stopped in front of a door. I knew he was trying to play dumb now, that he knew what I was talking about.

"Don't pretend you don't know what I'm talking about." I replied, a hint of annoyance in my tone. "The bathroom is in there." I pointed to the closed door we had stopped in front of.

I wondered if he knew what I was talking about, or if he was enjoying himself like he made it look to the rest of my family members. I realised then that I over-analysed everything; no matter what it was, I would always spend so much time thinking about it. I needed to stop thinking so much, but how do you stop something that comes naturally to you? Jase left the bathroom then, and instead of walking back outside, we continued to walk through the house.

"This place is massive." Jase muttered to himself, although I could hear it.

"It's not that big, really. I mean it's pretty big now that Daniel and Lucy don't live here, but- sorry I'm rambling." I said shyly.

"Well, it feels like a mansion to me. But I guess that's because I've practically lived in a shoe box my whole life." Jase said then, looking up the stairs. He sighed then, before turning to face me.

"We should probably go back outside, they might be wondering what's taking us so long." I nodded before we walked out the back.

Daniel spotted us almost immediately as we walked through the door, stumbling over and wrapping his arm around each of our shoulders. It was only then that I noticed how drunk he was. He smelled of beer and sweat; the strong smell of alcohol was almost enough to make my head spin.

"Come on, it's time to dance!" He slurred, pulling us towards the open space in the backyard that was perfect for a dance floor. I watched as Daniel ran up behind Lucy, grabbing her around the waist and spinning her around. They both laughed as they tried embarrassingly to dance, and from what I could tell, Lucy was a little tipsy too.

I had hardly noticed that it was getting dark now, and someone had turned on the lights throughout the garden. Now it looked magical. Mum had hung fairy lights around the trunks of trees and through the rose bushes, and some even dangled from the branches above. It transformed the garden, but it still looked just as beautiful as it had in the daylight.

Jase had disappeared some time during my daydream. At first I thought he might've left, but I knew he wouldn't do that. He was trying to make a good first impression, and if he were going to leave, he would've at least said goodbye to me. A hand grabbed me then, dragging me deeper into the dance floor. Daniel's arm wrapped around my waist, while his other held my hand in a firm grip. We stood in a waltz pose, before he began to spin the both of us around, carelessly bumping into other people. I felt dizzy, but mainly all I felt was happiness and my stomach muscles tightening as I laughed harder and harder as we spun.

* * *

It was about ten in the evening when majority of the party left. It had been such a long day, and I could see the exhaustion in my mother's eyes as she tried to clean as much as she could. I watched from one of the tables as Jacob grabbed her arms and told her not to worry about it, we would all help clean up in the morning anyway. It would be a lot easier to clean in the daylight as well.

I was surprised when Jase came and sat beside me; I had hardly seen him all night. I had actually started to think he had left without saying goodbye, but I guess I had been wrong. We sat together in silence for a while, just watching our surroundings. I could feel myself getting tired, and I knew I would fall asleep as soon as my head hit the pillow later that night.

"I thought you left hours ago," I said, trying to stifle a yawn. I looked over to him, realising he was already looking in my direction. He chuckled then, before yawning himself.

"I spent a lot of time with Jacob and your mother. I hardly realised the time until now." I smiled at the thought of Jase getting along with my family, even if he was acting some of it. If he wanted to make a good impression, then surely that meant something, didn't it?

He stood up then, grabbing my hand to pull me up beside him. "I think it's time for me to go."

After Jase said goodbye and my family finally let him go, we walked out the front together. It was a lot darker out here than out the back, the only light coming from inside the house. I noticed there was no car waiting for Jase, but figured his ride had to be on its way.

"Thank you for coming, Jase." I smiled, though he probably wouldn't have seen in the dim light.

"Yeah, yeah. Whatever, it was nothing." He looked down at his feet, before back up at me with his signature smirk.

"Jase, I'm serious. You don't understand how much it meant to my family that you came, and how much it meant to me. So, thank you."

"I had a good time, and you're family are pretty cool. I can tell that you all care about one another, see how close you all are. Makes me kind of jealous."

"Well, you know you're apart of the family now, so you don't have to be jealous."

He smiled, before looking out towards the road.

"Is someone coming to pick you up?" I asked then, following his gaze.

"Uh, no. I walked here." Jase replied as he turned back towards me, taking a step closer.

"Jase, you can't walk home! Let me take you!" I demanded, but he didn't listen. His hand came up to my face, slowly pushing my hair behind my ear. His hand came to rest under my chin, before his cool fingers began running gently down along my collarbone. His touch sent shivers through my whole body. It felt so intimate; it wasn't like when he held my hand earlier, this felt true and real.

"I never told you how pretty you looked today, but you did, you really did." His voice was only a whisper, but he was close enough for me to hear it clearly. I could feel my cheeks beginning to turn pink, before his lips touched my cheek.

I watched him, wide-eyed, as he slowly turned around and walked down the driveway. All I could do was stare after him; he had left me speechless and frozen, with my heart pounding against my ribcage. Maybe I wouldn't be sleeping tonight after all.

Chapter Fourteen

- -

It was strange how different I felt driving myself to school a few days later. It was as if driving a car to school made me twice as cool as I was before, not that I was very cool to begin with. It was hard to believe that two weeks had already gone, and that I was back at school again. So much had happened since I had been at school last. So much had changed.

Walking from the student car park I felt as though the school was different. Perhaps it was because I'd never really seen it from this angle before, or perhaps I was the one that had changed. I couldn't say which it was, but either way the walk felt good. No, it felt right. I made my way towards my locker, knowing that Claire's tiny figure would be leaning against it waiting for my arrival.

"Hey hot stuff," she grinned as I reached her. Her hair was in a tight topknot, and somehow she managed to make our uniform actually look decent.

Now that it was getting colder, we had to wear our winter uniform which unfortunately for me, meant stockings and a long skirt. Claire and a lot of the other girls at school always managed to dodge the 'must be to your knees' rule, though I never bothered trying to alter it.

"Hey, Claire," I smiled, before unlocking my locker.

"Guess what happened to me last night?" Claire said excitedly.

"If it's about your sex life, I'd really rather not hear it," I mumbled, though Claire either didn't hear or didn't care. She continued with her story nonetheless. I tried my best to zone out, though it proved difficult since Claire spoke so loudly.

She was in the middle of talking about something to do with a bottle of vodka and a pineapple, when I spotted him walking in my direction. He smiled as he walked past, and I gave him a small wave in return.

"Who was that?" Claire asked, seemingly forgetting about the rest of her story. "That wasn't Jase, was it? I won't be happy if it is and you never told me that he went to our school, Candy."

"It's not Jase, he- actually I have no idea what school he goes to." The more I thought about it, the more I realised that I still knew near to nothing about Jase. I had known him for weeks now, but I didn't really know him at all.

"So who is he? He's kind of cute," Claire said, her gaze following Ryan as he walked down the hallway.

"It doesn't matter if he's cute, Claire. I have a soul mate and so do you." Claire gave me a strange look, before shrugging.

"No need to get defensive, Candice. You can still think a boy's cute without wanting to stick your tongue down his throat." I shuddered at the image that popped into my mind; I could only hope my first kiss wouldn't be anything like that.

"Although I really couldn't blame you if you wanted to stick your tongue down his throat." She nodded in the direction Ryan gone in, before wiggling her eyebrows at me.

"God, Claire, please stop," I groaned. "That's not really what kissing is like, is it? It sounds painful."

"Sometimes I forget how innocent you are," she laughed.

* * *

I walked into the classroom for first period, scanning the tables to try and find an empty seat. My late arrival only caused stares and snickers from the other students in the room, and also left me with the table right up the front, which just so happened to be the seat right beside Duncan Phillips. I was never one to laugh at or bully other kids, mainly because I knew how it felt to be on the bottom half of the food chain, but being stuck beside Duncan Phillips for almost two hours wasn't going to be an easy task.

I placed my books on the table, before sitting down and trying to gain as much distance from him as possible. Already I could smell the body odour oozing through his school shirt. He looked up at me, surprised that someone had decided to sit next to him.

"Hi, Candice!" Duncan grinned, and I couldn't help but feel sorry for him. He wasn't exactly the most attractive boy in the school, or the skinniest either, but I'd never talk about him behind his back like the rest of the school's population did.

"Hi, Duncan," I smiled, before taking my sketchpad out and flipping to a blank page. I could feel his eyes baring into the side of my head, which made me super uncomfortable and want to scoot away even further, but I had already reached the end of the table. I silently cursed myself for not bringing my earphones, there was no way I could get my work done if he was going to try and hold a conversation with me the entire class.

I felt a small tap on my shoulder several minutes later. Turning around, I saw Ryan, who somehow had snuck into class a lot later than me and still managed to grab a better seat than I had. He gave me a small wave, before holding up his sketchbook. 'Need some saving?' was scrawled over the page in big, bold letters. I did my best not to laugh, before nodding my head and turning back around. I heard the legs of a chair screech across the wooden floorboards seconds later, indicating that someone had pulled their chair out. I was sure it had to be Ryan, so I waited to see how his plan was going to unfold.

"Hey, Duncan. You mind if I steal Candice from you? I need her for my artwork," Ryan, with his arm around the other boy, smiled politely.

I looked up at him, before attempting to hide a smile. I was positive that he didn't actually need me for his work, but if it was going to get me away from Duncan, then I wasn't going to complain.

"Oh no, of course you can. I don't mind." Duncan smiled at me, before dropping his gaze back down to his work. I could see that he was actually quite a good artist, but had to hold back a laugh at what he was actually drawing. I had kind of expected it from him, I don't know how, but he just seemed like the type to be really interested in dragons and mythical creatures.

"Thank you for saving me," I whispered once I sat beside Ryan. There wasn't really much room, seeing as there were three people occupying the small table. I barely had a corner, but I didn't mind. It was a lot better than being next to Duncan. The boy on the other side of Ryan, Justin, gave me a quick and short nod, as if to say hi. His spiky blonde hair, sticking out all over the place and clearly coated in a thick layer of wax, barely moved as he nodded.

Ryan chuckled, "Oh you know, it was nothing."

"I feel so sorry for him. If only he didn't smell so bad." I shuddered, the scent seemed to be embedded in the back of my nose. I opened up my sketchbook, staring blankly at the naked page in front of me. For once in my life I didn't actually know what to draw. Usually something would just pop into my head and I'd go from there, but I couldn't think of anything to draw today. Well, to be perfectly honest, I could think of something to draw, or someone. But I didn't want to draw Jase, or Ryan, especially since he was right beside me.

I turned to look at Ryan, whose pen already stained the starch white paper. It was hard to tell exactly what he was drawing, but I didn't want to ask either. I always felt like a person's artwork was somewhat private and personal. It was a way to release your emotions after all; to let out your frustration or passion onto a blank canvas and see what your mind truly wanted you to see.

"That looks nothing like me," I whispered, still unable to put together what he was drawing.

He looked up at me, his startling green eyes full of concentration. I instantly felt bad for breaking him away from his focus, but he didn't seem to have minded at all. He gave a small smile before shaking his head; his thick curls bouncing as he did.

"I'm not quite sure what you mean, Candy." His pen was still gliding across the paper, even though his focus was now all on me. I had always admired those who could still write or draw without having to pay their full attention to their work. It was as though it was completely natural to them, like a sixth sense, although every time I tried I'd end up with something similar to Picasso's work. I wasn't saying that Picasso wasn't a great artist, but I just never understood his paintings or why everyone loved them so much.

"You said you needed me for your artwork," I smiled. He grinned in reply, before flipping the current page he was working on over, to reveal a blank page. He began to draw again, but this time I recognised a figure forming.

"If you wanted me to draw you, you could've just said so," Ryan smiled without taking his attention off his work. I sat there and watched the paper come to life, all by the simple movement of a pen. I had never actually seen Ryan's artwork before; never realised just how talented he was. "It's not like I've never done it before, anyway."

I turned my attention from the paper in front of him to his face, though it was mostly covered but his dark hair. I wasn't sure if he had been joking, or if he really meant what he said. Not that it mattered if it was true, seeing as his face had shown up in my artwork several times before as well. I turned my attention back to his work, and knew then that he had been telling the truth. The way he drew without much effort or concentration, the fact that he hadn't looked up to study how my nose was slightly pointed at the end or that one of my eyebrows was more arched than the other. He drew as if he was drawing something that he had memorised completely, as though I were a familiar object in his house that he saw every time he walked out of his room.

"You said you weren't good at drawing people," I whispered after he put his pen down, now admiring his work. I saw the corner of his mouth twitch upward; like it had been attached to string and someone had just decided to pull it.

"No, I said I wasn't good at portraits." He looked up at me, before continuing. "This isn't exactly a portrait."

He was right. It had an almost animated feel to it, like I was a character out of a cartoon show. He had dressed me in a long dress, a ball gown; something I would never have thought to wear in my lifetime. Although he had made my figure a lot thinner and more beautiful than it really was, I could picture the dress on me, fitting like a glove.

"I never knew you were this talented, Ryan," I said.

"So you like it, then?" he asked. He sounded a little nervous, which I thought was strange coming from Ryan. He had always seemed so confident, not in the way Jase had been, but in a good way.

"Are you kidding? Of course I do," I replied.

We sat silently for a while, and this time I had finally connected ink to paper. I almost hadn't realised that I had began drawing until I was already half way through the sketch. It was a boy, though he didn't have a face yet. I was still trying to decide who he was, when Ryan spoke, interrupting my focus.

"How is everything, you know, with Jase?" I looked up from my work, not expecting a question about Jase from Ryan at all. He was one of the only people who knew how we had met, and he had been with me at the Police Station the night Jase had been arrested, but I hadn't spoken much about him since then at all. It felt strange to talk to Ryan about Jase now, and I couldn't pinpoint why it felt so awkward.

"Uh, good. Really good actually." I was going to leave it there, I should have. Something told me to change the subject, to talk about something else, but I didn't. "He came to my brother's wedding and met all of the family. I think they really like him, which is really great. I was so scared they wouldn't like him at all. And we have been hanging out a fair bit in the last couple of days too."

Ryan didn't reply. I shrugged it off, not thinking much of it at first. I continued on with my sketch, adding texture to his hair and detailing to his clothes. He was still faceless, but I had decided to leave him that way. I could come back to this piece some other time, and maybe then I'd know how to draw his face or who it was going to be.

I flipped to a new page, glancing briefly over at Ryan. He seemed to be adding some final touches to his work, but when I looked closer, I noticed exactly what he was doing. He had added a tiny strip to my wrist, but instead of leaving it blank or putting a bunch of numbers on it, he had picked up a red pen. The red line looked startlingly bright on the black and white image, but that's not what shocked me. He had made my Timekeeper just like his, like my mother's, and so many other unlucky people out there. The thick red line coated my wrist, becoming the main focus of the image.

I glanced away before he caught me staring at it, knowing he hadn't intended on me seeing it at all. The page was flipped over a second later, back to what he had previously started. I stared blankly at the page in front of me, unable to forget what I had just seen. Although it wasn't real, it spoke what Ryan was feeling, just like anybody else's artwork did.

Ryan hated Jase, so much so that he would rather me without a soul mate, than with Jase at all.

Chapter Fifteen

"Are you sure you want to go back in there?" He asked me as we stood in front of the café. "I mean, the last time we were here together we kind of made a scene."

I turned to look at him, his hair blowing in the strong wind. The day had been perfect earlier at school, and when I had decided on wearing one of the skirts Claire had bought for me. It was a pastel mint kind of colour that I believe Claire had called a 'skater skirt'. I wasn't particularly sure why you'd chose to skate in a skirt, but I wasn't about to say that to Claire.

The weather had dropped dramatically from the time I had left the house to arriving at the cafe, leaving me freezing my butt off while I waited for Jase to show. I didn't care if the skirt was cute, or even if I looked cute, at that moment I just wanted to slip into a pair of jeans and a big woollen jumper. I was relieved when Jace finally came around the corner, my bare legs and arms covered in goose bumps. He gave me a small smile, and quickly glanced at my outfit. At least he noticed it, so the mild hypothermia I had no doubt acquired by now was somewhat worth it.

"Aren't you cold?" He had said as he reached me, pulling his dark grey jacket around himself tighter.

"Freezing actually," I grinned through chattering teeth. "Can we please get inside now?" He chuckled, his whole face lighting up the way it always did when he smiled or laughed. It made my stomach tighten, my heartbeat quicken.

He was staring at me now, still waiting for my answer. "Yes," I finally said. "I'm sure."

Once we walked in, we made our way through the scattered tables finding one right in the back, closest to all the books. I hadn't come here on my own for what felt like forever ago. The last few times I visited I had been with someone else, the very last time being with Ryan. The thought of Ryan sent butterflies through my stomach. I tried to ignore them, like I always did, but knew they shouldn't have even been there in the first place.

I looked up at Jase, who was studying the menu intently. His eyes were almost a dark green as he gazed down, though when he looked up over his menu they changed back to their usual colour. It was strange how hard it was to describe them; I could never find the right words or anything similar to compare them too. I always thought they were like a rare gem; an emerald, that had blue flecks through it, somehow making the gem more beautiful.

"Hey Candice, what can I get you today?" Ruby said as she arrived at our table. She took a quick glance towards Jase, before raising her eyebrow towards me. She clearly still hadn't forgotten about our very public fight that I constantly try to push to the back of my mind. Now though, I could hardly believe that the Jase that sat in front of me now, was the same person that I had first met.

"I'll have a chocolate chip muffin and a hot chocolate, please." She gave me a nod as she mentally noted my order down, before turning to Jase.

"And you?" Her tone was sharp, and I knew she wasn't pleased to see him here again, especially not with me.

"Um, I'll just have a hot chocolate, thanks," he smiled, but Ruby had already began to turn away from him.

"I don't think she likes me very much," Jase mumbled, his gaze following Ruby all the way back to the front counter.

I laughed, "Yeah well you didn't really leave a good first impression last time, did you?"

"Yeah, I know. I've never been very good with first impressions. But you already knew that." He sighed, running his hand through his hair.

I wasn't sure how to reply, or if I was even supposed to. But thankfully, Jase continued talking.

"So," he began. "How was school?"

"Did you really just ask that?" I laughed. "It was fine, I suppose." I shrugged, just as Ruby came back with our order.

"Do you go to school, Jase?" I asked as Ruby left to attend another table.

The café was unusually busy for this time, and a lot of teenagers filled the tables. I didn't like it being so busy, and I worried that it was starting to become a popular place for teens to hang out. I came here because it was always quiet, and because their hot chocolates were to die for, but now it seemed that the usual Starbucks junkies had found my special place.

"I dropped out last year," he said as he played with the marshmallow floating on top of his drink like an iceberg.

"You dropped out or got kicked out?" I teased.

He glared at me, and for a moment I thought maybe I had crossed the line. I was working up to an apology when he started laughing.

"It's a funny story, actually." He went on to tell me how he and one of his friends had gotten into the roof of one of their main buildings and let loose about twenty or so rats.

"Nothing happened for almost a month," he explained. "But a massive crack had started to appear in the ceiling. They had tried to plaster it up, but one day when we had a school assembly, the crack burst open and hundreds of rats fell through, landing on the heads of the school choir. It was hilarious."

"Did anyone get hurt?" I asked. Jase looked at me, clearly not happy with my serious response.

"No. Well apart from the rats," he grinned, before taking a sip of his hot chocolate.

"But how did they know you were the one who done it?"

"Let's just say that I wasn't exactly the most well-behaved student at school," he laughed.

It had started to grow dark by the time we made our way outside. I hadn't realised just how long we had been inside for, and I don't think Jase did either. We must have been in there for a good few hours, since the road was now filled with headlights and people most likely on their way home from work.

"So, where did you park?" I asked, crossing my arms around my chest to try and keep myself warm. I silently cursed Claire for not offering to buy me anything warmer.

"Oh, um, I walked here," he muttered, almost under his breath.

I raised my eyebrows. "You walked here? Why didn't you drive?"

"I-I don't have my licence. Or a car for that matter."

I stared at him in disbelief. Maybe he lived close by, but I still thought it was strange. Most guys I knew got their licence as soon as they turned sixteen, because guys love cars, right? But Jase was the exception; Jase was always the exception to everything, I thought to myself.

"Well let me drive you home, Jase. It's way too cold to walk." He began to protest, but eventually started following me back to my car. He was silent as he hopped in beside me, his hair still dishevelled from the wind.

I pulled out of my park; unaware of which way I was supposed to turn until Jase gave me some directions. Apart from Jase's directions every now and then, the drive was pretty silent. I felt like I had been driving in circles, when he finally told me to pull over in front of a white weatherboard house. It was small, like Jase had said, but he had made it seem like he lived in a dump. The house was surrounded by hundreds of different flowers, which would no doubt look magical during the springtime. At the moment though, their petals had begun to drop and wilt.

"Um," Jase paused, before continuing. "Do you-do you want to come in?" he stammered. His gaze was out the window towards his house, but I could tell he was nervous. His hands lay in his lap, fiddling with each other.

It took me a while to register the question he had asked. It wasn't until he turned back to look at me that I really realised what he was asking. He wanted to invite me into his home; a place he never talked about and clearly didn't invite people into very often. I could feel the nerves jittering in my chest, like tiny little insects. My palms had begun to get sticky with sweat, but as nervous as I as, I knew the answer almost straight away.

"Yes-yes of course I do."

I stood a little behind Jase as he fidgeted with the keys, his hands not as steady as they usually were. As soon as the door had clicked open, there was a loud, repetitive thumping noise that grew louder and faster as we stepped inside. I realised what it was as the small figure darted around the corner, they were footsteps. She ran straight to Jase, wrapping her tiny arms around him as though she hadn't seen him for years.

"Hey Izzy," he laughed, crouching down so he was around the same height as her. "How was school today?"

"Good! I learnt about space!" she grinned, before going into great detail about what she now knew about space. It took her a while, several minutes actually, before she noticed me standing behind Jase. The moment she did she went quiet, her eyes studying me nervously.

"Jase." I heard her whisper. "There's a pretty girl behind you."

I then heard Jase chuckle, before he stood up and looked over his shoulder at me. He gave me a goofy grin, before grabbing my hand and pulling me forward so I stood beside him.

"That pretty girl is my soul mate, Iz." Was all he said back.

She had run off before I could even manage a hello. Maybe I had scared her? I wasn't sure, but Jase seemed to think it was funny anyway.

"That's my cousin, Isabel," he grinned, before looking back at me. "And clearly I'm not the only one that's bad with first impressions," he laughed, before tugging at my hand to make me move. We walked down a hallway before turning into one of the rooms that branched off it. I could tell what room it was before we even entered; it was the strong smell that gave it away. The smell was hard to describe, but it was incredible.

"Mummy, Mummy! Jase brought a pretty girl home!" I heard as we entered the room, the room a lot bigger than I had imagined. The dining table was square, and was already set for dinner. I hadn't realised the time until now, and felt a little rude for being there. Behind the stove stood a woman who looked about five years younger than my mother. Her hair was the same colour as Isabel's, a dark mahogany brown, and she was about the same height as Jase.

She looked up from the pan, almost dropping the wooden spoon she held in her left hand. Her eyes hid behind a thick fringe and dark framed glasses, though I could still manage to see her eyes go wide when she saw me. I wasn't sure what I had been expecting, but I guess she was just as excited to see me, as my own mother had been to meet Jase. She turned one of the knobs on the side of the stove, before hurrying towards us.

"Aunty Kath, this is Candice," Jase smiled softly, though he didn't take his eyes off me. He wasn't the only one; every pair of eyes in the room seemed to be staring at me, except my own.

"Hi," I smiled. I thought briefly about curtsying, mainly because I was wearing a skirt, but immediately decided against it. Who even curtsied these days?

"Why it's so lovely to meet you, Candice! I really didn't expect to meet you at all!" she grinned, Isabel now at her hip. She stared up at me, her eyes filled with curiosity.

Kath looked from me to Jase, before shaking her head. "Jase, you could've told me you were bringing her over earlier. I've already started preparing dinner." As if remembering that she still had food cooking, she hurried over to one of the many pots and saucepans on the cooktop.

"Oh, no. It's fine. I was just going to leave, anyway. I don't want to intrude," I said, receiving a raised eyebrow from Jase.

"Nonsense. It'll be fine, Candice. Please, do stay." The look in her dark eyes was almost pleading, and made it too hard to say no.

"Alright, I'll stay." I smiled, and somehow, I already felt like I belonged with Jase's family.

Chapter Sixteen

"How was community service today, Jase?" Kath asked as she cleared the plates off the table.

I was surprised she had brought it up, honestly. I hadn't thought Jase would tell his family that he was stuck doing community service, or the reasons why he was doing it. I figured he hadn't told them the entire story, since I was sure they didn't know he was a commonly seen face with the police.

"Wasn't too bad. I'm almost finished as well," he said proudly.

"Really? It feels like you only just started yesterday," I said, stunned.

"They're pretty pleased with me and my behaviour. They said I've changed a lot since I walked into the building on the first day."

He looked at me then, a little spark in his eyes. I knew they were right; he really had changed dramatically over the past couple of weeks. I felt somewhat responsible for his change, and felt a little guilty about it. I remember what he had said to me outside the police station, that I couldn't change him. And he had been right; I couldn't change him. He had to change himself, and that's exactly what he did. I think the homeless shelter was the main influence towards his change, though, which made me feel a lot happier.

"Well I'm very proud of you, Jase," Kath grinned, and you could tell that she really meant it, too.

After we helped do some of the dishes, even when Kath insisted she didn't need any help, we walked into the living room where Isabel sat at the small wooden coffee table. I couldn't exactly see what she was doing, but her face was filled with great concentration. As I moved to kneel next to her, I noticed she was drawing. It was a typical type of seven-year old drawing; and it reminded me of a painting my mother showed me that I had drawn when I was around the age of six.

There was a circle with a smiley face inside it, though the circle also seemed to be the body. Stick arms and legs stuck out the sides of its head, and it had bright yellow hair sitting atop it as well. I tried not to laugh, though it was hard not to. It seemed like all children this age had the same image of people in their heads, and they apparently didn't have a separate head to their body. Maybe that's how they saw people in the world, and wouldn't that be interesting.

I looked over my shoulder, only to notice that the space Jase had just been occupying was now vacant. I wasn't sure where we went, or when he even left, but I didn't want to follow him around like a lost puppy. I made myself comfortable beside Isabel, grabbing one of the spare sheets of paper spread across the table, and a coloured marker.

"What are you drawing there, Isabel?" I asked, trying to start up a simple conversation.

"My family," she replied, as though I should have already known what she was drawing.

I began scribbling around the edges of the paper, not entirely sure what I was going to draw. This had been happening to me quite a lot recently. I had once been able to pick up a blank piece of paper and know what I wanted to draw almost instantly, but now, it was as though my mind was too jumbled to be able to put together a solid image to transfer onto paper.

"What are you drawing?" Isabel asked me then, taking her eyes off her own work and gazing at mine.

"I'm not sure," I smiled at her. "What do you think I should draw?"

She was silent for a moment, her lips pursed and her eyes gazing away. She looked so much like her mother that it was almost freaky; I had even thought I saw a tiny bit of Jase in her, but it seemed to vanish as soon as she turned her attention back to me.

"You should draw Jase! We can both draw him!" She said excitedly. If only she knew how many times I had tried to draw him already.

We worked silently, side by side, nothing but the TV and the sound of markers sliding across paper filled the room. I had never actually tried to draw with markers before; my more preferred tool was the granite pencil. I had tried to experiment with charcoal once, but it just turned into a smudged mess. The marker was a lot thicker than what I was used to with a pencil, but it didn't smudge when my hand ran over the paper, which happened to me quite frequently.

I was so focused on the paper that I didn't even notice Jase slipping back into the room. I don't think Isabel did either, until he cleared his throat. We both spun around in unison, looking up at Jase who was seated on the arm of the couch.

"What are you two doing?" He smiled. He seemed to enjoy the fact that we were getting along, which was understandable. I had felt the same way seeing Jase getting along with my family members.

"We're drawing pictures of you!" Isabel exclaimed, holding up her artwork with a proud and satisfied grin.

It was almost identical to the other drawing she had made, but this one had a bright yellow sun in the corner and a couple of flowers sprouting out of the green grass. Jase took the drawing from her hands, pulling her into a hug as he spoke.

"Thank you, Iz, it's beautiful." Seeing him around his cousin made my heart melt. He was so caring, and I could tell that when she hit high school he'd be the overly protective figure that she would no doubt want to ignore.

"Candice's drawing is nice, too," she smiled as they broke apart.

"It's not as nice as yours, though," I said. I hadn't really been thinking when I started to draw him, but now I regretted it. The thought of Jase seeing my drawing of him made me want to throw up.

"Let me see it, Candice," Jase grinned, like he had read into my thoughts. I was tempted to rip it up when Isabel snatched it from the table and handed it over to Jase. His eyes grew wide, though I wasn't sure if he was admiring it or just surprised that I could actually draw something other than a stick figure.

"Wow, I-I wasn't expecting that." He looked up at me, a small smile spread across his lips. I was still unsure if he actually like the drawing or not, when Kath came into the room. She looked tired and worn out, the same way my own mother used to look when I was much younger. It made me wonder what had left Jase's aunt to be a single parent, though I didn't want to pry into her life when I had only just met her.

"Come on, Izzy, time for a bath," she said.

"But mummy, I'm having fun!" Isabel protested, but stormed off after her mother anyway. Her protests continued down the hallway, until the closing of a door silenced them. I turned back towards Jase then, who was still holding my drawing. It made me feel uncomfortable; it always had. Like when Ryan had asked me to draw him, while he sat there and watched every stroke and line I made on the starch white paper.

I remember Jacob had asked me to draw a portrait of one of his ex-girl-friends, once. I declined, telling him that my artistic ability wasn't a promising birthday present for his girlfriend. But really, I just didn't want my work to be displayed in anyway. It wasn't like I was ashamed or em-barrassed of my work, but more that it had always been a private hobby, something that I liked to do in the confines of my own bedroom with no one around.

"You never told me you could draw," Jase whispered suddenly, bringing me back to the present.

I shrugged, "It's not like it had ever come up in one of our conversations."

"But, you're amazing, Candice. This is amazing." He pointed to the draw-ing he still held between his fingers. My heart almost flew out of my chest; did he really mean the words that he spoke?

"Everyone has a talent. I guess mine is drawing," I smiled. I could feel my cheeks heating up, and could only hope that they weren't as red as they felt.

"I don't have a talent," he mumbled, placing the drawing back on the table.

"Of course you do, Jase." Kath said as she walked back into the room, Isabel trailing along behind her.

She now wore bright pink pyjamas, covered with blue polka dots. She held a stuffed rabbit tightly to her chest; half of its ear had been torn away and one of its button eyes had fallen off. Even though the rabbit was all battered and torn, it didn't stop the love she felt for it.

"Oh, yeah? And what is this so called mystery talent that you speak of?" Jase said, clearly amused.

This was really him, I thought. This was who he truly was. There were no walls up, no masks; this was him baring his true self, and it was hard not to like what had always been hidden underneath. He laughed with his family, and I watched as they teased each other, and reminisced about some wonderful time back when they were younger. He was truly happy with them, no matter what had happened in his past or with his biological parents, this was where he really belonged.

"Alright, missy. Time for bed, I think," Kath yawned, though I wasn't certain if she was talking to her daughter or herself.

"I want Jase to take me, please!" she pleaded, causing Jase to laugh.

"Alright, let's get you off to bed, then." Jase got up off the floor, where he had been previously sitting, stetching like a cat as he stood.

Isabel gave her mother a kiss and a tight hug, before she ran to me with her arms spread wide. I didn't have time to brace myself for the impact, and it almost knocked me over, but I was able to steady myself. Her head was buried into my shoulder, her little heart beating fast against my own.

"Thank you for being pretty for Jase," Isabel grinned as she let go. We all laughed, before Jase picked her up and headed down the hall. Kath's gaze lingered at the opening to the hallway, as if she wasn't sure if she should follow after them or not. She seemed to have decided against it, turning back to me.

"Thank you for coming over today, Candice," she smiled. I was about to reply, when her face became more serious. I wasn't sure why, or if I should've felt nervous or frightened, but she didn't look angry. The look that spread across her face was closer to sadness, than anything else.

"In all honestly I never actually thought we would ever met Jase's soul mate," she began to say. "He had always said how he didn't care about meeting her, that he didn't want his Timekeeper to stop. He practically hated the whole idea of belonging to someone, that his soul and another were connected. And I knew that it was because of me, he felt this way."

She sighed then, before lifting up the sleeve of her woollen jumper then, revealing her Timekeeper. I wasn't sure what I had been expecting; the dreaded red line, maybe twelve different numbers, still slowly counting down. It wasn't like that hadn't happened to people. They said most people met their soul mates young, around the ages of sixteen to the early twenties. But there were some people that had to wait a lot longer than that. The first three numbers would be stuck on nine hundred and ninety-nine, because that's as high as the Timekeeper could go. So if it were more than that, the numbers wouldn't move until you dropped below nine hundred and ninety-nine days.

Kath's wasn't still counting down, though. Neither did it have a horizontal red line. The Timekeeper was stuck on the twelve consecutive zeros, just like mine was. So she had met her soul mate, but that didn't make any sense. If they had met, then where was he now?

"His name was Andrew, and it was love at first sight. Well, for me anyway. We got married, had Isabel, and we seemed just like every other happy couple going around." She paused, pushing the sleeve back down with an anger that hadn't been there a second ago. "But then, one day, I found a note from him left on our bedside table. All it said was, 'Kath, I've found someone else, I'm sorry.' I cried for weeks."

She was staring blankly at the wall now, and I wasn't sure if she had finished speaking or if she was going to continue. She eventually did, though her eyes never moved from their spot on the wall.

"Jase was only around twelve years old, but he could understand what was happening. I practically had to drag him to the clinic to get his Timekeeper when he turned sixteen last year, and he only agreed to get it because I practically begged him."

"Why are you telling me this?" I whispered, unable to look up from my feet.

"Because his view on having a soul mate has changed completely, and I believe it's because of you."

Jase walked back into the room then, a small smile sitting on his face. I wondered if he had heard any of our conversation, but his face told me that he hadn't.

"She's asleep," he said softly, as though he didn't want to wake her. Kath gave him a smile, and it was like our conversation had been completely forgotten about. I stood up then, stretching my body out. I hadn't realised how sore my legs were from sitting on them for so long.

"Well, I better get going now. My mum's probably started to wonder where I am," I said, before turning back to Kath. "Thank you for dinner, and it was really good to meet you."

"You're welcome over any time, Candice," She grinned, before Jase lead me back towards the front door. He closed the door behind him, ridding us of the warm air that radiated inside the house.

"I'm really glad you were over," Jase said after a short while.

It was freezing cold out here now, though it didn't seem to bug Jase. It probably had something to do with the jeans and jacket he wore, keeping his body heat enclosed underneath the layers of fabric he was wrapped in. I hated to agree with her, but my mother had been right, as she usually was.

"Is that all your wearing?" She had said as I came down stairs and headed towards the front door. "At least take a jacket, sweetie. It isn't summer anymore."

I had regretted my decision the moment I had walked outside, but now, with the temperature having dropped what felt like another twenty degrees, I wanted to punch the past me in the face.

"I'm glad I came over, too. Your family is wonderful, Jase." He gave me a small smile, though he hadn't really looked at me since we stepped outside. Was he nervous? Was he thinking about the same thing I was? I had watched plenty of romance movies where the two characters had just spent a wonderful evening together, and now it was time for the goodbye. Were we just going to bid our farewells, or would we hug goodbye or, kiss? I wasn't sure I was prepared for either of the options, but the last one not only scared me, but also sent excitement through my whole body. Would this be my first kiss? Right here, on Jase's doorstep?

At that moment, Jase took a small step forward. Before taking another, and another, until the distance left between us was barely visible. I could feel the heat radiating from my body, and I wanted so badly to wrap myself into him to try and give my own body some warmth. He looked down at me, his gaze first locked on my eyes, before dropping down for just a moment, to my lips.

I knew then that he wasn't planning on hugging me, wasn't going to just say goodbye and walk inside. And he certainly wasn't planning for it to be just a kiss on the cheek either. He was about to kiss me, like really kiss me. The type of kiss girls my age dreamed about. The type of kiss some people waited years for, until they got to share it with their soul mate. I knew exactly what this kiss was, and what it would mean.

So why on earth did I dodge his pouted lips and give him a hug instead?

Chapter Seventeen

"So, let me get this straight," Claire mumbled through a mouthful of her doughnut. "He went in to kiss you, and you bitched out?"

I sighed, stirring the now cold cup of tea that sat in front of me. I had replayed last night in my head so many times it felt like I had been living the same day for years. I could still see his surprised face when I had avoided his kiss, and wrapped my arms around him instead. He didn't reject my hug, which I suppose was a good thing, but I couldn't help but feel like I had sent him the wrong message.

"I just, I don't know, Claire. I totally screwed up," I groaned.

"Oh, it's not that bad. I mean, maybe he'll just think you're all cute and innocent and find that kind of thing really sexy," she shrugged, before pulling her scarf tighter around her neck.

It was an especially cold Saturday morning, the coming winter evident on the dewy grass and foggy morning mist. Thankfully today I had prepared for the weather, and was quite cosy in my skinny jeans and thick, black woollen jumper. Claire, on the other hand, always cared more about appearance than comfort. She said she wasn't cold, with her navy blue t-shirt dress and extremely thick woollen scarf, but I could see the goose bumps travel all the way down her legs before vanishing is her ankle boots.

"So, you don't think he'll hate me?" I asked.

"I highly doubt it, Candy," she said as she spooned the left over doughnut crumbs into her mouth. "I mean, yeah you rejected him, but I don't think he's that heart broken about it. I'm sure he'll get to kiss you soon enough anyway."

I rolled my eyes, "it's not like we have to rush it or anything."

"Are you scared because you've never made out with a boy before?" she asked. She looked up then, and saw the look on my face. "Oh my god, you are!"

"Oh come on, is it really that bad that I am? I just want it to turn out perfectly."

"Well that's not going to happen," She laughed. "First kisses are never perfect; don't trust the books you read or the movies you watch, okay? First kisses are supposed to be fun and awkward and you shouldn't make a big deal out of them. Just start off slow, and let your lover lead the way."

"But if he's never kissed before either, well I don't know, it will just work out," she added with a shrug.

My phone buzzed then, thankfully, interrupting Claire as she began to go into great detail on 'the art of kissing'. My heart skipped a beat, and although I highly doubted he would want to talk to me, I wanted it to be Jase. It wasn't, which didn't surprise me. The message was actually from Ryan. I hadn't really spoken to him much since the other day in art class, so the message was quite unexpected.

'Hey Candice, can you meet me at the abandoned apartment in fifteen? It's important.'

"Has he forgiven you already? God, he must be really into you," Claire, who had clearly been watching me staring at my phone, smiled. I hadn't even noticed that she had stopped talking, but was thankful that she had.

"No," I sighed. "It's not Jase."

"Then who is it? Your mum?" She asked, impatiently. Though it was really none of her business who I was talking to, I felt like if I tried to keep it a secret, then it meant there was something to hide. There was nothing going on with Ryan and I that I needed to be messaging him in secret.

"No, it's Ryan." I glanced up at her, waiting to see what her reaction was. I had briefly told her about Ryan, but I was still unsure how she felt towards him.

"I don't know how I feel about this Ryan boy," she said through squinted eyes.

"You said he was hot the other day," I laughed.

"Yeah but that doesn't mean I would be texting him and inviting him over to come and play." She wiggled her finger towards me, as though I was a five year old she was telling off for being naughty.

"He's never been to my house!" I protested.

"I know. I was just saying, Candice. Just be careful around him." I had never heard her speak with such a serious tone before, but I knew it was just because she was trying to look out for me.

"He's not a serial killer, Claire," I sighed, pushing a loose strand of hair behind my ear.

"But he doesn't have a soul mate, so that makes him almost as dangerous." I laughed, before rolling my eyes. She always exaggerated things, no matter how stupid they sounded.

"Okay, okay. I'll be careful." She gave me a grin in return, before going on to talk about the party she had tonight. I zoned out, staring back down at my phone. I still hadn't replied to Ryan's message, and now I wasn't exactly sure I should. Despite what my mind thought, my fingers had other ideas. I watched as my fingers pressed the letters on the screen, before pushing send in the bottom corner.

'Okay', was all that my fingers wanted to send.

I left Claire soon after, which she was fine with. "I have to start getting ready for tonight, anyway," she had said. I wasn't sure how on earth it could take someone over ten hours to get ready, but I knew Claire would somehow manage to find a way to do it.

I walked along Wilson Street, my arms wrapped tightly around me. The streets were mostly deserted, which didn't surprise me. No doubt everyone had the same idea today; stay inside where it was toasty warm. It was where I wished I was right now, anyway. Beside a blazing fireplace with a good book and a pair of fluffy bed socks.

I turned down the side street then, where the door to the apartment was hidden behind bags and bags of rubbish and empty cardboard boxes. It wasn't the first time I had wondered how on earth Ryan had found this apartment; I mean it wasn't exactly an easy place to find, seeing as it was practically in the middle of nowhere. The door was left ajar, as it always was, when I reached it. I had half expected Ryan to be standing at the foot of the stairs when I entered, but he wasn't. He wasn't anywhere to be seen, not even as I made my way into the apartment.

It looked almost as it always did, dusty and empty. The single rotting couch still sat in the middle, a thin layer of dust covering its damaged fabric. The lonely dining table still stood in its usual place, though there were strange patterns covering it, where the dust had been disturbed. Everything looked normal, well, except for the millions of Christmas lights that were hanging from every wall and the high ceiling. I was taken aback; the place looked like some kind of magical planet where the stars were almost within reach. I felt a tap on my shoulder then, and spun to see Ryan, a wide grin on his face.

"When you said important, this is definitely not what I was expecting," I said, gazing back around the room.

He chuckled, "Okay so I may have lied about that, but what do you think? Do you like it?" He walked to the middle of the room, flinging his arms out wide and gesturing towards the lights.

Of course I liked it, it was beautiful, but I couldn't say that. This wasn't right, he and I both knew that, but Ryan didn't seem to care anymore. He had gone to all this effort to make it pretty, and it was just that. But it wasn't a place for friends just to sit around and laugh anymore, it was a place to take someone you loved on a romantic date.

"Why? Why did you do this?" I asked quietly, before sitting on the couch.

Ryan raised his eyebrow, clearly expecting a greater reaction from me than what I had given him. "Well, I thought you would like it-"

"I do like it, Ryan, it's just- why? You've made it into some sort of romantic hide away," I cut in, and received only silence in return. His hands were in his pockets now, and he was looking at the ground when he walked over to sit beside me. His hair fell in front of his eyes, as it always did, but this time he pushed it back.

"I don't know what you were expecting from me, but it can't happen. I'm with Jase," I said, quietly.

"Do you even like him?" Ryan whispered, after what felt like several minutes of silence. I glanced over at him, trying to find a sign to tell me he was joking. But his face was as serious as ever.

"Is that a serious question, Ryan? Of course I like him, he's my soul mate." Something inside Ryan snapped then, and I could see the anger beginning to flare up behind his eyes.

"But how do you know you don't just like him, because he's your soul mate?" Ryan exclaimed. "Would you still feel the same way about him if he wasn't your soul mate? If that damned thing on your wrist hadn't told you he was your soul mate?"

I was taken aback. How could he even ask me such a question? And what did he mean by it? I hadn't even realised that I had been rubbing my thumb over the piece of plastic on my wrist, but it seemed like Ryan had.

"But he is my soul mate, Ryan. Nothing else should matter," I protested.

"If you took away the Timekeeper, and the knowledge that Jase is your soul mate, would you still want to be with him?" Ryan looked back at me then, a scary fierceness in his eyes. "Well? Would you?"

I looked away, unable to stare into his eyes any longer. I had never thought of it like that, but then again, I never needed to. Jase was my soul mate. It didn't matter if the Timekeeper's existed or not. I would've still met Jase when I did, and even if we didn't meet again for another few years, that wouldn't make a difference, he would still be my soul mate.

"Of course I would, Ryan." I said, almost as a whisper. He didn't reply, only got up off the couch and walked over to the window. I could see the reflection of his face, though I couldn't read what he was feeling. At first I thought he had been angry, but now he almost seemed sad.

"Why does all this matter so much to you, Ryan?" I asked quietly. I wasn't sure if he heard me; his face was half hidden by the reflection of the Christmas lights now, but he didn't turn around. I was about to ask again when he turned and began to walk back towards me.

He sat down, not leaving any space between us. He was looking down into his lap, his hands resting on his knees. His Timekeeper was hidden as it usually was, under the hem of a jumper or long-sleeved shirt. Today it was a dark blue zip-up jacket, though the sleeves were a bit short for him, and occasionally displayed the small strip of plastic he had learned to hate.

"You're going to think I'm crazy, Candice." He was looking at his hands, which lay in his lap.

"The thing is, I can't stop thinking about you. My mind is full of thoughts about you, and even when I sleep all I seem to dream about is you. We have a connection Candice and I know you've felt it too. Don't tell me you haven't, because I've seen it in your eyes."

I couldn't look at him, couldn't even find the words to say back to him. My mind was racing as fast as my heart, and I wasn't sure if it was because he was right or it was just the way he was looking at me. I had felt the connection; though I pushed it aside saying it was nothing more than the feeling of a strong friendship. I knew I was lying to myself, that friends didn't make each other feel this way, but how could I feel this way? I had a soul mate, a soul mate that I really liked and that caused my heart to speed up just through a single touch. How could I have the same feelings towards two boys, when I knew I was only meant to be with one?

His hand brushed my cheek then, and it was at that moment my whole body seemed to shut down. I was not in control anymore; my whole body was paralysed. I felt like I was watching someone else in my body, and I was left to watch on standing by on the sidelines. I watched as my body let him turn my face towards his, which now sat only centimetres away from mine. I knew this was wrong, I knew I should move away or slap him across the face, but I couldn't move. My mind screamed at my body, though it wouldn't listen.

His face pulled mine even closer, and before I knew it our lips were touching. It had happened, my first kiss. It was soft and gentle, like I had always imagined it to be. Claire had been wrong; it did feel perfect, well for a short moment, anyway. Until I was back in control of my body again, and I actually realised who I was kissing. I broke away, standing up so suddenly my legs had hardly been ready for it. I felt dizzy, like I had just been spun violently around on a crazy rollercoaster ride.

"Candice? Are you alright?" Ryan asked, concern filling his eyes. I shrugged off his touch before he could even lay his hand on me, but said nothing. I was speechless, and I felt nauseous. This wasn't right; this wasn't even supposed to happen. What were you even thinking, Candice? But that's just the thing, I wasn't thinking at all.

"Candice, it's alright. It's going to be okay-" I spun around before he could finish his sentence, unable to keep the worlds from spilling from my no longer virgin lips.

"Don't even try that on me, Ryan. I can't even believe-" I cut myself off, feeling angrier and angrier the more I thought about what had happened. The anger wasn't at Ryan; it was at myself for letting things get this far out of control. Claire had seen it before I had, she warned me, but of course I hadn't listened, and now I had to pay the biggest price of all.

"I have to go," I croaked, turning away before Ryan had a chance to protest.

I ran out of the building, the cold air hitting my face immediately. My head was still spinning, and I could feel my body shaking right down to my toes. I was still struggling to piece together what had just happened, though all I wanted to do was wake up from this nightmare. But how could something so wrong, so utterly wrong, feel so right? I could hear Ryan calling out to me, though it was faint, I knew he would catch up to me soon enough. I started running again, unsure of where I was going or where I really was at all. I twisted around to see if Ryan was still chasing me, which turned out to be a really stupid idea.

I didn't even get to try and stop myself before I crashed into him. We both fell to the ground, my elbow scrapping the hard concrete floor. I felt pain shoot up my arm, but I did my best to ignore it. I scrambled to my feet, mumbling an apology under my breath as he brushed himself off. I thought he was going to start cursing at me for not watching where I was going, but then he looked up, and I saw his face. He was stunned, though I wasn't sure if it was from being knocked to the ground or because it was me who knocked him over.

I couldn't believe my luck. Of all the people in the world, it had to be him. And of all the goddamn days to crash into him, again, it had to be this one. Jase stood opposite me, with his hair pushed back from his face, his signature smirk sitting on his mouth, and his eyebrow raised.

It was quite obvious that the universe was not in my favour at all today.

Chapter Eighteen

"Candice," he smiled, and I felt my heart shatter. He was truly happy to see me, his eyes lit up almost the second he noticed who had crashed into him. "I was actually just going to call you."

His phone sat in the palm of his hand, the screen still lit. He slid it back into his jeans pocket then, before taking a small step towards me. He reached out and grabbed my hand, pressing it in between his palms. I had never seen him this relaxed and comfortable around anyone but his family, which just made me feel ten times worse than I already had.

"Really, why?" I asked, though I wasn't really listening. All I could think about was what had just happened with Ryan, and the more I looked at Jase, and how genuinely happy he looked, the more I hated myself.

"Well, about last night-" he began, but I cut in before he could go any further.

"Look, Jase, I'm so sorry. I just freaked out. I've just never been kissed before." Those un-kissed lips aren't so innocent now, though, are they? The thought drifted through my mind, making me shiver.

"It's all right, I'm sorry if I made you uncomfortable," he said, pushing his hands into his jacket pockets.

"No, of course not!" I exclaimed. "Can we just forget about last night?"

He looked at me, really looked at me. He could tell I was trying to avoid the conversation, but I had to. I had to get as far away as possible, before I spilled everything then and there. I knew I should tell him, he deserved to know how much of an awful soul mate I was, but I couldn't bring myself to do it.

"Are you alright, Candice? You look like you're in a pretty big hurry-" he was cut off by another voice, from a fair distance away.

"Candice! I'm sorry, okay? Please!" I saw him running towards us, and silently cursed myself. This was exactly what I didn't want to happen. He slowed as he saw me, and somehow he hadn't spotted Jase yet. Jase had spotted him though, and looked utterly confused as Ryan stopped in front of me. He glanced over at Jase then, and they locked gazes. Ryan's eyes growing wide and his face turning a shade lighter as he finally noticed who Jace was.

"Oh," Ryan puffed, clearly working out the situation in his head. I had never imagined the two of them to be in the same situation, especially not in a situation like this. It was strange to see how completely opposite they were from each other, and how I was interested in them both still confused me. There was an awkward silence for what felt like several minutes, before Jase spoke.

"Sorry for what?" His gaze hadn't moved from Ryan since he got here, and the more he stared the more I wanted to disappear.

"I, um-" Ryan stuttered.

"Wait a second, you were with Candice that night at the police station, weren't you?" Jase said, raising his eyebrow. "I thought you looked familiar."

Ryan didn't say anything, just put his head down and stared at his shoes. Jase looked at me then, before back at Ryan. His hand turned into a fist then, but they didn't move from his side.

"Candice, did he hurt you? Is that why you were running?" he said through gritted teeth.

"N-no, Jase. He didn't hurt me," I whispered, though I wasn't planning to, but it seemed to be all I could manage. He was staring at me now, his face filled with confusion.

"Then why were you running? And why was he chasing after you? I highly doubt you were playing a game of tag."

I opened my mouth to speak, but no words would come out. He knew I was hiding something from him; that there was something I wasn't telling him. He had never asked about Ryan before, though I wasn't sure if it was because he didn't care or didn't really remember him. Now, I knew it had to be because he hadn't really noticed him at the police station that night.

"Well?" He was still waiting for an answer, for me to say something. I knew I had to do the right thing and tell him the truth, no matter what happened because of it. It was easy saying it in my mind, admitting what I had done, but when it came to actually speaking the words, it was a struggle.

"I-I'm so sorry, Jase, I-" I began to say, but before I could say any more, Ryan spoke.

"I kissed her," he mumbled, still looking at his feet. I hadn't expected him to be so forward, or so truthful. Actually I hadn't really expected him to say anything at all. I thought he would've ran away the moment he saw who

Jase was, but he didn't. Maybe he was brave, or maybe it was stupidity, but I couldn't really tell which.

Jase's face paled, and his fists tightened. He looked from Ryan to me, too angry to speak. I wasn't sure how I had expected him to react, not that I had been given much time to think about his reactions, but him not saying anything at all wouldn't have been one of them.

I wanted so badly to be in my bed then, the warmth of blankets surrounding me as I woke up from a horrible nightmare. I would be able to go on with my day and plan it out perfectly, so that this situation never had to happen. But this wasn't a dream that I could just forget about, this was reality, and I had really fucked it up.

"So," Jase began, his attention completely focused on me. I knew how he was feeling then, angry. No, it was way beyond anger. He had reached a level of fury I don't think I'd ever seen anyone reach before. "You can kiss him? But you can't kiss me?"

I bit my lip as I remembered our awkward goodbye last night. I had almost forgotten about it in the short amount of time it had been when Jase brought it up before. Last night when I laid restless in bed, that's all I could think of, but now my mind was filled with so much other junk it had been pushed to the corner. How strange it was just how quickly things could change.

"Is he the reason why you didn't kiss me last night?" Jase glared at Ryan then, who was too shocked to speak. "I can't fucking believe this."

"Jase, I'm so sorry," I said, but he wasn't listening, he wasn't even looking at me. He was still looking at Ryan, who was looking at me now. I couldn't read his expression, but it didn't matter, because Jase moved then, so fast that I wasn't able to stop what was about to happen from happening.

His fist collided with Ryan's jaw, knocking him to the ground. It had happened so quickly I almost missed it; it was mostly just a blur and a mix of colour. Ryan's hands flew up to his face, and I could hear him crying out in pain. My body was in complete shock; and all I could do was stand there wide-eyed and watch Ryan lay helplessly on the hard, concrete ground.

Jase turned to me then, his right fist covered in blood, though I wasn't sure whose blood it was. I could see cuts on his knuckles, but there seemed to be a lot more damage to Ryan's face than to Jase's hand. I could see the anger in his eyes, and for a split second I thought he was going to punch me, too. But his fist loosened, though the expression on his face stayed the same.

"This is exactly why I never wanted to get one of these fucking things on my wrist!" He held his arm up, baring his Timekeeper to me. I felt myself flinch at his sudden movement, though he didn't seem to notice it. I could feel tears burning at the back of my eyes, but I refused to let them run down my cheeks.

"Jase," I tried to say, but no noise came out. It was like my voice box had been shattered into tiny pieces, and I was unable to fix it.

"I can't believe I fell for this stupid soul mate crap. After all this time of saying I was never going to get it and let myself fall for it's stupid game, I- I can't believe I was stupid enough to opened myself up to you! To think I actually might've had feelings for you, boy, what was I thinking?" He spat, his words like venomous poison.

I thought of his aunt then, and what she had told me last night. His view on having a soul mate has changed completely, and I believe it's because of you. Her words drifted into my mind, though this time; her tone was full of anger, like she already knew what I had done. All this time I had thought Jase was the one that needed changing, but what I should've done was looked in the goddamned mirror. I shouldn't have ignored the warning signs my brain was sending me about Ryan, and I should've stopped it as soon as I noticed how he felt towards me. But it was too late now, if only the scientists that created the Timekeeper's could create a time machine, too.

"I didn't mean for this to happen, I'm so sorry, Jase," I whispered; glad to have finally found my voice.

"I did a lot for you, Candice. I stopped stealing, did the community service, practically changed myself for you, and this is what I get in return?" I felt a tear slide down my cheek then, and hoped Jase hadn't seen it.

"Well, you know what? I want you to do something for me this time." He stepped closer, and I sucked in a breath. He smelled of blood and sweat, and underneath that, the spice of men's cologne. My heart crashed against my ribcage, and I couldn't even bring myself to look him in the eyes.

"Stay away from me, okay?" Each word felt like a knife being pushed through my chest. I felt my lip begin to tremble, and another tear escape from the corner of my eye. Jase turned around then, glancing once down at Ryan, before he looked back at me. I wasn't sure if he was waiting for a reply, or if I was even able to create a response, but it didn't matter. It was too late; Jase was already walking away.

The tears had finally begun to fall down my cheeks, and they wouldn't stop. I wanted so badly to go after him, and beg for forgiveness, but I couldn't bring myself to do it. I knew it would be pointless anyway; all I would do is stare at him, because there was no way my voice was going to work for me. I turned back to look at Ryan, who was still holding his jaw. He was sitting now; the blood had thankfully stopped dripping from his lip. His shirt was splattered with blood, as was the ground all around him. I knelt beside him as he looked up at me.

"Are you okay? Do you want me to call someone? I'm so sorry, Ryan," I managed between sobs. I put my hand out to touch his face, only to have him jerk away from me.

"Candice, don't," he grimaced, before leaning to the side and spitting blood. "You shouldn't be saying sorry, I should be."

He looked down for a second, or so I thought. He grabbed my arm, twisting it at an awkward angle that caused pain to shoot through my elbow. I looked down, only to see the skin around my elbow was cut and bleeding, and the surrounding skin already turning purple.

"That looks painful, Candice. What did you do?" Ryan mumbled.

"I fell on it, when-when I crashed into Jase," I sniffed, my face soaked from the tears. Thankfully they had subsided, but I knew I still looked like a mess. I guess it didn't matter since Ryan had seen me like this before anyway.

"God, I've really messed everything up, haven't I?" I whispered, more to myself than to Ryan, though he answered anyway.

"It was my fault, I shouldn't have done what I did. And even though it felt right in the moment, we both know it wasn't." He stood up then, sticking his hand out to help me up as well. I wiped my face with my sleeve, attempting to dry it.

"Are you going to be okay, Ryan?" I asked, before looking back in the direction Jase had left. My heart ached, my stomach felt like it was a tangled piece of jewellery, and my mind couldn't stop racing. Just when I thought things were really going well with Jase, I had to ruin it. Heck, I probably ruined our whole relationship, because the look on his face as he left, told me that he wasn't planning on forgiving me anytime soon.

Ryan made a strangled noise then, which I realised, once turning back around, was actually a laugh. "Are you?"

Chapter Nineteen

I heard my mother yelling for me to get out of bed from downstairs, but refused to leave the warmth of my bed. I felt bad for lying to her, telling her I felt sick and that's why I couldn't go to school yesterday. But I wasn't sick at all; I just couldn't risk running into Ryan at school, or the questions Claire would be asking me. It was so much easier lying in bed all day, blaring music to drown out my problems, even if I knew that wasn't the right way to deal with things.

"Honey, you've got to get up for school," my mother said as she walked into my room. She pulled my blankets off; the crisp morning air hitting my bare legs instantly sent a shiver through my whole body.

"I'm not going," I groaned, attempting to grab the blankets back off her, and failing miserably.

"You have to go to school, Candice," she sighed, before sitting on the edge of my bed.

I had hardly left my room since Saturday night, when I got home from my run in with Jase and Ryan. It felt like an awful nightmare that I just couldn't forget about, but it had been real. I had kissed Ryan, not Jace, and I was still struggling to come to terms with that. I had a number of missed calls from Ryan, but I didn't know how to talk to him or if I even wanted to. Jase, on the other hand, hadn't replied to any of my messages. I hardly expected him to, after what I did to him, but I still felt the need to try.

"I don't want to, not today anyway." I had class with Ryan today, and although I really wanted to go to art class, I knew I couldn't. I wasn't sure what he would say to me, probably just 'I'm sorry' like his messages, and I didn't know what I would say to him, either. I wasn't sure how I felt towards him, mainly because I had been trying to focus on Jase.

"Sweetie, you didn't go yesterday either." She gave me a concerned look only mothers could give. "Were you even sick? What's going on, Candy?"

I sighed, "I've screwed things up, mum. Like, really, really badly screwed things up."

"Is this about Jase?" She asked, leaning over to pull my curtains open. I nodded, not really wanting to go into further details about what happened. What would she even think of me? Knowing that I kissed someone who wasn't even my soul mate, especially since her soul mate was gone now. I thought I couldn't possibly feel any worse about the situation, but I guess I was wrong.

"Was there another guy?" she said suddenly, as if reading my thoughts. She sounded relatively calm, which surprised me. If you thought your daughter had cheated on their soul mate, shouldn't you be lecturing them and telling them how disappointed you are in them? I shot her a look, and was about to deny it with a shake of my head, but it was like she already knew the answer. She walked to the door, stopping to look back at me. I thought she was going to be mad, or even disappointed, but her face was barely readable.

"I was hoping it wouldn't happen to you as well." She was out the door before I had a chance to ask her what she was talking about. I scrambled out of bed, tugging a jumper on as I followed her down the stairs and into the kitchen. The kettle was already boiling; mum grabbed two mugs out of the cupboard, placing a tea bag in each before she looked up at me. I sat down at the table, waiting for an explanation of what she had said before, but only receiving silence in return.

It wasn't until she sat down beside me, placing the steaming hot cup of tea in front of me, that she finally sighed. Her hands hugged the mug in front of her, so tightly her knuckles turned white.

"I was nineteen, and it was a few months before I was going to meet your father," she began, staring into her cup. "I was at a party and met this handsome boy, Darren, and it felt like I had bet the Timekeeper in the countdown to my soul mate. He was perfect; and we hit it off almost instantly.

"We would catch up all the time, and we thought that maybe, our Timekeeper's were wrong. He was due to meet his soul mate a couple of weeks before I was to meet your father, but we almost convinced ourselves that we were soul mates."

She gazed out the window; though the early morning fog made it impossible to see anything outside, it was like my mother was watching her memories unfolding in front of her.

"I was with him when he met her," she said quietly. "I saw the look on his face when he saw her, and knew they had to be soul mates. We hardly talked after that, and then it was my turn to meet my soul mate."

"But, you said when you met dad it was-" I began, but she had already started talking over me.

"Love at first sight? Oh, it was. I never lied about that, Candice. I knew your father was my soul mate, I didn't know how or why, but I just knew. I hadn't heard from Darren in months, when I got a random message to meet him one day. I wasn't sure what he wanted, and was surprised that he even remembered who I was, but after that, we caught up in secret more and more. We both knew it was wrong, but we couldn't stay away from each other."

I couldn't believe what I was hearing. I couldn't believe that my mother had done such a thing to my father, and for a short moment I couldn't help but feel angry. It didn't last long, though, because the thought of Ryan and I, and Jase's face, drifted back into my mind where they had been living for the past few days.

"Then what happened?" I whispered. She turned back to me, before putting her head down.

"I ended it with Darren, but your father had already found out. It was rough; he didn't talk to me for well over a week, but he did forgive me, and I never heard from or saw Darren again." She finished, taking a sip from her mug.

We sat silently for several moments, mainly because I wasn't quite sure what to say. I wondered if I was the first to hear about this, or if my brother's already knew and everyone had been keeping this from me all this time. Would my mother ever have said anything about it if I hadn't have messed everything up with Jase? I knew then that I had to tell her what had happened, everything that had happened. From when I first met Jase, to the police station, to community service, to the other day; I needed to tell her everything.

It felt good to be finally letting it all out, even if I had told Claire some things already. I had been hiding all of this from my family for so long, that I didn't realise how relieved I would be once I finally told my mother. I wasn't sure what I was expecting her to say, or do, when I finally finished talking. I might've expected her to be mad, for not telling her all of this earlier, I mean, I was mad at myself for not telling her beforehand. Maybe she could've helped guide me in the right direction, and maybe I wouldn't be stuck in the situation I had found myself in now. All she did was reach up and wipe my cheeks with her sleeve, which to my surprise, came away wet. I had no idea when I had started crying, but I hadn't even noticed it.

"So," my mother finally said. "You really think you like both of them?"

I nodded. I never told myself that I liked either of them, never once said those words aloud, until then. It was so strange, to think that I liked two boys, when I was only supposed to like one. How did that even happen? Why did my body think it was okay to like two boys at once, especially when I already knew I was supposed to be with one? Maybe it was a genetic flaw in my DNA; a single cell carrying a simple message throughout my body, 'your soul mate isn't as easy to find as you first thought.'

"I know it's hard, sweetie, but you've got to decide who you want to be with."

"Do I really have a choice?" I whispered. Jase was my soul mate, not Ryan. So what choice was there? I was meant to be with Jase, and that should've made the decision a whole lot easier, but it didn't.

"Of course you do; you always have a choice, Candice. Even when you think you don't." She got up from her seat, taking our empty mugs into the kitchen. How could I still have a choice? I didn't understand what my mum was trying to say, or what she meant, because it made little sense. She came back to the table then, but just hovered behind the chair she had been sitting in.

"You're still not going to go to school, are you?" she sighed, clearly already knowing the answer. Or maybe her question was rhetorical, and didn't really require an answer, I wasn't sure. She grabbed her keys from where they sat in the centre of the table, before leaning over and kissing the top of my head.

"You better not make a habit of this, Cand. I want you back to school tomorrow, no excuses." She walked out of the room then, and I could hear the front door close seconds later. Sighing, I went back up stairs, having lost my appetite for breakfast.

I wasn't exactly sure how I was going to spend the whole day, seeing as nobody was home to talk to, and it didn't help that the one person I wanted to talk to didn't want to talk to me. I had a quick shower, and changed into an old baggy shirt and some track pants. I wasn't planning on leaving the house, so track pants seemed like a pretty good option for today. I checked my phone then, seeing it light up with a message alert. My heart skipped a beat, as it had almost every time my phone lit up the past couple of days. It wasn't Jase, though, which I knew even before I saw who it was from.

The message was from Claire, just wondering where I was and why I wasn't at school. She didn't seem too concerned, and I was pretty surprised I had even received a message from her. She rarely messaged me when I was at home, sick, but maybe this time she knew I wasn't really sick at all. Maybe she knew something had happened, or maybe Ryan had asked her about me? A shocking thought came into my mind then, what if the whole school had found out what I had done? I tried to shake the thought away, knowing that I was just being paranoid now. There was no way the whole school would find out, because I knew Ryan wouldn't say anything, would he?

I turned my phone's volume up as high as it could possibly go, knowing that it was going to send my music throughout the entire house. But I didn't care, and there was nobody home that it would bug anyway. Music now blaring from the speaker of my phone, I sprawled out atop of my bed, grabbing the sketchbook off my bedside table. I grabbed a pencil, and flipped it open, hoping to start a fresh page. The page that lay in front of me was not blank though; a body had been sketched into the starch white paper, a male body, but the face was left empty. It was similar to the sketch I had started at school, and a lot of other's I had tried to draw recently. I would always end up staring at the face, and not knowing whose eyes or lips to draw on it. I sighed, it was a lot easier when I had just merged the faces together.

I flipped to a blank page, and tried to imagine Jase was sitting in front of me. I thought of his blonde hair, and the way it curled around his ears. The way his eyes sparkled when he talked about something he was passionate about, or the way one side of his lip rose slightly higher than the other when he smiled. Or the sound of his laugh, or just how he made me feel with a simple look, like there was nothing else he would rather look at. Thinking about him made my heart ache, and I could feel tears stinging the back of my eyes.

I glanced down at the paper, only to see that it was still bare. The only thing that had seemed to hit the paper had been a few tears. I threw the sketchpad against the wall, before burying my face into my thick blankets. How could I ruin something that had once felt almost perfect?

Chapter Twenty

"Just try it on!" Claire yelled from behind the curtain.

"Claire, I've told you already, I'm not going!"

The curtain drew back then, and Claire became visible. The dress she wore was a stunning red, though the main focus of the dress was it's extremely low V-neck. She pulled it off though, just like the other five or so she had tried on.

"What do you guys think of this one?" she asked, twirling in front of Alex and I.

"Baby, you look perfect," Alex smiled.

"You're really no help at all, you know that, right?" she grinned, before leaning over to kiss him. I rolled my eyes, before getting up from the sofa, which sat facing the change rooms, and began walking around the shop. I wasn't looking for anything in particular, but it gave me something else to do, rather than sit there and watch Claire and her soul mate make out.

She had dragged me here after school today, even though I told her there was no chance I was going to this stupid dance. The 'Annual Soul Mate

Gala' was on Friday night, two days from now, where people of all ages would bring along their soul mate and dance and drink and party until the sun began to rise. If circumstances were different, I'm sure I would be beyond excited for the dance, but why bother if your soul mate wasn't even talking to you?

I sighed, turning back towards Claire and Alex, who had, thankfully, stopped kissing. Claire glanced over to me, before picking up the dress she had placed on the sofa and shoving it towards me.

"Just try the darn thing on, please?" she groaned.

"Fine, but I'm still not going." I grabbed the dress off her and hopped into the change room adjacent from the one Claire had been using. The dress was a muted yellow colour, a colour I would've never pictured myself in. When I pulled it on, it finished around my mid thigh. It only had one strap, thick and draping over my left shoulder. Once the zip on the side was done up, I allowed myself to take in my appearance. The dress fit me perfectly, the colour, the size, everything. It was like the dress was made especially for me. It wasn't revealing like the dresses Claire had tried on, nor did it stick to my body like glue. It flowed outwards nicely, and for the slightest moment I imagined what it would look like as Jase spun me around on the dance floor.

I yanked the curtain open, shaking the thought out of my head. Stop thinking up scenarios you know aren't going to happen, I thought to myself. Claire looked up as I walked out of the change room, her small smile turning into a wide grin.

"I knew it would be perfect for you," she said triumphantly.

"It doesn't matter, Claire. Because I'm not going to be wearing it," I sighed. I felt like a broken record, one that Claire refused to listen to.

"Why? Did you find one you like more?" She raised her eyebrow.

"Have you not heard what I've been saying for the past hour? I'm not going to the stupid dance!" I yelled, causing the few customers in the store to look my way. Claire fell silent; I had never yelled at her like that before, and already I felt horrible for it.

"Look, Claire. I know you're trying to be positive about this whole situation, but it's not helping. If anything, it's just making things worse."

It was hard telling Claire what had happened, what I had done. I wasn't sure how she was going to react, or if she would even want to speak to me after I told her, but she hadn't really said much when I did finish telling her. It might've been because we were at school at the time, and she didn't want to cause a scene by slapping me on the face or screaming at me.

She got off the sofa then, grabbing my arm and dragging me into the change room I had just come out of. I raised my eyebrow as she pulled the beige curtain shut behind her. She still wore the last dress she had tried on, the bulky tag sticking out from under her arm. She took a short glance at her appearance in the full-length mirror, admiring her slender frame in the dress, before turning her attention towards me.

"Candice, you screwed up, you know that, right?" she sighed.

"If you're trying to make me feel better this isn't exactly helping," I mumbled.

"I am trying to help you, don't you see?" She placed her hands on my shoulders, her gaze steady on me. "You've got to win Jase back over, and that dress is going to help you get there."

"Jase won't even return my calls, or reply to my messages. How am I supposed to get him to the dance?"

"You've just got to try again, be more persuasive. Show up at his doorstep, or outside his window like in all those cheesy teen movies," she shrugged, before smiling.

"If only life were as easy as one of those movies," I laughed.

After finding some shoes to match the dress, and waiting for Claire to finally decide on which dress she wanted, we left the shop. Unfortunately, I couldn't afford the dress, but the storeowner said I could hire it out for the night, which was a lot cheaper. I trailed behind Claire and Alex as they walked hand in hand through the shopping mall. I had left Jase a message about the dance and how nice it would be for us to go together, though I wasn't at all surprised that he still hadn't replied. I already knew the answer, but I wasn't going to give up on trying.

I looked up from my phone then, and locked eyes with a familiar face. His eyes widened when he saw me, and began to walk towards me. His dark curls looked unwashed and matted, and the greying circles under his eyes told me he hadn't slept, either. Was he punishing himself as much as I was myself? I turned away before he reached me, unable to look at him any longer.

"Candice! Please, I just want to talk!" Ryan pleaded. I sighed. I knew I couldn't ignore him anymore; I'd have to face him sooner or later. I may as well get it over with now.

"Fine," I said. Claire shot me a look, a look that meant this was a bad idea; I ignored it and turned back to Ryan. "But only for a couple of minutes."

We walked towards a short bench seat sitting in the centre of the mall, leaving Claire and Alex watching from a distance. I hesitated before I sat down, still trying to work out if this was a good idea or not. According to Claire, it was a bad idea but if I told Ryan that whatever we might've had together was over, then it wasn't such a bad idea, was it?

"I'm really sorry, Candice. I didn't mean-" Ryan began as he fumbled with the drawstrings of his hooded jacket.

"You can't say you didn't mean for this to happen. You knew exactly what would happen if you kissed me," I cut in, my tone bitter. I knew I should've been nicer, but I couldn't help it. Half of me blamed him for the whole situation, where the other half, knew that it was just as much my fault as it was his.

I watched a couple walk by then, the girl resting her head on the guy's shoulder. Their fingers were interlocked, and they looked like every couple was meant to look, happy. The way the guy looked at her, the sparkle in his eyes when he laughed at something he just said, he was completely in love with her. I felt my heart crumble in on itself, knowing that that could've been me if I hadn't gone and ruined everything.

"I thought you wanted me to," he mumbled, still avoiding my gaze.

"I have a soul mate, Ryan," I said, as though that answered the underlying question. I thought you wanted me? Though he seemed too shy to ask it directly.

"But what if he-" he looked up as I cut him off before he could finish, his eyes full of sadness.

"If he wasn't my soul mate? Ryan, we've been over this before. It still couldn't work out between us, I'm sorry." I looked down then, the hurt in his eyes unbearable to look at.

"Why not?" he asked softly.

"Because it just can't, okay?" I looked down at my hands, knotted in my lap.

"You're-you're lying," he stuttered. "You're just taking the easy way out of this instead of what you really feel, which is really unfair on me."

My mouth opened, but nothing came out. I wasn't expecting him to say that, and had no idea how to reply. What was worse, what he said was somewhat true. The easy way out was Jase, because he was my soul mate and therefore it wouldn't make things complicated. It wasn't like I didn't want to choose that pathway, because I did, but a small part of me wanted to defy the rules and what was right, to be with Ryan.

"I don't like you in that way, Ryan," I whispered finally. I tried to make myself sound as convincing as possible, though I wasn't sure who I was actually trying to convince, Ryan, or myself?

"I don't believe you," he said, looking away from me.

"Just, give me some space, please. I just need time to figure this out." He looked past me, his face unreadable. He stood up abruptly, startling me. He shoved his hands in his pockets, but kept his head looking down. His curls completely hid his face, until he lifted his head slightly.

"It's funny isn't it?" he said then. I gave him a questioning look, not quite sure what he was saying.

"What is?" The situation we were in definitely wasn't funny, not in the slightest. I was sure that Ryan didn't find it funny either, but what on earth could he be talking about then?

"Time," he finally said. "It's supposed to help us find love, but with me, it only helped me in losing it." He turned away then, leaving me to stare after him.

Claire was by my side the instant he disappeared from sight, asking what felt like twenty questions at once. I answered her the best I could, though I didn't want to tell her everything. She may be my best friend, but that didn't mean she needed to know every little detail about me or what had just happened.

We started walking again, heading back towards the car. I let Claire and Alex walk ahead of me, giving me a chance to watch them. I know it sounds creepy, but I wasn't watching them in a creepy way, more just observing how they acted around each other. Claire babbled on about something as she always was, but Alex didn't really seem to be listening. He was staring at her as she twirled her finger around a strand of hair, a nervous habit of hers. His face turned into a wide smile, his hand brushing her cheek.

"What?" I heard her ask as she brushed her own hand over her cheek, as if she was trying to remove something that wasn't there.

"You're so beautiful," Alex said then, leaning in and kissing her forehead. She giggled, and at that I had to force myself to look away. I could feel tears stinging the back of my eyes, but I wasn't about to let myself cry.

Everyone's relationship with their soul mate seemed so perfect. Claire and Alex, the young couple that walked by before, even my brother's relationships; they all had exactly what I've always dreamed of having. And then there was my relationship, shattered to pieces, and it was all my own, stupid fault.

Chapter Twenty-One

And once again, my phone went straight to voicemail. I sighed, putting it back in my pocket. I had called Jase about five times while I sat at home and waited with Claire. I knew she was getting impatient, that she wanted to leave to go pick up Alex, but she still refused to leave my side. I wasn't sure why, maybe she felt I needed some kind of support, but she insisted she'd wait with me until JaSe showed up.

It was Friday night; the night of the dance, and like always Claire had helped me get ready. My hair was pulled into a bun at the back of my head, secured by what felt like hundreds of bobby pins. My eyelashes touched my brow bone when I looked upwards, though she hadn't added any fake eyelashes.

"We don't want you to be too over the top or he'll think you're trying too hard," Claire had said as she ran the mascara brush through my lashes. "I'm thinking we do all natural, but it's not exactly natural because you'll be wearing make up."

Claire had made tonight all about impressing Jase, though I had told her over and over that he still hadn't replied to me. She refused to think I'd be dateless on a night that was all about you and your date. I, on the other hand, had fully prepared to spend the night home watching episodes of One Tree Hill and eating multiple blocks of chocolate.

Claire looked impatiently at her phone as another message popped up from Alex, most likely asking her where she was or why she was taking so long. She looked stunning tonight, though she always did, really. She had straightened her frizzy locks, which I knew would've taken her at least three hours to get it the way it looked now. She wore a red floor length gown, which I hadn't expected her to pick, especially from all the other dresses she had tried on. It made her look like some kind of princess, the way the bottom half of the dress turned to tulle and bounced out around her.

"You don't have to wait for me," I sighed suddenly, startling her as she gazed down at her phone.

"Don't be silly, Cand. I'm not leaving." she shook her head, her long dangling earrings shimmering. "And there's no way I'm missing out on a chance to meet this bad boy."

"He's not coming, can't you see that?" I croaked, unable to hide how upset I was becoming.

"You need to be a little bit more positive, just call him again."

"He won't answer," I argued.

"Just do it!" she cried, the frustration of being late finally showing.

I picked up the phone, dialling Jase's number once again. Claire stared at me intently, and I could see the hope in her eyes. She was equally as disappointed as I was when the phone went to his voicemail, once again. I sighed, flinging myself back onto my bed.

"Claire, don't worry about me, okay? Just go. I don't want you to miss out on a special night because of me," I mumbled, hoping she could hear me.

"Alright, I'll go, but Candice?" She stood up then, smoothing down her dress. "You can't give up just yet. It's time to take things to the next step."

I had no idea what she meant at the time, until I found myself sitting in my car, Jase's house across the other side of the road, an hour later. Driving over here and demanding to see him seemed like a good idea at the time, even Claire had thought so, but now I wasn't too sure. My fingers tapped the steering wheel, the nerves finally hitting me. What if he didn't even bother to open the door? Or slams it in my face? I guess that's exactly what I deserved, but it didn't make me feel any better.

I had a sudden burst of determination, knowing I had to do this if I ever wanted things to be right again. Even if Jace didn't forgive me, I still needed to try and explain what happened and apologise again. I wasn't sure what I was going to do if he didn't forgive me; I hadn't really put much thought into it. What did one do with a soul mate that didn't want to be your soul mate?

I got out of the car, locking it as I began to walk towards the house. Why hadn't I prepared myself more for rejection? I knew now that it was the most probable outcome, rather than forgiveness, and cursed my past self for being so spontaneous and not thinking ahead earlier tonight.

I was facing his front door now, my hand hesitating as I held it up to knock. Was I really ready to face him? To face what I had done? I was so sure I was, but now... My knuckles hit the dark wood, before I stood back and took a deep breath. Nobody answered. I shrugged and knocked again, louder this time, but still after several minutes, nothing. Had Jase told his aunt what I had done? That I turned out exactly how he imagined his soul mate would?

I sighed after the third knock, knowing no one was going to answer the door anytime soon. I turned to walk away, only to pause half way down the steps. I pulled my phone out of the small clutch my mother had found in the back of her wardrobe, saying it would match perfectly with the dress. I dialled Jase, hoping this would be the call he would finally answer, but it went straight to voicemail. I was about to hang up, when I had a sudden idea. I wasn't sure if he ever listened to the voicemail messages I left him, but maybe this was the only, if not last, chance for me to explain myself.

"Hey, Jase, It's me again. I know you're still mad at me, I mean I'm still mad at me, but I really just want to talk to you," I began. "I feel like I can explain myself now, and I really want you to give me that chance. I know I don't deserve it, heck; I deserve a big slap across the face for what I did to you. We were supposed to be at the soul mate dance right now, or at least, I was, but I couldn't bring myself to go without you. So here I am instead, standing outside your front door, too scared to knock because I don't know if you will even answer or not, and if you don't I don't want to think what that means for us. Anyway, I'm not sure if you'll ever get this message, or if you will even care, but I just wanted to say-"

The door opened then, warm light pouring out onto the steps. Jase stood there, his phone to his ear, his other hand on the door. My heart pounded against my chest; this was the first time I had seen him in almost a week. His hair was shorter, hardly an inch shorter, but it somehow now sat differently on his head. It didn't look bad, not at all. Actually I rather liked it better this way; it made it easier to see his eyes.

"Hi," I finally managed to say, before hanging up my phone. Jase slid his phone back in the pocket of his jeans, which also looked fairly new, too.

"Hi," he mumbled, looking down at his feet. We stood staring at each other for what felt like hours, but only seconds had passed before I worked up the courage to speak again.

"Can I, ah, can I come in?" He moved to the side, allowing me to move past him and into the house, before he shut the door behind me. I followed him as he walked silently into the lounge room, which was empty. The only noise in the house seemed to be coming from the Television, but otherwise, it didn't seem like anyone else was home. He sat down on the two-seater couch, making sure to leave plenty of room between us as I sat down after him.

"Where is everyone?" I asked moments later, trying to avoid the real reason I had come over.

"Out." Jase said bluntly. We sat there, barely looking at each other, before Jase spoke again. "Why are you here, Candice? If you're here to get me to go to that stupid dance, you may as well leave right now."

"No, I'm not going to the dance," I sighed. Jase looked up at me then, before raising an eyebrow.

"Why not?" he asked.

"What's the point in going to a soul mate dance without your soul mate?" He looked away then, his fingers fiddling together in his lap the way they always did when he was nervous.

"Look, Jase, I know you're still made at me, and I know I screwed things up, but I just want you to know that Ryan is completely out of the picture now, promise."

"You shouldn't have to promise something like that to me, don't you see? This whole soul mate thing is fucked. How can you have feelings for two guys, when only one is supposedly your soul mate?"

"My mum told me she fell for two guys when she was younger," I stated, hoping it would somehow make my actions less horrible.

"Huh, must be a genetic thing then," he said bitterly, still avoiding my gaze.

"Jase, I really am so sorry. I wish I could take it all back, I really do." But do you, though? Do you really? The small voice drifted through my head, jumbling my already puzzled thoughts.

"If only these stupid things were time machines, instead," he muttered.

"Jase-" I began, but he bet me to it.

"No, Candice. You don't understand what it's like to be thrown away, to be the second choice. Let me just tell you that it sucks, like, really fucking sucks. My parents left me; decided I wasn't worthy of their time and moved on with their lives. Nothing has ever gone right for me, ever. And then my aunt took me in and gave me a roof over my head, and things were going great."

"And then I met you. I didn't want you to see me like that, stealing and trying to support my family, but it happened that way anyway. At first I didn't want anything to do with you, but as I got to know you, everything changed. My thoughts were always of you, my heart would beat a little faster when I saw you, and I had no idea what was happening to me. Was I sick? Was this normal? To feel this way about another person you still hardly knew? And then I realised that I really liked you, and although that scared the shit out of me, I didn't care, because I thought you felt the same way back. But then-"

He went quiet, and I knew he was thinking about Ryan and I. I should've said something, to really show him how sorry I was and that I meant everything I said. But I couldn't speak. Jase turned to me then, a completely different expression on his face now. I had expected him to be mad, to start yelling at me and kicking me out of the house, but his face told me otherwise.

"You know, it's really hard to stay mad at you," he whispered after a while. "Well, it was easier when you weren't right in front of me, but now..."

His eyes flickered downwards, taking in my appearance for what I had thought to be the first time all night. "And when you look like this-"

He pulled me up from the couch then, placing one hand on the small of my back and the other still resting in my hand, before pulling me in close so that our bodies were just touching.

"Can I have this dance?" he whispered, taking my hands and placing them around his neck. I felt my heart pound against my rib cage, as his hands touched my hips. And we started dancing. I had never been a dancer, never even tried it due to my lack of coordination and fitness. But somehow, dancing with Jase worked perfectly. Our feet found their way through the other's legs, and moved around the coffee table soundlessly.

He stopped near the couch we had been sitting on, spinning me around and back into his arms. He reached behind me then, startling me. He smiled softly, and I felt his hand in my hair. He pulled at the bun Claire had spent hours on, although to his surprise, it didn't budge. His fingers began pulling at the pins keeping the bun in place, before he laughed.

"They make it look so easy in movies." Finally my hair came loose, spilling down my back and around my shoulders in waves. He grinned then, raking his fingers through the loose curls.

"You should wear your hair down more often," he whispered. His hand cupped my cheek then, bringing my face closer to his. Being this close, I could see how his eyes had brown flecks through the irises, and now they looked bluer than ever before.

"Are you sure you're ready for this, Candy?" he whispered then, his gaze focused completely on my lips. I didn't move, nor could I speak. His lips brushed mine, and I could hear my heartbeat pounding against my eardrums. His lips parted then, but only into a smirk.

"Are you sure you want me to kiss you?" he whispered, pulling his face back so our lips were no longer touching. He was driving my body mad, every inch of me wanted to kiss him, to touch him, and yet, he seemed to be enjoying watching it happen in front of him.

"Because the last time I tried-" I couldn't stand it anymore, I closed the gap between us. I felt him smile beneath my lips, clearly happy that I was the one that caved, before his lips pushed back against mine. My mind whirled, my heart raced, my body felt like jelly. Where Ryan had been soft and gentle, Jase was hungry and rough. It didn't mean that Ryan was better, oh god no, Jase wasn't a bad kisser at all. In fact, he was quite the opposite.

His palm was warm against my cheek, as it tried to pull me in even more. He lifted me up, sitting me on the couch next to him. My hands wrapped around Jase's neck, attempting to pull him impossibly closer. I must have misjudged my strength, because suddenly I was lying on the couch with Jase on top of me, our lips still moving together. I felt Jase's stomach muscles vibrate as he chuckled, before our lips broke apart. His face was flushed, as I suspected mine would be as well. His arms held him up now, placed either side of me like a barrier.

"Was that as scary as you thought?" he breathed, his forehead sticky with sweat. I laughed then, shaking my head. His eyes looked twice their size from this angle, and I could see the muscles bulging from his arms as he kept himself propped above me.

"Not at all," I whispered, before wrapping my fingers around his neck once more and pulling his face back down towards mine.

(A/N: firstly, the pic on the side is the dress candy is wearin, and i'm sorry you can hardly see it i couldn't find a better picture but if you've seen the spectacular now then you know what it looks like anyways. and also the song is for when they are dancin, bc it's been stuck in my head all night and it seems to fit it perfectly (and i just love the song so ya)secondly, i just wanted to ask y'all, who do you ship? jase and candice (aka jandice) or ryan and candice (aka randice) i wanna see where your little hearts are at hehehehe dedicated to my hsm bestie @argentile bc she's nice. mwah i hope you wonderful people enjoyed this and don't forget to vote and comment xxxxxx)

Chapter Twenty-Two

"Candice! Claire's here." My mother called from the bottom of the staircase. I quickly pinned some of my hair back, letting the rest fall down my back. It wasn't something I was used to, but all I could think of was what Jase had said last night. You should wear your hair down more often. The thought sent shivers down my spine, just making me want to see him even more. Although, I knew the moment the wind hit my hair and sent it every which way, I'd instantly regret leaving it down.

"Come on, we've got to go!" Claire said, suddenly appearing in the doorway. Her hair was still straight from the dance last night, though her curls had started to appear around her ears.

"Alright, alright, I'm coming," I smiled, following her out the door and down the stairs. Alex was lingering around the front door, looking almost too afraid to move just in case he touched something he wasn't supposed to.

"Hey Alex," I grinned as we approached him, receiving a small wave in return. He was always shy around me, though Claire said he would never shut up when it was just the two of them together. It was funny how you acted so differently around certain people.

I quickly said goodbye to my mother, before we headed out the door and piled into Claire's car. She was recounting the dance to me, telling me how amazing it was and that I really missed out on a great night. I didn't mind that I'd missed the dance, my night still turned out to be pretty good.

"I can't believe you couldn't convince Jase to come! I was so sure that dress would steal his heart," she sighed. I hadn't yet had the chance to tell her that things with Jase were back the way they should be, but she could tell something was up by the smile that had been plastered on my face all morning.

"I think he really liked the dress, Claire," I smiled, thinking of the way his eyes kept flicking down my body.

"Well obviously not enough if he hasn't even-" She looked at me then, her eyes flicking from the road in front of us back to me. All I could do was grin and nod repeatedly. "He forgave you? Well then, this calls for a celebration!"

The car jerked suddenly, almost cutting off the oncoming traffic as Claire turned down a narrow side street. I had no idea where she was planning on taking us now. At first I had thought she would just be going back to her house, or down to the shops for some retail therapy, but we were too far away for either of those options right now.

"Where on earth are we going?" I asked finally, afraid we might've been lost.

"To Jase's house, of course," Claire grinned, taking another sharp turn, throwing Alex and I around the car like ragdolls.

"Wait, what? Claire-" I warned, knowing already that this couldn't possibly be a good idea. It wasn't that I didn't want to see Jase, because of course I did, I mean I could barely stop thinking about him, but Claire's plans were always a bit crazy.

"What? We can't double date if you don't have your date, now can we?" she smiled, unable to wipe the grin off her face.

"I never agreed to this," I said, looking out the window towards row upon row or residential houses.

"Either did I," Alex called from the back seat. He wasn't particularly happy that he drew the short straw and missed out on the passenger seat.

"Oh shut up, the both of you! It's going to be fun!" She rolled her eyes, turning down a small court that suddenly seemed extremely familiar to me. I wasn't sure how she knew where Jase lived, though I wasn't about to ask. She probably followed me here last night, making sure I had actually gone to his house and not to sulk at the café.

Before I knew it she was ushering me out of the car, towards Jase's house. My foot caught on the road, making me stumble as neared the home, hoping nobody saw it. Though when I turned around back towards the car, I could see Claire laughing, proving me wrong. I made a face, before turning back around just as I entered the small path that lead to the front door. I thought back to last night, when I stood here pathetically hoping for forgiveness, and for the door to open. This time, the door opened on the first knock.

"Hey, Jase," I smiled. Jase stood, his chest bare, with only boxer shorts to cover his bottom half. I felt my cheeks burn as I raked my eyes across his chest. He didn't have muscles protruding from his abdomen, something that a lot of girls seemed to find dreamy, but he was definitely not over-weight, either. He somehow fit in between, though he was much closer to the skinnier side of the scale, and to me he looked perfect.

I had always hated the word; perfect. How could anything ever be perfect? Everything had flaws, cracks, pieces missing; nothing could ever really be defined as perfect. That was until just recently, when I found something that finally fit the definition. Jase. Though some people wouldn't agree, that his smile wasn't perfect because it was slightly crooked, and his arm had a scar from some childhood injury. But to me, those little things were what made him perfect.

"Hi." He looked startled, and for a second I worried that maybe he didn't want to see me. Maybe I should've called him before I just showed up to his door, not that Claire had really given me much of a chance to let him know.

"I'm sorry, I should've told you I was coming by," I apologised.

"No, no, it's fine, Candy! Surprise visits are always much better," he smiled, moving back to let me through.

"Oh, wait, I can't stay long. I've actually just come to get you," I said, almost forgetting about Claire and Alex waiting in the car.

"Get me? And take me where?" He looked puzzled, his eyebrow raising.

"To, um- Actually I have no idea where we're going, but Claire says you have to come along."

"Claire?" His face was full of confusion, and I realised that I had never really talked to him about Claire before. I felt like I'd known him for such a long time now, but there were still parts of each other that we both had no idea about.

"Oh, don't worry, just hurry up."

We walked out the front door several minutes later, and towards the car waiting across the road. I could see that Alex had moved into the passenger seat, leaving Jase and I to sit in the back. Not that I didn't want to sit next to Jase, but the back seat of Claire's car barely had room for one person, let alone two. She was quite possibly the messiest person I had ever met.

"Finally! Gosh, what took you guys so long?" Claire exclaimed as she started the car. She turned around then, a wide grin spreading across her face. "Or do I really want to know?" She wiggled her eyebrows, receiving a slap on the arm from me and a strange look from Jase.

The car ride consisted of mostly Claire talking and asking Jase questions, Alex sitting quietly, and Jase just feeling awkward from the bizarre questions he was trying to answer. I couldn't help but laugh, and in a way, feel kind of grateful. I ended up finding some more about Jase that I didn't know before, and that I would never have thought to ask either.

"Okay, but if Dinosaurs still existed-" Claire was saying, but stopped suddenly as the car turned an abrupt corner and a huge sign appeared in front of us. 'Welcome to the Zoo,' it read in bright green bolded letters. I saw Claire's face light up through the rear view mirror; she'd been nagging me to go to the zoo with her for months now, which probably sounded strange for a sixteen-year-old girl. But Claire had an insane love for animals, and I knew one day she'd choose a career that would keep her close to them.

Jase looked at me, raising an eyebrow. The zoo was probably the last place he was expecting me to take him, and honestly, I hadn't been expecting to end up here either, though I really should've.

"Really?" he said as Claire parked the car. I laughed, getting out of the car and watching Claire practically run to the front entrance, Alex struggling to keep up behind her. "Why the zoo?"

"Why not?" I smiled, before heading towards the entrance.

* * *

"Come on, I wanna go see the tigers again!" Claire nagged, pulling at Alex's arm. He rolled his eyes. Sometimes I wondered how he could put up with Claire so often. I mean, I did it too, but there was only so much enthusiasm and energy one could handle. Alex always just went along with whatever

Claire said, and I felt as though he would literally do anything for her, even if it were to jump into the tiger cage and use himself as bait just so Claire could snap a good photo.

"Claire, I think we should go home. We're all exhausted," Alex insisted, trying to pull his arm back.

"Well I'm not, so let's go!" We all groaned as she half skipped, half dragged Alex behind her. Jase and I walked together a few paces behind, watching as Claire attempted to jump on her soul mate's back for a piggy-back ride, but failing embarrassingly.

"Do you think she'll notice if we go through here?" Jase whispered then, not wanting Claire to hear him, though she was much too far away to even see us now. I didn't even get to answer when Jase grabbed my hand and jerked me onto a small path branching off the one we were on. Although it was a rather sunny day, the path was quite dark due to the forest of trees that enclosed around the narrow path. It almost felt like we had transported to a real rainforest, minus the rain.

The path eventually opened out to a body of water that was too small to be called a lake, but much too big to be called a pond. Jase let go of my hand, walking over to the sign that would tell us what animal lived here.

"What is it?" I asked, staring out into the water to try and spot any movement.

"Otters," Jase said, walking to stand beside me. We both stood by the edge of the water, searching and waiting for something to appear. We had almost given up when an otter scurried to the water from behind a large rock. It was followed by another one, only seconds later. They dived into the water, swimming around in circles as Jase and I watched on.

"Aw, they're holding hands! How cute!" I said as they floated past, holding the other as close as possible. Jase grinned then, before turning to look at me.

"Do you know why they hold hands?" he asked. I shook my head. "They do it when they're sleeping, because they don't want the other to leave them."

"How did you-" I began, though Jase cut in before I could finish.

"It said it on the sign," he grinned, taking my hands and pulling me closer to him. His hand ran up my arm, sending small jolts of electricity through my veins and through my whole body. I shivered, though thankfully Jase didn't notice. His hand reached my shoulder, then my neck, and before I knew it, he was pulling me even closer towards him. His lips were only centimetres from mine; I could feel his breath, could almost taste his lips. I leaned up slightly, making the space between our lips disappear. It was a sweet kiss; full of joy rather than hunger like last night. I couldn't pick which one I enjoyed more, maybe last night's since it lasted longer.

"There you two are! We thought we lo-" I heard the voice before I saw her, breaking away from Jase and instantly feeling my cheeks heat up from getting caught. "Oh, sorry for interrupting, but we're going to leave now."

I looked back at Jase, who just shook his head, his mouth pulled into a smile. We walked back to the car, the sun beginning to set as we drove off.

I got home just in time for dinner, and to my surprise, the whole family had decided to show up. Mum had cooked a huge roast lamb, which was a sort of family tradition when we could all be together at the table. It was great seeing Lucy and Daniel, since I hadn't seen them since their wedding. They had just gotten back from their honeymoon; some remote island with an expensive resort and an all you can eat buffet. Everyone had exciting news to share, everyone was happy. It was like my world was finally falling into place, and everything was finally going right.

When I went to sleep that night, I felt completely fine, happy even. That was until I woke to a strange beeping sound, loud and close by. I restlessly checked my phone, only to see that the battery was dead. I struggled to flick the lamp on, squinting as light flooded through my room. Once my eyes finally adjusted, I could see that it was exactly as it had been when I fell asleep. The noise stopped suddenly, and that's when I felt it, a strange jolt of electricity starting from my wrist and going through my entire body. It wasn't painful, and it only happened once, but it did surprise me. I thought about going back to sleep, seeing as the noise had vanished, but something still felt wrong.

I lifted my arm then, pulling it free from the tangle of blankets it had gotten caught in. I turned it over, not at all expecting to see what was there. My Timekeeper had changed; the twelve consecutive zeros had disappeared, or maybe a better word was replaced. My heart leaped out of my chest, and my throat tightened. I felt nauseous, like I wanted to throw up, but my body wouldn't move. It was in complete shock, the only part of me moving was the tears slowly rolling down my cheeks.

What stood in place where the twelve consecutive zeros once were, was a thick, blood red line.

Chapter Twenty-Three

I don't think I had ever gotten dressed and out of my bedroom so fast in my life. I ran downstairs, almost tripping over my feet on the way down. My mind was going a millions different ways, and my heart was beating so fast I worried that I might go into cardiac arrest.

I reached the front door just as I tugged on my brother's jumper that I had found in the middle of the hallway. It was way too big for me, especially with only my pyjama shorts on. But I didn't care. I didn't care how cold it was when I opened the door, nor did I care that it was the middle of the night. All I cared about was getting to Jase's house as fast as I possibly could.

"Candice?" I heard from behind me. I cursed myself for not caring enough to be quiet on my way out, before turning to see my mother, still looking half asleep.

"What on earth are you doing?" she yawned, though she sounded very serious.

"Mum, I'm sorry I woke you, but, I really have to go." She must have finally processed what I had said, because her eyes went wide.

"You can't be serious, Candice. It's the middle of the night! I'm sure whatever it is you're hurrying off for can wait until morning," she said firmly.

"No mum, you don't understand! This cannot wait, or else it might be too late!"

"Cand-" she began. She took a step towards me just as I threw my arm out, baring my Timekeeper to her. At first she just looked confused, and I really couldn't blame her. She had just caught her daughter- who never breaks the rules or does anything remotely rebellious- trying to sneak out of the house in the middle of the night. But then she really looked at my Timekeeper, and I saw the colour drain out of her face. I could feel my eyes getting teary again, even though I told myself I wouldn't believe it until I saw it with my own eyes.

"Oh. Oh, Candice, sweetie," she whispered, not because she didn't want to wake the others, but because that's the only noise she could manage.

"So please mum, I have to go. I-I have to see him." It was silent for a moment. I could hear the faint sound of rain hitting the roof, but thankfully, as I looked out the open door, I saw that it was only a light shower. My eyes stung with tears now, though I wasn't exactly sure when I had started crying again.

"Okay, but let me drive you there. There's no way I'm letting you go alone," she said at last.

We got to the car, mum in her dressing gown and slippers, me bare foot and barely clothed. It should've been freezing out, there was no doubt it was, but I couldn't feel it. I couldn't feel the wind breeze through my tangled hair, couldn't feel the stones digging into my feet as I walked, I couldn't feel anything. It was like my body had gone into such shock that it forgot how to function normally. Mum fiddled with the keys, finally unlocking it and hopping in the drivers seat. She reached over and pulled the lock up on the passenger door, allowing me to get out of the rain.

Most of the drive there was silent, my leg's impatiently bouncing as my mother drove. I caught her glance over at me ever now and then, like she wanted to say something but wasn't quite sure what. I wasn't sure I really wanted her to say anything; I just wanted to get to Jase's house and for the line on my wrist to disappear. I had never really thought about what it would be like to not have a soul mate, but I've never had too. Why would you ever want to think about the death of the person you belonged to?

"Mum, can you drive any faster?" I yelled, unable to keep my emotions under control.

"Sweetie, I'm already over the speed limit. Just breathe, everything will be okay." I shot her a look, and I knew I was being horrible, but I didn't care. Not right now, anyway. My body ached to see Jase, to touch him once more, before it might be too late.

"Don't even try that on me, mum. How can you even say that?" I choked, the tears spilling down my cheeks again.

"When you're father died-"

"Don't. Just stop, please. You don't know he's gone, not yet." I knew I sounded crazy. This whole situation seemed crazy, surreal even. I was being wildly optimistic, or I was just trying to deny the truth that sat on my wrist. I refused to look at it now, pulling my brother's jumper down to cover the small strip of plastic.

"Candy-" she began to protest, but stopped when she saw my face.

"Please, mum. I just need to see him," I whispered. "I just need to see him."

She didn't reply, though I felt her foot press down further on the accelerator. I wasn't sure how fast she was going now, but to me it still felt much too slow. I just wanted to wake up, because surely this had to be a nightmare. Surely something like this couldn't happen to me? Not when things were going so well? Was it my fault this had happened? Should I have invited him around for dinner? Or dropped in to see Kath and Isobel? Not that any of that mattered now, I couldn't change the past no matter how much I tried.

"Turn down here, and then it's the third street on the right," I mumbled, hoping my mother was still able to hear me. She nodded, and followed my instructions without another word. Was she afraid to say anything? Or maybe she just didn't know what to say? What did you say to a person who had just seen the dreaded red line appear on the inside of their wrist? 'I'm sorry' didn't even seem like the right thing to say.

I pointed to Jase's house as we began down his street, and was out of the car before my mother could even put it in park. I sprinted across the road, my bare feet stinging from the damp ground. I heard mum call out after me, but I wasn't about to stop now. I was too close to him, if he was even home. I almost tripped up the footpath as I realised I really hadn't thought this through. What if Jase wasn't even here? What if was at a hospital? Or maybe he never made it to the hospital, and maybe he was out there somewhere-

I shook the thought from mind, not liking the images that came along with it. Just think positive, Candice. Despite my minds request, I struggled to stay positive. The image of the bright red line slicing through my Timekeeper kept reappearing in my head, almost every time I closed my eyes.

I was at the door now, pounding as hard as I possibly could on the hard wood. My knuckles ached, my head was throbbing, and all my body wanted to do was lie down and rest. The door finally opened, revealing a very tired and quite furious looking Kath. She did a double take, not expecting the obnoxious doorknocker to end up being me.

"Candice? What are you-" She started, still in complete shock that I was standing at her doorstep. I gave her a sideways glance. She obviously hadn't been awake when I came banging on the door, so she really had no idea why I was here. I half expected to see Kath as a blubbering mess, but she just looked very annoyed.

"Is Jase here?" I asked impatiently, trying to see if anyone had appeared from behind her. The hall was deserted though, to my surprise. How my loud pounding on the door hadn't woken Isobel up was truly shocking.

"Of course he is? He's sleeping, sweetie. It's the middle of the night." I felt another tear trickle down my cheek, unable to stop them falling now. "What's wrong?" Kath asked, clearly seeing how upset and worried I was.

I pushed past her, unable to stand there any longer. Every second I wasted was another second Jase could be- I couldn't even bring myself to say it. I hardly wanted to think it, to believe that such a thing could be true. Not after everything we've been through, and not now. Not now that our relationship was finally a true relationship.

I ran down the hall, swinging the door to Jase's bedroom wide open. It took my eyes a few moments to adjust to the dimness of the room, and it was then that I realised this was actually the first time I had ever been in his room. It seemed like a typical teenage boy's room to me. Clothes thrown carelessly on the floor and on top of a wooden desk that sat on one wall, a smell you could only associate with a boy, and a couple of posters of bands I had never heard of. But what was different, was the shelves filled with books. I could see some that I was familiar with, Game Of Thrones, Harry Potter, but there were also some I'd never seen before.

Jase was sprawled out on his bed, the blanket's supposed to be covering him lay at the base of his bed in a tangled mess. I squinted, trying to see even the smallest of movements, something to indicate that he was alive, but I was unable to see anything. I switched the light on, the brightness almost blinding. My legs almost gave way, my hands shook as though I'd been standing in the freezing cold for far too long, and my heart was beating so fast I thought I might faint. Somehow though, I managed to walk towards the bed.

I heard Kath's voice from a distance, or so I thought it was. I had shut out everything that the whole world around me seemed to have disappeared and my vision was blurred. My only focus was on the body lying in front of me, his chest seemingly unmoving. I found myself climbing onto the bed and kneeling next to Jase. My face felt wet, and I realised that I had been sobbing so hard my vision had become blurry. I wasn't sure when it had started, but there was no way it was going to stop now.

"Jase," I whispered through tears. "Jase, please wake up."

He looked so peaceful lying there, as though he really was asleep. It was the most beautiful and awful thing I had ever seen, and I wasn't sure how that could even be possible. How could something so beautiful possibly cause so much pain and grief?

"Jase, you can't leave me. I can't lose you, please!" I cried, almost pounding my fists on his chest. I was suddenly leaning down by his face, my lips almost touching his ear.

"Jase. Jase, please. Please just let this be a horrible nightmare, and I'm going to wake up now. Please don't let this be real. It can't be real. What I feel for you is the realest thing I've ever felt about anyone. Nobody else makes me feel the way you do, Jase. Not Ryan, not anyone. And I know it's too late, that you won't even be able to hear this, but I love you. It's probably crazy that I am saying that, but I do, I know I do."

My head lay on his chest now, and I could almost imagine his chest rising and falling underneath my cheek. But I hadn't imagined that, there was no way I had imagined it. I shot up, staring down at his peaceful face. My heart was beating even fast than it was before, though I didn't think it was even possible for it to beat this fast.

"Jase?" I whispered, but received nothing in return. I grabbed his shoulders then, and started shaking him. His whole body shook, his hands falling limply to his sides. I felt hands on my shoulders then, trying to pull me away from his body. I could hear myself screaming, tears still falling down my face. I was in hysterics, and gripped onto Jase so hard I thought his seemingly fragile body might crumble underneath me.

It was then that I felt a movement so tiny it could only be one thing. A heart beat. I looked up at the face that lay below me, just in time to see his eyelashes flutter open.

I couldn't believe my eyes. He was alive. Jase was really alive.

(A/N: I'M SORRY FOR PUTTING YOU GUYS THROUGH THAT HORRIBLE CLIFFHANGER IN THE PREVIOUS CHAPTER. I HOPE THIS ONE MAKES UP FOR IT! (also dedicated to @thepurplerose because she's one of the sweetest, kindest people here on wattpad and you should all go follow her and love her) DON'T FORGET TO VOTE AND COMMENT YOUR THOUGHTS. WHAT DO YOU THINK HAPPENED WITH CANDICE'S TIMEKEEPER?????)

Chapter Twenty-Four

His eyes finally landed on me after adjusting to the brightness of the room. I could see that he was searching for a snarky comment to say, trying to find the right thing to say as I sat on top of him staring down in complete shock.

"Well," he croaked. "This is not what I had ever expected to wake up to."

I stared wide-eyed at him. His eyes were blinking, his chest was moving; he was as alive as a person could be. I burst into tears, though it was more like tears on top of tears, since I hadn't really stopped crying since I got here. He raised his eyebrow, clearly confused at both the fact that I was here on top of him in the middle of the night, and that I could barely look at him without letting out another sob. I hated crying in front of people. It was like they were seeing the real you, the raw, unedited version of yourself that you hid from the rest of the world.

"Candice? Are you okay?" Jase asked when the tears had started to recede. He attempted to sit up, and before I knew it was I was wrapping my arms around his neck, almost knocking him back down. I hadn't thought I would ever be in this position, never thought I'd be so close to losing my soul mate, well at least not for another fifty years. And now that he was here- in my arms and unmistakeably alive- I couldn't bear the thought that if I let him go, I might really lose him this time.

"I-I thought you were- it said you were-" I blubbered into his shoulder, unable to string a proper sentence together.

"Thought I was what?" he asked after I finally let him go. The tears began streaming down my face as I remembered seeing his body lying on the bed, unmoving and peaceful. I looked down at my wrist, even though the sleeve of my brother's jumper covered it. Was it still there? Had the red line even shown at all, or had I just imagined the whole thing? I pulled up my sleeve and showed him my wrist, waiting for his reaction. It would either tell me this had all been a misunderstanding, that I had just imagined what I saw, or it would tell me I wasn't so crazy, but that meant a whole other problem. He gave me a funny look, before he really looked down at my wrist.

"Wait, what?" He asked moments later, confirming that I was, in fact, sane and hadn't imagined the line. His fingers traced around the small strip of metal on the inside of my wrist, as if he was trying to fix it, trying to make the red line disappear. It didn't move though, just sat there like a bloody stain. His touch sent shivers through my body, as though my body wasn't yet used to him. "What do you think this means?"

"I-I don't know," I stuttered after a while. My heart, although it had slowed, was still beating faster than normal. My body seemed to be still in shock, unable to process what had happened within the last hour. It felt like so long ago, like a lifetime had passed, since I first saw the red line. It was strange that time could feel longer or shorter, depending on what was happening in the world around us. When you were sitting in maths class, the time seemed to stop and drag on forever, but when you were catching up with an old friend who you haven't seen in years, time would fly by.

"Are we not soul mates?" Jase asked softly. I gave him a funny look, before really registering what he had actually asked. I hadn't even thought about that possibility yet. That would explain why Jase was still alive, but then again, our Timekeeper's had lead us to each other. They had chimed as both our countdowns reached zero, which was exactly what was supposed to happen when you met your soul mate.

"Maybe your Timekeeper just broke?" Jase questioned, unable to take his eyes off my wrist.

"I've never even heard of them breaking before," I yawned, suddenly feeling extremely tired. The adrenaline that got me here was clearly wearing off, and now my body was trying to tell me to get back to sleep. 'It's the middle of the night, why on earth are you awake?' I could imagine it telling me, though obviously my body doesn't have it's own mind or way of talking. "I didn't think that was even possible."

"Maybe it will just go back to normal tomorrow?" His eyes flicked up from my wrist then, though his hand stayed wrapped around the Timekeeper. He looked tired, but his eyes looked hopeful. He really believed that it would go back to normal, that this was just a small glitch and would all be fixed by the morning. It was as though this kind of thing had happened to him before, and he knew that everything was going to be all right.

"I don't know, Jase. It did exactly what it was supposed to do once a person loses their soul mate, the beep and everything." He looked down at his own wrist, and stayed silent for a while. It was then that I heard murmuring from the door, and realised that Kath and my mother were standing there watching us. I was sure Kath probably followed after me once I stormed past her and ran towards Jase's room, but when had my mother arrived? It was stupid of me to think she would just wait in the car until I came back, which I hadn't really thought about either. What if things had turned out differently, if I had walked into Jase's room and was greeted with a dead body, rather than a sleeping one? Would I have run back to the car? Ran to his body and held him so tightly that if he were alive, I would've squeezed him to death?

All these crazy thoughts began rushing through my mind, so fast and hard that I thought I might pass out. I tried to calm myself, to think of other things. It took several seconds before my mind began to clear, and when Jase spoke again, I had almost missed it from being so caught up in my own thoughts.

"Have you-ah, spoken to Ryan?" Jase asked suddenly, which caught me by surprise. I looked at him, trying to see if he was joking, but his face seemed as serious as ever. It took me a moment to realise why he asked this. At first it seemed like a completely random question, maybe a question he had wanted to ask me for a while, but now didn't really seem like the right time for it. But then I realised what the actual question was implying.

"No, why would I?" I knew exactly why he was asking, and it honestly shocked me that he brought it up in the first place. I had only just now truly wondered if Jase was even my soul mate; that maybe somehow my Timekeeper had gotten mixed up with someone else's, and my real soul mate was out there somewhere, lifeless. For the slightest second I thought that maybe my Timekeeper was paired with Ryan's, because how could Jase possibly be alive if my wrist said he wasn't? And maybe, just maybe, that would explain the feelings I had thought I felt for him.

"Well, maybe your Timekeeper is working and your soul mate is- well, you know- really gone." It only took me a moment or so to completely cancel out the theory, mainly because I suddenly remembered that Ryan's Timekeeper had already shown him that his soul mate had passed away. But then again, if my Timekeeper had malfunctioned, what if Ryan's had too? What if I wasn't the first person that this had happened to? What if there were hundreds of people out there, depressed, sad lonely, because they believe what the Timekeeper told them? That their soul mate is dead?

"No, that can't be possible. Ryan's Timekeeper showed the red line before I had even met him," I explained. "He's not my soul mate, Jace, he can't be."

Relief washed over his face, a small smile playing at his lips. He was thankful that Ryan couldn't be my soul mate, and I knew I should've been thankful, too, but there was still no explanation for what was happening, for why my Timekeeper had clearly malfunctioned. It wasn't as though I wished that it were telling the truth, I was quite happy that it had been just a glitch, quite happy indeed. But if it had malfunctioned, then why? And what if it had happened before? What if the Timekeeper's couldn't actually be trusted?

"Well," Kath said, attempting to break the now silent room. "Since we're all awake, I'll make some tea." She clapped her hands together before walking down the hall. My mother began to follow her, and Jase quickly grabbed a shirt and some track pants off his floor to chuck on. I looked away, even though he had been almost naked this whole time. I cursed myself for not even taking the time to check out his body, but the moment had passed now, as he ruffled his hair with his hands.

I felt his hands fall onto my hips, and almost jumped out of my skin. I heard him chuckle, before he spun me around to face him. Our faces were only inches apart, and my heart began beating uncontrollably fast again. I wasn't sure if it was just because of the intimacy, or if it was the fact that his heart was beating, his lungs breathing, and his brain sending millions of messages around his body. I never thought I would be this happy to see someone so healthy and alive.

He lifted his hand, letting his fingers brush my cheek. It was then that I suddenly became conscious that I probably looked hideous. I could tell my cheeks were bright red, and my eyes were no doubt swollen from all the tears I had shed. My nose was pretty blocked, and I thought for a moment that if he were to kiss me, I wouldn't even be able to breathe.

"Come on you two," I heard Kath call from the kitchen, "out of the bedroom." Jase gave a small pout, though it didn't last long. It turned into a smirk, his signature smile, before he placed his hand in mine and began walking out the door.

Kath and my mother sat at the dining table when we walked into the kitchen, their voices hushed once they saw us. I wasn't sure what they were talking about- probably something to do with the two of us- but I couldn't bring myself to ask. It wasn't like I was afraid of what they might say, but I had reached a point of exhaustion that it made it hard to even open my mouth.

"Tea?" Jase asked, grabbing a pair of bright yellow mugs from one of the cupboards. I nodded.

We sat in the lounge room, just Jase and I. I could still hear Kath and my mother talking, but I wasn't able to make out what they were saying. I held the steaming cup of tea with both hands, attempting to steal the heat. I felt utterly exhausted, and I knew if I laid my head down, even just for a second, I'd drift to sleep.

Jase placed his mug on the coffee table, the coffee table that Isabel and I sat at for hours drawing together. I was actually surprised that with all the noise and commotion going on, that she was still asleep. Kath had gone to check on her earlier, and said she was somehow fast asleep still. It was hard to believe that so much had happened in only a short amount of time, it felt like I'd lived another two days within the past few hours. I lifted my jumper up slightly, just enough to see the Timekeeper. The red line still appeared, and I couldn't help but slightly worry that maybe Jase wasn't my soul mate, and whoever my real soul mate was, he was really gone. How awful that would be, to die lonely and without someone to love you.

"Stop staring at it, Candice. It's not going to make it go away," Jase said softly, placing his hand over my wrist.

"I know, I just- what are we going to do?" I sighed, leaning back into him. He grabbed the now empty mug out of my hands, before he wrapped his arms around me, pulling me in closer. His chin rested on top of my head, slightly digging into my skull. I didn't really mind; at this point I was too tired to really even know what was going on around me.

"I wish I knew, babe."

"Babe?" I giggled.

"Don't like it?" he chuckled, running his hands up and down my arms, sending shivers through every movement.

"Not at all," I said, shaking my head.

"Not even a little bit?" I just laughed, before trying to snuggle even closer to him. My eyelids felt too heavy to keep open now, and I could feel my whole body relaxing. There was no way I was going to stay awake for much longer.

"Did you mean what you said?" Jase asked suddenly, almost startling me. I could feel his chest rising and falling, and couldn't help but smile. Jase was alive, and whether he was my soul mate or not, I didn't even care. All that mattered was that he was miraculously alive.

"What did I say?" I said, or at least tried to. All that I could really manage was a mumble, but Jase seemed to understand what I had said anyway.

"You told me you loved me, when you thought I was dead. Did you really mean it?" I could barely remember it now; it felt like it had happened so long ago. Did I say I loved him? I wasn't even sure anymore. My brain was beginning to shut itself down, ready for a rest before another day of nonstop work tomorrow.

"Candice?" Was the last sound I heard before I drifted into a deep sleep.

(decicated to @algort for making the beautiful cover xxx)

Chapter Twenty-Five

Two days had passed since my Timekeeper had malfunctioned. Two days, and still nothing had changed. The red line still stuck prominently on my wrist, and every time I saw it, I would have a mini freak out. I wasn't quite used to seeing the dreaded line, even though it meant nothing to me. I had called Jase almost every hour of every day since; just to make sure he was still alive and breathing. I know it sounds stupid, but I couldn't help it. The longer I'd go without speaking to him or hearing from him, the worse my paranoia would get. I hated it, and knew I was being extremely annoying, but I just couldn't help it.

I sat on the couch, eating some toast and flicking through television shows. There was never anything on before school, only a bunch of educational children shows. This one in particular seemed extremely old, and involved Count Dracula singing about numbers and playing the piano. Sighing, I got off the couch and strode into the kitchen, finishing the last few mouthfuls of toast and washing the crumbs off of the plate.

The house was relatively empty now. Jacob had left for work already, and Patricia had a business meeting on the other side of the city so she left last night and stayed at a nearby hotel. I wasn't sure where my mother was, seeing as she would usually be up by now. Maybe she was outside in the garden, or upstairs taking a shower. I knew she'd pop up sooner or later to remind me that I have school today, as she does every school morning, just in case I may have forgotten.

I took the stairs two at a time, almost tripping on the last step and falling flat on my face. But I managed to keep my balance, and walked into my bedroom. I flopped down onto my bed, which isn't the most graceful thing to do when you're wearing a skirt, even with tights underneath. I grabbed my phone from underneath my pillow, and frowned slightly seeing I had no messages. My fingers padded across the screen, pushing numbers and doing so without a moment's hesitation; I now knew Jase's number off by heart. It wasn't an extremely difficult number to remember, seeing as a lot of the numbers were the same. The phone began ringing as I gazed down at my wrist, a habit I had begun doing long before a red line cut through the metal strip.

"Hello?" The voice on the other end was deep and groggy, making it obvious that I had just woken him up. A rush of relief flew through my body as soon as he spoke, and I was reminded yet again that he was healthy and alive.

"Did I wake you?" I laughed as a yawn slips from his mouth.

"Candice? What time is it?" Jase asked, clearly irritated from being woken up.

"Around half past eight," I smiled, just happy to hear his voice.

"And you decided to wake me up at this ungodly hour because?" he asked with a sigh.

"You can't sleep the day away, Jase," I laughed, though feeling slightly guilty for waking him up. It's not like he had to be up this early, he didn't have school and had finished his community service last week. I knew he was applying for jobs around the city, but he'd been unsuccessful so far.

"There are twenty-four hours in a day, I think I'm allowed to sleep for more than eight of them." I laughed, ready to reply, when I heard my mother calling my name downstairs. She's probably just making sure I'm up and ready for school, like every other morning.

"Yes, Mum, I'm awake," I yelled, before trying to turn my attention back to Jase. But I could still hear my mother's voice calling me from the stairs, and her tone was starting to sound more urgent. I got up off my bed, almost falling back down again as my body tried to adjust itself to the sudden change of position, before walking out of my bedroom and down the stairs.

"Candice, you can't just wake me up and then not talk to me." Jase's voice drifted through the phone that still sat by my ear.

"Sorry, Jase. I-" I stop mid-sentence, unable to force another noise out of my mouth. My mother is standing in the living room, TV remote in hand, the volume on the TV turned up so high I am surprised I couldn't hear it earlier.

"Candice? Are you still there?"

'Breaking News', the headline flashed across the top of the screen as a middle-aged man sat at a desk facing the camera, facing me. I could see my mum's face from the corner of my eye, her face filled with concern.

"The Timekeeper on her wrist had shown her the Mark, although her soul mate was still, unbelievably, alive." It took me a few moments to register what was coming out of the man's mouth, but when I did, I almost dropped my phone. Me. The man on the Television was talking about me.

"Candice?" The voice seemed to float into my mind from nowhere, and it took me a few seconds to realise that I was actually still on the phone to Jace.

"Jase, turn on your Television right now," I croaked, struggling to speak.

"What? Cand-" He began, clearly starting to worry.

"Just do it." I hear him shuffle around, and moments later hear the muffled voice of the same reporter that I'm seeing. A photo of my face popped up in the corner of the screen then, as the reporter continued to talk, though I wasn't sure what he was saying. I had completely zoned out, unable to hear anything except my heartbeat. I suddenly hear a gasp through the phone, as my hearing decides to come back into focus. A photo of Jase has appeared beside mine now, and I began to wonder how on Earth they got these photos? Heck, how on Earth did they even know about us?

"This just leaves the question, do the Timekeeper's really work? Or have we been fooled by love all this time?"

We hadn't told anyone about my Timekeeper other than our families; I hadn't even told Claire yet. But somehow people had noticed, and some-one told the whole world. Surely our families hadn't gone and told without consulting us first? But I guess it didn't really matter how it got out or who had done it, because it was already too late. The whole world now knew that my Timekeeper had glitched, and they didn't just know a name, they had a face to search for too.

"Candice?" Jase whispered through the phone.

"Yeah?" I whispered back as Mum turned the volume on the TV down. The news broadcast had finished now, and my mother was staring at me with concern. I couldn't believe what I had just seen, I didn't want to believe it. How did they know? How was I going to show up to school and act like I always had, invisible?

"What are we going to do?" What were we going to do? Everybody knew, which meant the whole student and staff population at school also knew, and every person I would pass on the street knew as well.

"I don't know, Jase," I sighed. "I don't know."

* * *

After a lot of persuasion and physically trying to push me out the door, my mother finally managed to make me give in. School was the last place I wanted to be right now. Already I could feel the stares of my peers as I walked through the yard, whispers following my every move. I knew even if I took the day off today, that tomorrow would probably be the same, if not worse. 'Better to get it over with sooner' my mother had said in her attempt to drag me off the couch.

And I knew as soon as I pulled up in the parking lot that today was going to be an excruciatingly long one. The moment I hopped out of my car, I felt like all eyes were on me. A group of girls stood by a silver Commodore, giggling and squealing about God knows what. It literally looked like a scene pulled from a typical high school movie, where they began to introduce the stereotypical groups found in every high school. At the sound of my car door shutting, they all looked up. I had seen their faces around before, and knew all of their names, but I knew that they definitely didn't know who I was.

I began walking past them, trying to avoid looking in their direction in case it prompted a conversation from one of them. I wasn't up for conversation today, especially not about what they no doubt wanted to ask me. 'Can we see your Timekeeper?' 'What happened?' 'How did you find out?' 'What did you do?'

I could hear their whispers now that I was closer, and wondered if they were speaking purposely so I could hear them. I mean, if you really didn't want someone to hear what you were saying, you'd wait until they passed or weren't around. But these girls didn't seem to care that I could hear every word that escaped their glossy lips. It wasn't long before almost every single person I passed would stare at me, or whisper to their friend about me. Even Mr. Cassidy couldn't keep his eyes off me when I walked passed him in the hallway. I was about ready to scream, to yell at the next person who's eyes landing on me and sat there for more than three seconds, when I heard someone calling my name.

"Candice Renee Smith!" The shrill voice was hard to miss, as Claire rushed up to me, causing even more people to look in my direction. I might as well have had 'YES I AM THE ONE WITH THE ZOMBIE SOULMATE' written on my forehead, since it's the answer to all the curious, staring faces.

"Is it true?" she asked as she caught up to me, slightly out of breath.

"Is what true?" I asked, even though I knew exactly what she was asking. It was the same reason people I passed couldn't keep their eyes off me.

"You know exactly what I mean, Candy. Don't play dumb with me," she said, slapping my arm just hard enough to make me wince. I glared at her even though she wasn't looking at me anymore. She seemed to notice that everywhere we went, hundreds of eyes were following. It was pretty normal for Claire to have a few guys goggling over her as we walked through the school, but never this many eyes. And it was never me they were all staring at.

Instead of replying to her, I flicked my wrist over, baring the pale, almost translucent skin underneath. My Timekeeper sat atop it, the red line hard to miss against the pale glow of the skin surrounding it. I lifted my arm up and in front of Claire's face, blocking her view as she walked. She stopped abruptly, as though she had slammed into an invisible wall. Her fingers gripped my arm, her gaze hard and focused as she stared down at my wrist.

"He's really still alive?" she whispered after several seconds of silence. I could see a few people beginning to surround us, some trying to get a look at my Timekeeper and other's just whispering amongst each other. I was never comfortable being the centre of attention, and right now I felt like

I was going to throw up. It didn't take long for a full circle of people to form around us, with around one hundred kids staring and waiting to see what was going on. Claire didn't notice, or maybe she just didn't care, but I could feel my breakfast stirring around my stomach and knew that if I didn't get out of here soon, there'd be much bigger and juicier news to share around than my Timekeeper.

"He is, Claire. Do you really think I'd be at school if he wasn't?" I sighed, pulling my arm out of her grip. She looked up then, clearly just now realising we were surrounded by people.

"Alright guys, nothing to see here," she yelled. "Come on, move along." She managed to make a big enough gap to allow us to squeeze out of the circle and out into the seemingly deserted hallway. I took a deep breath, glad to be free of hundreds of staring faces and unblinking eyes.

"It's going to be a long day," I sighed just as the bell sounded, making me late for first period.

The art room was relatively empty when I walked through the door, and thankfully Mrs. Nelson hadn't yet arrived either. I quickly scanned the room, trying not to look as all heads started to turn my way, finding a spare table near the window. I hurried across the room, afraid someone might want to ask me a question or see my Timekeeper. Thankfully, the class remained quiet; the only sounds to be heard were pens and pencils staining the paper, and a few whispers here and there. I wondered if those whispers had anything to do with me, or if now I was just overreacting.

"Look who's the talk of the school once again?" The voice sent a jolt through my body, instantly recognising whom it belonged to. I hadn't seen him sitting in the class when I walked in, but I didn't see him walk in either. I wasn't sure how long I had been staring down at my paper for, but it must've been s little while. I didn't want to turn around; I couldn't deal with him right now. As if things in my life weren't already complicated enough, he decides now is the right time to try and talk to me again.

"Ryan, I'm really not in the mood," I sighed, unable to take my eyes from the page. Don't look at him, don't look at him. Maybe he'll go away. I curse myself for choosing a table that had two spare seats at it, knowing he is going to want to sit beside me.

"Fine, we'll talk about something else, that's fine with me."

"Ryan, I don't think-" I started, but he doesn't let me finish.

"Come on, Candice. Just a simple chat." I didn't want to chat, and he knew it. I had been ignoring him all week; avoiding him at school, ignoring his calls and texts at home. He had to have some idea that I didn't want to speak to him, and it couldn't be a coincidence that the day he decides to try to talk to me is the day that the whole world found out about my Timekeeper.

"May I?" He asked, gesturing towards the spare seat beside me. I sighed, before nodding my head in approval. I couldn't really say no; it was either Ryan or Duncan, and there was no way I was sitting next to Duncan again.

I flipped open my sketchbook to a blank page, my mind unable to decide on something new to draw. It seemed the only thing my mind wanted to draw was Jase. Jase, Jase, Jase. I couldn't say that was such a bad thing, but I felt like all I had been drawing for the last month or so were Jase and Ryan, and I needed something different, something fresh and new.

My hand dragged across the page, leaving behind a trail of thick dark lead. I knew even before the shaped formed that I was drawing a face, and I knew exactly whom it would be. My mind could hardly think of anyone else lately, even when I tried not to. I could see Ryan watching my hand move swiftly across the page from the corner of my eye, though he didn't say a word. He knew whom I was drawing, he had to. It was too obvious to not know now. His hair was there, his eyes, his lips; all that was left were his nose and a few smaller details on his face, like the few freckles he had on his nose and the tiny scar above his eyebrow.

I felt Ryan's fingers wrap around my wrist, as he gazed down at my Time-keeper. I almost jumped out of my skin, not at all prepared for the sudden action. He placed his arm beside mine; the two Timekeeper's sitting perfectly aligned. For the first time since I'd met him, our wrists matched.

"They match," he whispered, as if he had just read my thoughts. I began to pull my wrist away, but his grip tightened.

"Don't you see, Candice? This has to be a sign." I looked up from my paper, raising my eyebrow at the boy sitting beside me.

"What are you talking about, Ryan?" I asked, before looking down at his hand that grasped my wrist. He followed my gaze, and instantly let go. His eyes flicked back up to meet mine as he spoke.

"Our Timekeeper's are the same; they're matching. This doesn't happen often, if at all. It can't just be a coincidence that we both have feelings for each other and now your Timekeeper is in sync with mine," he whispered, his gaze unwavering.

"No, Ryan, that's not true. You made me believe that I had feelings for you, and I thought I did, but the truth is I didn't and I never have. I had never had any guy treat me like you did, no one confess they liked me. So when you told me, I didn't know what to do. My mind knew I was with Jase, but some small selfish part secretly wanted to have the two of you. I was confused and flattered, but I never meant for anything to happen between us. I'm sorry it's taken me this long to say all this, but there never was anything between us."

He let out a tiny gasp, as though he really wasn't expecting me to say that at all. I cast my gaze away from him, unable to look at him for much longer. I couldn't believe I was saying all this right now, and to his face. I had never been good at confrontation, and all of this had been bottled up inside me all week, I wasn't sure I was going to be able to let it all out.

"Wh-what about the kiss? I know you felt the connection, Candice. You can't deny it," he stuttered, his hands now gripping the other so tightly his knuckles had turned white.

"I won't deny that the kiss wasn't special, Ryan, it was my first ever kiss. Of course I regretted it the moment our lips were apart, but it was still, and probably always will be, special."

"No!" he yelled, his hands slamming on the table. The whole class turned to look at us, and I could feel my cheeks getting hotter by the second.

"Is everything alright, Mr. Hawkins?" Mrs. Nelson asked, peering over her glasses at Ryan. Ryan wasn't looking at her though; he wasn't looking at anyone else in the classroom. His eyes never left me, and now I could see that they were pleading with me. He stood up abruptly, almost knocking the table over.

"Mr. Hawkins?" she said louder, standing up from her desk. Ryan finally locked eyes with her, before looking down at his feet.

"I, uh-" He turned back to me, taking once last glance before he practically ran out of the room.

Chapter Twenty-Six

The next day I somehow managed to avoid Ryan, or maybe we were avoiding each other, I wasn't sure. But I didn't see him in the halls or classrooms as I passed by. I knew I had upset him, but I didn't expect him just not to show up to school the next day. It made me worry slightly, hoping he hadn't gone and done anything he would regret. But there wasn't much I could do now, except give him space and hope he would move on eventually.

Ryan wasn't the only one that I was trying to avoid though. The whole school population knew about my Timekeeper now, with thanks to almost every single radio station and television channel. I thought I would get home and be able to escape all talk of it, but when I got home I had my whole family firing question after question my way. But if I thought yesterday had been bad, today was a heck of a lot worse. News reporters had dug around and somehow found out which school I attended, where I lived, and where my brothers worked. They had spent the entire day stalking the school grounds with everyone else, all trying to find me. If this was what it was like to be famous, I think I'll pass.

I wasn't sure how long I had been curled up in the corner of the Cleaner's room for, but I had basically missed most of my classes. A bell sounded on the other side of the door, though muffled and hard to hear, I knew it meant that the school day was finally over. I heard multiple footsteps race up and down the hall, cringing slightly every time one sounded too close to the door. I knew it still wasn't safe out there; they would all be waiting out in the car park for me to show up, expecting me to think I had escaped all the questions. So instead, I waited even longer. I wasn't sure how much longer I could last. My legs were cramping, my stomach grumbled, and my bladder was on the brink of bursting. I hadn't left this spot all day, and I was beginning to face the consequences.

Once the hall outside became quiet, and I was sure enough time had passed, I tried to get to my feet. My feet weren't quite prepared for the change unfortunately, and I almost fell into the shelves behind me. I had to make it to my locker, stop at the toilets and then make it to my car without being spotted. It might've sounded pretty easy, but my locker and the bathroom were on the complete other side of the school to the car park.

I silently headed for the door, waiting several moments before I opened it just a crack. The hallway seemed pretty deserted, but that didn't mean the school was completely empty. I knew there would still be the odd few students that stayed back to study, or the ones who had to suffer the silence of detention. I took a deep breath, before slipping out into the open. I sprinted down the hall, thankfully not passing anyone as I neared my locker. If only I had thought to bring a hoodie or a beanie to try and hide my face, but all I had was my stupid school blazer that wouldn't help hide me at all.

The short distance from my locker to the girl's bathroom should've been easy to go unnoticed, until I realized that the detention room was close by. Relief washed over me as I managed to slip through the door just as someone walked out of a classroom across the hall. I waited in the bathroom several minutes after I had emptied my bladder, before I entered the hallway again. I hurried down the hall, my backpack slapping loudly in between my shoulder blades. Reaching the courtyard, I prayed that the car park was empty by now. But it seemed my streak of good luck had ended.

There were five or six cars scattered around mine, and at first glace I thought I had made it. There didn't seem to be anyone around, not even on the football field that I sprinted across to make it to the car quicker. I shrugged my bag off my shoulders as I approached my car, shuffling through the contents to try and find my car keys. It was then that I heard a car door slam behind me, followed by another, and another. My heartbeat quickened as I frantically searched my bag, knowing I was almost out of time. My fingers hit the bottom of my bag, before finally closing over the car keys.

"Hey, Candice!" A voice called from behind me. I shivered at the closeness of it, but still refused to turn around. My hand shook, making it extremely difficult to unlock my car as I could hear the footsteps getting closer.

"Hey-" A different voice spoke this time, but I didn't get to hear what else they had to say. My door flung open, I threw my bag into the passenger seat, spilling its contents all over the place, before I jumped in and slammed the door behind me. The group of people stood beside my car, yelling at me to come out and talk to them. I jammed the key into the ignition, twisting it to life. The engine roared, and I sped straight towards the road, not glancing back once.

I let out a cry of relief when I finally got home, flopping down onto my bed. I had expected the group to follow me home, or to be bombarded by more news reporters when I drove up the driveway. Thankfully, they hadn't gotten that desperate yet. I stared at my ceiling, raising my arm so that it came into my view. My Timekeeper sat there, almost innocently, though the red line still gave me a slight heart attack no matter how many times I'd seen it. How could something so small cause so much drama?

I had almost forgotten my phone was in the pocket of my blazer until it started vibrating against my hip, almost making me jump out of my skin. I pulled it out of my pocket, instantly smiling once I saw who was calling.

"Jase," I grinned.

"Hey, Candy," Jace said, making my heartbeat a little faster from hearing his voice.

"What are you doing at the current moment?" he asked then, and I could almost see the smirk on his face as he spoke.

"Nothing exciting, really. Unless you count staring at my ceiling as exciting," I sighed, placing one arm behind my head.

"Oh, of course I do. That sounds extremely riveting." I laughed, just as a knock sounded at the front door. Startled, I walked out of my bedroom and headed down the stairs. I stopped in front of the door, unable to see out and afraid to open it. What if it was a news reporter, or a whole mob of them? What would I do? Nobody was home to help shoo them away, and there was no way I was going to welcome them into my home.

"You still there, Candy? Or did the ceiling become so exciting to stare at that you passed out?" Jase chuckled through the phone, but when I didn't reply, I could almost sense his concern. "Candy?"

"Jase, there's someone at my door," I whispered.

"Well? Answer it?" he laughed, clearly not understanding why I was so freaked out.

"I can't! It's probably a mob of news reporters or something," I sighed, taking a step back from the door as another knock sounded.

"Just answer the door, and if it's a news reporter then tell them to go away." I sighed again, taking a step forward and placing my hand over the doorknob. I took a deep breath, before I pulled the door towards me. Thankfully, it wasn't a news reporter, nor was it anyone who I would've expected it to be.

"What are you doing here?" I laughed, before shaking my head. "You almost gave me a heart attack!"

"Is that how you always greet your guests?" Jase grinned, hanging up the phone and slipping it into the pocket of his jeans. I punched his arm softly, unable to wipe the smile from my own face. He stepped through the door, closing it behind him. We stood staring at each other for several moments, taking in each other's appearances. It was at that moment that I realized we were home alone, for the first time since the night of the dance.

"What are you actually doing here, Jase?" I asked, breaking our gaze and turning my attention to the floor. My last thought had made me blush nervously, which was something I didn't want Jase to see.

"Well, I have a question to ask," he said as he began to climb the stairs, before stopping halfway and turning around to face me.

"A question? You couldn't have just asked it on the phone?" I laughed, looking up at him from the base of the staircase.

"It's a very important question, Candy, and I thought maybe you could take a break from all the ceiling-staring you were doing." He moved down a few steps, reaching out his hand to me, I grabbed it and we walked upstairs together. Would he want to go into my room? Oh, gosh, what if he did? I hadn't cleaned it since last week, and had I known Jase would be stopping by, I probably would've hidden my sketchbook that was currently sitting on my bedside table, opened onto a drawing of him.

"Well then, what is it?" I asked, turning around just as we reached my bedroom door. Jase's smirk faltered, his palms rubbing on his black jeans as he looked at me nervously.

"Um, well, do you-" he stuttered, before continuing. "Do you have plans tonight?"

I stared at him in surprise; was he asking me out? Or did I misinterpret the question?

"Are you asking me out, Jase?" I asked quietly, afraid that if he hadn't, that I had just made a fool of myself.

"I guess, I am, kind of," he stammered, unable to string a sentence together. "Yes, Candice. Will-will you, uh. Will you-" I laughed, causing him to look up at me. Confusion fell across his face, though I knew he was still nervous as I reached out and placed my hands in his. He didn't need to finish the sentence, and I didn't need time to think about my answer, either.

"What's the plan?" I asked, receiving a wide grin in return.

We walked along the street, hand in hand, heading towards a restaurant that Jase had apparently booked prior to showing up at my door.

"What if I had have said no?" I had asked before we left the house. Jase shrugged, clearly not fused about my question.

"I could still eat dinner by myself, I suppose." He grinned, though I wasn't sure if he was being serious or not.

It was chilly out, the autumn breeze breaking through my thin jumper with ease. Jase didn't seem fazed by it, seeing as he only wore a t-shirt and jeans. Maybe it was a guy thing, seeing as most males we walked past also didn't sport any jackets or jumpers. We were almost at the restaurant; I could see the name across the street flashing in neon lights. There were other flashing lights as well, though they were coming from the front of the restaurant. I wasn't sure what they were, until we got closer and realized that they were cameras, and they were flashing at us.

Jase gripped my hand tighter, quickly spinning us around and hurrying back in the direction we came. The mob followed us, the flashing lights never seizing.

"It's like they were waiting for us!" I yelled over the voices shouting at us from behind.

"They probably were," Jase replied, before breaking out into a run. I stumbled, almost losing my footing, as I tried to keep up with him. I was struck with a feeling of déjà vu, as I remembered the very first time Jase and I had met. I almost had to laugh; things were so different now it was as though I was thinking back to a time over a year ago, when it had only been a couple of months since we had met. What if I hadn't have pursued him that day? What if we hadn't worked things out?

I pushed the thoughts aside, trying to focus on what was going on around me instead. The flashes behind me had become less frequent, and it didn't seem that there were as many as when we had first been caught. I refused to turn around and check, and tried to sprint a little faster to fall in step with Jace. I reached him just in time for him to grab my arm and pull me hard to the right, slamming my body through a door. Before I could see where we were, or turn to Jace and complain, he pushed me forward until we were right at the back of the room.

I fell to the floor, gasping hopelessly for air. I had done so much running and hiding in the past twenty-four hours I was sure my body was going to repay me painfully the next morning. I looked up as Jase moved towards me, and began to see the familiar surroundings. The sound of a coffee machine, the rows of book shelves, the chalkboard wall. I couldn't help but smile and feel a little relieved, seeing as our pursuers hadn't spotted our little hideout.

"Stay here," Jase said, still slightly breathless. "I'll go see if we're safe."

I nodded, unable to form any words to reply. Jase disappeared to the front of the café then, leaving me to catch my breath. I peered through the shelves, spotting a few tables here and there occupied. It wasn't a very busy night, which had always been my favourite nights here. I turned around, using the closest shelf to lean back on. The chalkboard wall had hardly changed since the last time I had been. There was a small love-heart drawn towards the left, the initials A.L and T.P written in its center, which hadn't been there before. The quote I always found myself reading was still there, right in the middle of the wall. I had practically memorized it now, and still longed to ask Jase if it was actually his piece of work. As if on queue, Jase appeared from the shelves carrying a tray of food and drinks. It wasn't until then that I realized just how hungry I was, and was grateful to see he had ordered their famous hot chocolate as well.

"I'm sorry our date didn't turn out the way it should've," Jase sighed, running a hand through his messy locks as he sat down beside me, placing the tray in between us.

"It's not over yet," I smiled, reaching out and squeezing his hand. He gave me a small squeeze in return, before turning his attention towards the food.

"Well, bon appetite," he smirked, as he picked up one of the grilled cheese sandwiches and took a large bite. I could see he was a little upset that our night hadn't turned out perfectly, but I didn't mind. I was never one to fantasize about huge, extravagant weddings or dream dates; I had always much preferred a quiet night in, watching a movie and pigging out on junk food. Though that didn't mean I didn't appreciate what Jase had planned for us tonight, I was still just as happy to be here with him.

"What a crazy day," I sighed, wiping my greasy fingers on my jeans and picking up my hot chocolate. Jase was staring up at the wall, either not hearing me or choosing to ignore me. I shifted slightly, allowing my head to fall onto his shoulder. He didn't move, not so much as a blink.

"Jase," I started, just as he began to speak.

"I'm sorry, Candice. I thought we could do something special tonight, but I ruined it. If we had have just shown up to the restaurant without a booking, those reporters and paparazzi wouldn't have been there waiting." His head fell against mine as his fingers ran along my arm, causing shivers to go through my body.

"Hey, it's okay. You don't need to spoil me or treat me to fancy dinners, I'm perfectly okay with what were doing right now," I smiled.

"But that's what soul mates are supposed to do." I shifted my arm, turning it over so my Timekeeper was visible to the both of us.

"I don't think we're really like other soul mates, Jase," I said softly, causing a small chuckle from him in return. He lifted his head then, his hand sliding under my chin and pulling my head towards his. I gazed into his eyes, looking bluer than ever, just as he closed them and leaned in. His lips were soft and gentle, though my heart still wasn't used to their touch. His palm cupped my cheek as our lips moved together effortlessly. Our lips broke apart for a moment, though I wasn't sure who caused it, and my eyes opened to see Jase already staring at me.

"I think I'm okay with that," he whispered. It took me a moment to realize that he was referring to what I had said before, but it was too late for me to reply. Our lips had found each other once again, and I was almost certain that this was the best and possibly most bizarre date I would ever go on.

Chapter Twenty-Seven

"J ase!" Isabel screamed as she opened the door, making me jump. "Candice is here!"

She gave me a huge grin before running off down the hall and out of sight, leaving me alone in the doorway. I wasn't sure if I should just walk inside or wait where I was. Although I was sure Jase and his family wouldn't have really cared if I just helped myself around their home, it still felt wrong to me. I was spared by making a decision when Jase appeared around the corner; his smile almost as wide as Isabel's.

"You know you didn't have to wait outside," he laughed as he approached me. "I think Isabel left the door open for a reason."

"Well I didn't want to be rude and just invite myself in," I smiled before pulling Jase towards me. He seemed surprised by the gesture, but didn't pull away. His arms slipped behind my back, pulling me even closer towards him. And just like that, my heart had started beating ten times faster. Surely only soul mates could have such an effect on each other, right?

We still hadn't really mentioned anything more about my Timekeeper, both choosing to avoid it as if it would just magically return to it's normal self. It hadn't though, much to my annoyance and astonishment. I just wanted it to go away, and maybe then I could have a somewhat normal life without being constantly chased down and questioned by crazy news reporters. I couldn't do anything anymore without catching the attention of one of them.

Jase must have sensed the drop in my mood, pulling my chin up so I looked into his eyes. I thought he was going to speak, tell me not to stress so much about it just like everyone else had, but instead he pushed his lips to mine. It's not like his choice of action disappointed me, God no. But it definitely wasn't what I was expecting him to do, catching me so off guard that I actually flinched back from him, just as his lips touched. He backed up a little, still holding me in his arms, and gave me a quizzical look.

"What?" he asked, a hint of annoyance in his voice.

"Sorry, I didn't mean to. I guess I've just got a lot on my mind lately," I sighed, placing my arms around his neck.

"Maybe you need something to distract you then," Jase chuckled, running one of his hands up and down my spine. I shivered, though whether it was due to his touch or the crisp breeze coming from the open door behind me, I couldn't be sure.

"Try again, I'll be ready this time," I whispered, moving my face closer to his.

"You ruined my element of surprise. I can't do it now that you know about it." I moved ever so slightly closer, knowing that sooner or later, one of us would give in to the temptation of the other's closeness.

"I can pretend to be surprised if you really want," I murmured, my lips now only centimeters from his.

I wasn't even sure this was working as I wanted it to, but I was now close enough that I could practically taste his lips, and it was killing me. I didn't want to be the one to give in though, but if this lasted much longer I wasn't sure I could hold myself back. Jase didn't answer; he didn't need to. He filled the gap between us, causing me to smile beneath his lips. It was as though we were kissing for the first time; sweet, passionate, and breathtaking. I wondered if every kiss felt like this, or if it just depended on the person you were with. Maybe it only felt this way with your soul mate, with the person you were meant to be with. I didn't know, but I was too focused on the way his mouth felt on mine to really care.

His lips broke away from mine much too soon, but I realized that there was a reason for it. Isabel stood behind Jase, staring wide-eyed up at us.

"Mum!" She yelled, in that typical 'I'm telling on you' voice that sibling's used on one another. "Jase and Candice are kissing!"

Jase and I both laughed, but didn't bother continuing. The moment had passed and become a lot more awkward with Isabel watching. Breaking apart from Jase's hold, I closed the front door; glad to rid the cold breeze. We walked down the hall and into the lounge room. The television was switched on to some children's show Isabel seemed to be really intrigued with, while Kath sat beside her attempting to braid her thick hair.

"Isabel," she sighed, placing her hands on her daughter's shoulders. "Would you just sit still for five minutes?"

She looked up as we entered, her frustration changing into delight.

"Oh, Candice! I'm so glad you're here!" she grinned, and I could tell she genuinely meant it.

"So am I," I smiled. And it was true. After everything that had happened recently, it was nice to be able to have a welcoming place that I could use as my personal hideaway. Lucky for Jase, the media hadn't yet found his home, making it the perfect place when I got sick of the constant clicking of cameras and numerous questions thrown at me.

"Jase told me how crazy it's been for you lately. Gosh, I can't imagine what it must be like to not even feel safe in your own home." Kath threw her hands up in defeat as Isabel squirmed away, running out of the room.

"I better go help her get ready," Kath sighed before walking out of the room.

"Ready for what?" I asked Jase, now that we were alone.

"Kath has to go to school to have an interview with Isabel's teacher," Jase said, his eyes focused on the empty couch in front of us.

"Is Isabel in trouble?" I asked.

Jase laughed, "most definitely not. I think she's just struggling with some of the work they're doing."

He took a seat on the couch his aunt and cousin had just vacated, gesturing for me to sit beside him once he found a comfortable position. Once I sat down, he placed his arm around my shoulder, drawing me in to rest on his side. I took in the faint smell of soap, the way his hair brushed my forehead ever so slightly, and the way the bare skin of his arms felt around my neck. In that moment, everything felt perfect. It was just the two of us, and nothing else happening in our lives or the world mattered.

It wasn't long after Kath and Isabel left when a loud thumping on the front door startled the both of us. We hadn't expected them to be home so early, and had made ourselves quite comfortable with the fact that we would be alone for a few hours.

"She probably left her purse," Jase sighed, slowly pulling himself off the couch. "She does that a lot these days."

He walked out of the lounge room and presumably towards the front door, seeing as the knocking hadn't receded. I sunk back onto the couch, trying to shake the feeling of annoyance that our moment had been spoiled once again. I couldn't be mad at Kath; it wasn't like she left her purse on purpose.

I could hear muffled voices from the door, though nothing recognizable. There were sudden shouts and a loud crash, followed by heavy footsteps pounding down the hall. Before I had a chance to go see what had happened, a man ran into the lounge room. I froze, my heart crashing against my rib cage. He looked around, but thankfully, hadn't spotted me just yet. Maybe I still had a chance to run and find Jase, but then his eyes landed on me. Jase ran into the room then, the side of his head turning purple and bruised. He moved closer to me, and I felt slightly safer with him by my side.

The strange man said nothing, his eyes flicking between Jase and I. Before I even had a moment to react, he lunged for my arm. I screamed as he pulled me up from the couch and pushed my jumper sleeve up my arm. I tried to pull my arm out of his grasp, but his hold was much too tight. Jase was beside me in an instant, trying to get between the strange man and me. My first thought was that he must have been a news reporter, but there was no sign of a camera or recorder on him at all.

I tried to pull my arm back again, but failed once more. Still holding my arm, he grabbed Jase's, which looked as though it was about to make contact with the strange man's face. Jase gave a startled grunt, but even he wasn't able to free his arm from the man's grip. He pushed our arms together; our Timekeeper's perfectly aligned with each other.

"Impossible," the man whispered after several seconds. I looked up at Jase, who shrugged, before turning back to the man.

I decided then to take in his appearance, now that I felt he was pretty harmless. He wasn't here to hurt us or take us away to some Newsroom to get us to talk, well not yet anyway. If anything, he may just be a bit crazy, though I'm not really sure if that was any better. He was taller than Jase by at least three inches, towering over me with ease. His dark hair was pulled back in a slick ponytail, though several strands had become loose around his thin face. Thick, black-rimmed glasses framed his dark blue eyes. Dark circles surrounded his eyes, as though the man hadn't slept for several days.

At that moment, he looked up at me, making me quickly look away to avoid his eye contact. He released our arms then, stepping back and rubbing his eyes. Jase and I stood there, unsure of what to do. Should we run to call the police? Hide? Ask him politely what he wanted? Ask him to leave?

"No," he mumbled, more to himself than to anyone else. "No, no, no, no, no!"

He pulled a phone out of the pocket of his trench coat, his fingers moving swiftly across the screen. I then realized that his trench coat wasn't actually a trench coat at all, but rather a laboratory coat. Instant recognition hit me. I had seen this man before, multiple times. Never in person, or in such a poor state of wellbeing, but I was certain he was who I thought he was. The creator of the Timekeeper, the scientist who we studied every year at school until we were sixteen, Dr. James Creswell.

"I know you," I gasped, earning a surprised look from both Jase and Dr. Creswell.

"You do?" Jase exclaimed, clearly not expecting to hear me say I knew this crazy guy.

"Well of course she does, and so should you." Dr. Creswell eyed Jase over his glasses. "Do you not go to school?"

Before Jase could reply with a snarky comment, I jumped in.

"Dr. James Creswell, creator of the miraculous Timekeeper," I recited as though the history textbook was right in front of me.

"Miraculous, huh?" He snorted. "Well clearly it's worked somewhat for you two, eh?"

"What are you talking about?" Jase exclaimed, taking a small step back and gesturing for me to do the same. "How do you know anything about us?"

"Please," he shrugged. "You two are all over the news, and have caused quite a stir in my laboratories and factories."

Of course he was here about our Timekeeper's, or more likely my Timekeeper. But was he here to fix it? It never occurred to me that someone would be able to fix it, mainly because I had been trying to pretend that nothing was wrong with it in the first place. Or maybe I would have to get it replaced? The thought of going through the excruciating pain again sent shivers down my spine.

"I knew this would happen eventually, but I expected it to last at least another fifty years." He shook his head, seemingly lost in his own thoughts. He paced the room, unable to stop fidgeting. Jase and I looked at each other, more confused now than when he first entered the room.

"Dr. Creswell, would you mind telling us what is happening?" Jase asked, the calmness in his voice surprising me. "Like maybe starting with why Candice's Timekeeper says I'm dead?"

Dr. Creswell stopped pacing, before looking up at us over his glasses. He studied us intently, but stayed silent. I could see Jase's frustration growing out the corner of my eye, his hands slowly curling into fists.

"Tell us, damn it!" Jase yelled, causing me to jump. Despite his demand though, Dr. Creswell remained silent and unmoving.

I knew Jase was getting close to breaking the gap between Dr. Creswell and us, and I knew that I couldn't let Jase make any contact with him or we might never find any of the answers we- and everyone else in the world- needed so desperately to know.

"Is Jase really my soul mate?" I suddenly blurted out, causing both pairs of eyes to move towards me. I wasn't sure it was the question I actually wanted an answer to, or if I really even wanted to hear the answer, but it was too late now.

Dr. Creswell cleared his throat and fixed his glasses, and I mentally prepared myself for an answer I didn't want to know. Would I be able to stop the tears from flowing? How would Jase react? Turning my attention around to him, I saw that he looked just as nervous as I was.

"Well, you see that's the thing," Dr. Creswell spoke after many silent minutes passed. He paused briefly, as though needing to add some sort of dramatic effect to the already dramatic situation. He smiled then, his mouth spread wide across his face almost creepily. "There is no possible way to know who your soul mate is, so what I'm trying to say is that these stupid little devices, don't mean anything."

Chapter Twenty-Eight

I hadn't left my room in days, nor had I spoken to anyone other than my mother. My phone was constantly buzzing beside my pillow, but I refused to answer it. I knew I was being foolish, ignoring everyone, but I didn't know what else to do. I just kept repeating Dr. Creswell's explanation in my head, trying to make sense of it all. But no matter how many times I replayed that day, I still couldn't believe any of it was real. I wanted it all to be a dream, but it wasn't. The truth was, the Timekeeper was a useless device that we all now had stuck within our skin.

I could hear the sound of the Television from downstairs, although I wish I couldn't. I was positive my mother had turned the volume up just so I could hear it from my bedroom. One of the voice's speaking belonged to a woman, while the other belonged to Dr. Creswell. It was easy to tell, seeing as he was trying to explain to the woman, and the whole country, what had happened with the Timekeeper's. I pulled the blankets over my head, attempting to drone out his voice, but unfortunately it did nothing but make it harder for me to breathe.

"So, I think the question everybody wants to know here is, what does the Timekeeper actually do? You know, seeing as it doesn't actually find our soul mate." The woman asked.

"Well, you see they are quite sophisticated devices." Dr. Creswell began; barely paying any attention to the awful way the woman was talking to him. "When we began designing them, we created them with a matching pair. We made it so that the two matching Timekeeper's would begin a countdown until they would reunite, using very advanced scientific technology. Obviously the matching pairs were then split up and given to two people, who would then become 'soul mates'."

"I see," the woman said, before continuing. "What you're really saying is that we are just matched up with any random person, anywhere in the world? That who we're paired with complete strangers and no thought at all goes into that? There's no connection or matching done to make it seem like the two people are actually soul mates?"

As the woman questioned Dr. Creswell, I realised that she sounded quite similar to me. I had bombarded him with question after question, and even then I didn't believe him, I didn't even want to try. He had spent probably all of his life working on a device that did nothing for us at all, and yet he was perfectly fine with that. How you could live with such a lie was beyond me, I definitely wouldn't be able to do it.

"Technically, no, but we do factor in age and gender and sometimes a person's place of living to try and get the best results for the matching pair. Then once the pair is matched, the mind begins to believe that your pair is, in fact, who you're meant to be with, and that's how the statistics of Timekeeper love are so high."

"So, you're saying that it's just mind over matter then? Our soul mate is chosen by our minds?"

"Yes and no." Dr. Creswell answered. I waited for him to elaborate on the second part of his answer, but he didn't.

"Dr. Creswell, how do you explain the Timekeeper's control over the body?" The woman asked then. She was staying relatively calm throughout the interview, unlike Jase and I. But how were you supposed to stay calm when you are told that the one thing you've learned about and grown up around and are supposed to trust turns out to be a lie? Of course Jase and I were mad, but so was the whole country. There had been riots outside the Timekeeper factories and headquarters already, and that was just the beginning of the chaos. Employers had closed their businesses until further notice, schools had shut down, and half the town was deserted.

"Well," Dr. Creswell began before clearing his throat, "it's as we've always said. The Timekeeper connects to your brain and nervous system, where it then can control your body's movements and lead you towards your pair. We never lied about that."

"I suppose one of the big questions here is, why? Why did you lie to the whole country about this? And why are we only finding out about this now?"

I sat up in bed a little, eager to hear what he had to say in response to that question. Strangely enough, I hadn't even thought about asking the whys. I just wanted Dr. Creswell to tell me that he had been joking, that my Timekeeper had just malfunctioned and he would reset it and everything would be normal once again. I left Jase's shortly after Dr. Creswell begun to say sorry, knowing I needed to be alone. Jase had called after me, but I ignored him and hadn't seen or spoken to Jase since.

"It was a tough decision, with many of my colleagues against it. But as you all know, fifty years ago the divorce rates were through the roof. This was causing multiple health issues, mainly mental health, and hundreds of people were giving up on marriage and even just love altogether." Dr. Creswell paused, though I'm not sure why. Maybe he was showing some graphs of the statistics he'd mentioned or was trying to make himself seem more dramatic, but he started speaking again before I could think too much more on it.

"We wanted to create something that would fix this epidemic, and when we started the Timekeeper, we were so sure it would succeed. After the first few trials though, we realised what we were trying to do was impossible. Science would never be able to find true love, but we couldn't give up. News had already spread about our mysterious invention, and people were thrilled to hear about it. So we kept working on them, regardless that they didn't necessarily work the way we wanted them to."

"And why did you feel now was the time to let everybody know about this?"

"It was never going to last," he sighed. "Hell, we were surprised they had actually lasted this long without one malfunctioning. We thought that maybe they could last at least another decade, but then we heard about the young girl who's Timekeeper told her that her pair had passed away when he hadn't. I first had to see the Timekeeper for myself, to make sure that it was really buggered, but then it was time. There would have been no other way to explain why or how the Timekeeper had malfunctioned without letting everybody know it never really worked in the first place."

I sat there, shocked. I hadn't expected to be brought into this interview at all. Knowing that my Timekeeper was the first to malfunction was a surprise, even though it shouldn't have been. I kept pretending that a faulty Timekeeper was a relatively normal thing, rare but still occurring. The whole hype surrounding it and the crazy paparazzi should have told me otherwise, but I was in denial. My life was finally falling into place, I want ready for it to spiral out of control again.

"I guess I have one more question to ask you then, Dr. Creswell," The woman asked then.

He didn't answer, well at least not verbally or loud enough for me to hear. The woman interviewing him either didn't need an answer or wasn't expecting one, because she continued anyway.

"Is there even such thing as a soul mate? And can we find true love?"

I held my breath, waiting for an answer. Why I was so eager to find out, I couldn't be sure. But I didn't get to hear his answer, because the house was thrown into silence. Someone had turned the television off, or at least muted the volume. Annoyed that I couldn't listen to what his reply was, I hopped out of bed and headed downstairs, determined to turn the TV back on. I got as far as the top of the staircase, when Jase stopped me. He stood at the bottom of the stairs, looking as he did the last time I saw him. His facial expression was unreadable, though I knew he had to be pretty mad at me for ignoring him for the past few days.

"Hi," I uttered, unable to look at him directly. He didn't reply, but rather made his way up the rest of the stairs. When he reached me though, he didn't stop but rather grabbed my arm and pulled me along behind him. We walked back towards my bedroom, stopping halfway as Jase let go and spun around to face me.

"Care to explain why you've been ignoring me for the past few days?" he demanded, and I could now see just how he was feeling. Angry, yes, but what surprised me the most was how upset he looked. I instantly felt guilty for being so selfish, not realising how much it would actually affect those around me.

"Jase, I'm sorry. I know it sounds stupid, but I just thought I needed time alone. I didn't take it well," I sighed, unable to look anywhere but at the carpet at my feet.

"And you think I took it well? You think anybody is taking it well?" he said through gritted teeth.

"It was all too much, I just- I didn't know what to do." I looked up briefly, and regretted it almost instantly. He looked about as angry as he had been the night I had tried to 'save' him in the police station. It hurt to see him that way back then, and it hurt even more now. The worst part was that I was the one causing this anger. I wasn't sure what was worse, the anger or the sadness I had caused him.

"And ignoring me was your best option?" he asked quietly, his voice serious and unwavering.

"I was scared, okay?" I replied in a whisper.

"Scared?" Jase laughed. "Scared of what?"

"That you wouldn't want to be with me anymore knowing that we might not really be soul mates," I mumbled, though it was barely audible and I wondered if Jase had even understood what I said.

I regretted the words almost as soon as I had spoken them. I was sounding more and more like a selfish child as the day went on, and I felt horrible for it. I wasn't sure how Jase was going to reply, and I honestly didn't really want to find out. Throughout our short relationship, we hadn't really been overly intimate with each other. Sure we kissed and hugged every now and then, but we hardly ever spoke about our feelings. It was strange really; when you thought about everything we had been through. There was a long pause before either of us spoke again, and I began to worry I had been wrong to say anything at all.

"How do you think I've felt these past few days, Candy?" Jase finally spoke, though his gaze never moved from the floor. "I thought- I thought you might've went back to Ryan. I thought-" he couldn't finish his sentence, and I didn't want him to. I had no idea Jase had been so worried about me getting back with Ryan; it hadn't even occurred to me that he would think that at all.

"Jase," I began, urging him to look at me. "I wouldn't do that to you. Whatever happened between Ryan and I was never meant to last, and I never felt the same way about him as he did for me."

He finally lifted his head, a small smile playing on his lips. He wrapped his arms around me then, allowing me to sigh with relief. I hadn't even been thinking of Ryan the past few days, though he had tried to contact me. Obviously he had been thinking about me and possibly hoping, now that the Timekeeper's weren't really a reliable source of finding a soul mate, that I would choose him over Jase. I couldn't help but want to laugh at that, which sounded really mean. I did feel sorry for Ryan, but whatever feeling's he had for me will eventually disappear and he'll move on. I hoped that one day he would be able to find his soul mate, because everyone deserved somebody to love. Jase pulled back, keeping his hands wrapped around my waist, and looked down at me.

"So, we're good then? The two of us?" he asked.

I smiled, before answering in a way that spoke better than I ever could. I pulled his face towards mine, gaining a surprised reaction from him. My lips pressed against Jase's, and I knew in that moment, that whatever happened with the Timekeeper's or with the rest of the world, it wouldn't matter. Because I had found my soul mate, the one I wanted to be with; and to me, that was all that really mattered.

Epilogue

- -

Three weeks later...

I had been staring at the wall for the past ten minutes. I'd been waiting for this moment for such a long time that I was still unsure about what I really wanted to write. I always wanted it to be perfect, but I knew now that nothing was ever really perfect. My fingers still held the small piece of chalk, though they were now coated in a thin layer of chalk dust. I took a deep breath and closed my eyes, trying to will the right words to come to me. Letting out the breath, I felt like giving up. I'd wanted to write something on the wall since I first discovered the café, but I still couldn't do it. Arms wrapped around me suddenly, and without having to open my eyes or turn around I knew exactly whom they belonged to.

"Hello, Jase," I smiled as I opened my eyes and leaned back into his chest.

"How? You didn't even turn around?" he exclaimed, resting his chin on top of my head.

"I'm a pretty smart girl." I turned around, swinging my arms around his neck and pulling his face down closer to mine.

Jase let out a chuckle, "that you are," he grinned before placing his lips softly on mine.

It was only quick, and I pouted when he pulled away, but it only made him smile. There was nothing wrong with his smile, gosh no, it always somehow managed to send butterflies fluttering through my stomach. But I had wanted him to give me another kiss, or at least a longer one, though Jase had other plans. We walked over to a couple of bean bags resting against a bookcase nearby, settling in just as a waitress came by to ask if we wanted anything.

"Just a hot chocolate for me today, Ruby," I smiled, remembering the first time Jase and I had come here together and the scene we had made in front of everyone, including Ruby.

She had given Jase a hard time ever since then, and I couldn't help but laugh. It was crazy to think how much things had changed since that day, since our first proper meeting. We had been through so much since then, especially within the last month. Since the Timekeeper was found to be a fraud, the country went mad. Riots broke out all over the country, mainly in front of the Timekeeper clinics and factories, though I never understood what they were trying to get out of it. Of course everyone was furious at being lied to for fifty years, but there wasn't anything we could do that could change the past. It took a little while for people to just accept what had happened, but now everything was somewhat back to normal.

"What about you, Jase?" Ruby asked, giving him a genuine smile now. It was clear she had forgiven him for how he had treated me, thankfully, since we were both regulars here now.

"I'll just grab a hot chocolate too, thanks," he replied, surprised by Ruby's change of heart.

"I don't think she hates you anymore," I grinned once she had left.

"I was thinking the same thing," Jase laughed before shifting in the bean-bag.

He glanced towards the blank spot on the wall where I had previously been standing in front of, before turning back to me.

"Still can't figure out what to write?" he asked.

"No," I sighed, slumping back into the beanbag. "Why is it so hard to think of something?"

Jace chuckled, before shaking his head, "You can't force it, Candy. Just let the words come to you on their own."

"That could take forever though," I groaned.

He laughed, before leaning forward and kissing my cheek. "You'll figure it out. You're a smart girl, remember?"

I rolled my eyes at him, pushing him back into the beanbag. He acted like it had hurt, and pretended to ignore me as he grabbed a book from the shelf behind him and started flicking through the pages, and I couldn't help but admire him. His blonde hair was just long enough to fall into his eyes, which annoyed his Aunty Kath so much she had threatened to cut it herself if he didn't hurry up and do something about it. Jase had laughed it off, but I was pretty sure she was being serious about it. Isabel then proceeded to chase him around the house yelling that she was going to shave all of his hair off, which had only made Jase laugh harder. He had tried to hide behind me, but I was only an obstacle for Isabel to try and jump over. We had ended up in a pile of bodies on the floor, laughing so hard our stomachs had started to hurt.

The sound of a phone interrupted my thoughts and jolted me back to the present. Jase had the book in his lap as he checked his phone.

"Wanna go to the movies later?" he asked after a few minutes, his eyes still on his phone.

"With who?" I asked, trying to peak at his phone screen but noticing the mug next to his beanbag instead.

Some time within my daydream Ruby had come by with our hot chocolates, though I never heard her. I picked up the mug, breathing in the warm chocolate aroma before taking a small sip.

"Claire, Alex and Ryan," he replied, his fingers moving across the phone screen rapidly even as he looked up at me.

"Sounds like fun," I smiled, receiving a smile in return.

Within the first week that the Scientists had broken the news to the world about the Timekeeper's, Ryan had called me. I tried ignoring it at first, thinking that he wanted me to choose him over Jase. After ignoring a few calls and texts, I ran into him once the school reopened. It was impossible to avoid him when he was in my class, and I was planning on telling him straight away that even though the Timekeeper's don't work, I still believed Jase was my soul mate. He surprised me though. Instead of trying to explain how we should be together, he apologised for everything that had happened. I was shocked, but relieved. He explained how he wanted to be friends and was moving on, which was a lot easier now, knowing that he didn't have to worry about a Timekeeper getting in the way. We had become good friends since then, though Jase and Ryan becoming best friends had taken a little getting used to.

Jase stood up then, startling me as he bent down and planted a soft kiss on my forehead.

"I'll be back," he said, before walking towards the front of the café.

I watched him turn down the small corridor adjacent to the counter, heading towards the bathrooms. I turned back around, looking back up at the chalkboard wall. With my mug in my hands, I eyed the blank space where I planned to write my piece. I closed my eyes and started to think about everything that had happened within the last few weeks. From the Timekeeper announcement, to Ryan, to Jase, so many thoughts rushed through my mind and slowly, piece-by-piece just like a puzzle, the words came to me.

I placed my mug next to the beanbag before standing up and walking towards the wall. I picked up the piece of chalk I had discarded earlier, rubbing it between my fingers as I walked the length of the wall. There were so many stories to tell, so many different lives within them. I came to a stop in front of the spot I would soon call my own. Turning around, I checked to see if Jase had returned yet, but he was nowhere to be seen. I closed my eyes and took a deep breath, before turning back around. This was it, the moment I had been waiting for since I first discovered the café.

My eyes opened, and I began to write. The chalk squealed against the wall, making me cringe. I didn't stop though, the words just kept pouring out of me through my fingers. It was strange and slightly embarrassing how much joy writing on the wall was giving me. But I had wanted to do this for the longest time, and now that I was finally doing it, I couldn't help but smile.

I stood back, staring up at the wall. My eyes trailed over the hundreds of different quotes and poems and names that had been left there over the years, each one different from another, and each with a different meaning to the owner of the words. My eyes finally fell on the piece in front of me, and my smile grew wide. It was only a couple of months ago that I had been standing in the same position, but now the piece that was written had been changed. The piece Jase had claimed as his own no longer existed, someone had rubbed it off. Now, the space had been replaced with new words, words that I could relate to, words that I had written.

Jase's hand slipped into mine then, startling me slightly, though my eyes stayed glued to the words in front of me. I could see him reading the words out the corner of my eye, and I felt strangely anxious. What if he hated it? What if he thought it was stupid and laughed? But I didn't have to worry about that, because he smiled and then stood in front of me, covering the words I'd spent forever trying to find. His face moved closer, now inches from mine. I could feel his breath on my lips, practically tasting the chocolate left behind from his drink.

"We should get going before we miss the movie," he whispered, though doesn't move.

"Yeah," I breathed, my voice even softer than Jase's.

I closed my eyes, hoping he would lean in and bring our lips together. He placed his hands gently around mine, before lifting them up and guiding them behind his neck. I wrapped my fingers together, securing the hold around his neck. He took a slight step forward, his hands moving down to land on my waist. He pulled me towards him, closing the small space between us and allowing our lips to collide. That was how I had wanted him to kiss me earlier, though I was quite content that it was happening now. His mouth parted against mine, and I could feel the passion intensifying between us rapidly.

I pulled away, as he cupped my face in his hands. Opening my eyes, I was reminded suddenly of where we were. A blush crept into my cheeks, and I hoped nobody had been paying attention to the young couple at the back making out. Jase noticed my blushing and let out a low chuckle, before wrapping his arms around me and pulling me tight to his chest. His lips kissed the top of my head, and in that moment, I couldn't think of anywhere I'd rather be than in Jase's arms.

"Come on," Jase grinned, as he let me go. "We're late."

He grabbed my hand as he began to walk towards the door. We got about half way through the café when I stopped, turning back to look at the wall once more. I could still see it from where I stood; my words finally up on the wall for everyone to see. I read through them once more, making sure I felt like they were right.

"People ask me how I know, that I've met my soul mate. Why it's easy, I say. Our souls are in sync; they are connected to each other long before our first meeting. What does it feel like, they ask. Indescribable, amazing, beautiful, are the words that come to mind. But I don't say those words; instead I smile wider and explain how I just know he's the one. I feel it with every touch, every look, every kiss. I feel it in my stomach, my mind, my heart. There's just something there that isn't present with anyone else, nobody else but him."

I turned back around, smiling to myself as I walked hand in hand out the door with my soul mate.

The end.